MAD SCIENCE INSTITUTE

A NOVEL OF CALAMITIES, CREATURES, AND COLLEGE MATRICULATION

SECHIN TOWER

Siege Tower Entertainment

Published in the United States of America
By Siege Tower Entertainment, LLC, Everett, WA

ISBN 978-0-9848507-0-9

Printed in the United States of America
First Edition published 2011
Version 1.1 published 2012

Cover art by Christopher Maddon
http://chrismaddenart.com/contact.html

Interior art by Christopher Martin
www.christopherlm.com/

Edited by Jane Kenealy

WWW.SECHINTOWER.COM

For my ancestors: you are all in this story.

For the Institute's first class:
Laura, Jim, Heather, Jen, Chris, Haili, Peter, Alan, and Gary.

For Jane
who got this book down to fighting weight.

And most of all for Katie
who makes everything seem possible.

"SO ALL THAT WAS GREAT IN THE PAST WAS RIDICULED, CONDEMNED, COMBATED, SUPPRESSED — ONLY TO EMERGE ALL THE MORE POWERFULLY, ALL THE MORE TRIUMPHANTLY FROM THE STRUGGLE."
— NIKOLA TESLA

Chapter 1 ~ Soap

My experiment exploded. Again.

Now I'm thirty feet above a concrete sidewalk, dangling from the railing of a gigantic, burning doomsday machine designed to bring civilization as we know it to a sudden and very messy end. Oh, and BTW: my fingers are slipping.

My name's Sophia, but people call me "Soap." They also call me a mad scientist, which I hate. Everyone knows mad scientists are old men in white coats who build monsters and death-rays and stuff and then laugh like maniacs while trying to conquer the world. I'm a sixteen-year-old girl, and whoever heard of a girl being a mad scientist? Besides, I don't mean to keep blowing things up. For me, explosions are just a bad habit, like talking with your mouth full or chronic butt-dialing. The only difference is that my bad habit causes widespread property damage.

So how did I end up here? It sort of started when one of my gizmos accidentally caused a couple dozen cell phones to explode while they were still in people's pockets. On the up-side, that experiment got me a college scholarship. On the down-side, it set off a chain of events that included chasing a lizard monster through a radioactive basement and being kidnapped by a motorcycle gang. And now I'm stuck between burning alive and falling to my death.

To be fair, half of the story belongs to my cousin, Dean. For him, it started 16 days ago, when the woman he loved showed up out of nowhere. This was the same woman who offered me admission to the college, so it's probably fair to start the story with them.

September 1st
(Doomsday minus 16 days)

Chapter 2 ~ Dean

As the curtain of black smoke pulled back, Dean yanked the oxygen mask from his face and dropped his heat-warped helmet to the pavement. His fellow firefighters rushed in to offer assistance, but he didn't need any. He was on his feet, and so were the rest of his crew. One man had a hurt shoulder—a broken clavicle, Dean guessed—but the fire was out and their job was done.

He unclipped the air-tank from his back, and when he shucked his insulated jacket from his shoulders, a light rain of charcoal chunks and burned brick chips fell from him. The late summer Los Angeles wind was hot and tainted by the coppery scent of smog, but it still felt refreshing as it hit his broad chest and played through his short, black hair. He was not the tallest firefighter at his stationhouse, but he was far from the shortest, and his sturdy frame was wrapped in ample muscle and minimal fat, allowing his body to shed heat with the greatest possible efficiency.

His colleagues gathered his discarded clothing as he dropped it and one of them shoved a canteen into his hand. Dean upended it over his head, then accepted a second canteen and gulped down the chilled water. By the time he finished, the station chief arrived and swapped Dean's canteen for another full one.

"Not exactly the best-case scenario," the chief said, pointing with his chin back towards the remnants of the building from which Dean had just emerged.

"I've seen worse," Dean said with a shrug. He had once remained on his feet for three days to battle a jet-fuel fire at a hanger outside of Bagdad. By comparison, today was easy. Half the building may have fallen down, but he had read the impending collapse in the sagging interior walls in time to hurry his men to safety. The apartment building was lost, but the fire would not spread.

"Take a rest," the chief said, jerking his thumb towards an awaiting ambulance. "I don't want to see you back on the line for thirty minutes, minimum. That's an order."

Dean had a seat and allowed the paramedics to record his vitals before he found a shady spot to watch the clean-up operation. Exactly thirty minutes later, he got up and went to lend a hand.

He took only three steps before he saw someone who stopped him short. There, across the street, stood a figure he instantly recognized but couldn't believe: Professor Denise McKenzie. She was standing on the far corner, just past the ring of plastic cones that marked the civilian safety zone, with the other spectators. It was her hair that made her so easy to spot: orange-red, the color of a daffodil's heart, and vivid even at a distance as it flowed over her shoulders. Her arms were folded across her chest, and she wore an earth-toned pants suit that allowed his eyes to follow the long journey of her legs all the way up from her black pumps.

Dean felt a surge of happiness at seeing her, followed almost immediately by a cold splash of regret. He had known her since their first day as college freshman, and since then he might have measured his life by the cycle of intense love and bitter heartbreak they traded with one another. The last time he had seen her had been two years ago, when she rejected his marriage proposal for the second time. All that seemed like so long ago, and his mind raced to come up with an explanation for why she might be here, now, standing on this very street corner.

She saw him and waved, then pushed past the other spectators to follow the safety line closer to him.

"McKenzie," he called out as he ran to her. He had always called her by her last name, ever since they had first met as freshman in college. Originally it had been a sort of joke, a jock's nickname for someone who couldn't have been less jock-like in attitude or upbringing, but the name had stuck with her. Even years later, her new acquaintances mistakenly believed that it was her given name because that's what everyone else called her.

He raced her to the edge of the safety line, but when he reached her he suddenly felt awkward and unsure of what to do. When they had last seen each other, they had been enemies after another ferocious break-up. By their usual pattern, they would now be lovers again, but Dean didn't want to make any assumptions. McKenzie, however, had no reservations as she flung her arms around him. He laughed, scooped her off her feet with a bear-hug and inhaled deeply, finding that even the clinging stench of the smoke was powerless to cover her scent of jasmine and honeysuckle—scents he couldn't name, but which he had learned to love. It meant they were about to re-discover all the ways they were so perfect for each other. Maybe, if they were lucky, this would be the time they would forget to explore all the reasons it could never work out.

"Sorry," he said, releasing the hug. "I'm all sweaty. But I'm so glad to see you. What are you doing here? And—how did you find me out on call?"

"I just followed the smoke," she said. "Wherever there's disaster, there's Dean."

When she looked up at him he saw deep, dark circles under her green eyes. She was smiling, but her mouth was strained. "What's wrong," he asked. "Is it your heart?" Her blouse covered the scar that had long since faded into a nearly invisible white line down her chest, but he knew it marked the implantation of the tiny electronic pacemaker that corrected her congenital heart defect.

"My heart's fine. Listen, I have a lot to tell you and not much time. First of all, I sent a letter of acceptance to your cousin, Sophia. She should be getting it any day now."

"Is that what this is about?" Dean rolled his eyes. "Look, I told you, I'm not that close to her or anything. You didn't have to take her on my account."

"That's not why I accepted her. Believe me, she's more than qualified. She's…extraordinary."

"Okay, you didn't come all the way out here just to thank me for the recruiting tip. Spill it."

She seemed hesitant to speak, hesitant even to look at him. "I need a favor," she finally said. "A really, really big favor. Dean, I need you to run my school for me. I need you to be the Dean of Students at the Mechanical Science Institute."

Dean just looked at her. He couldn't imagine why on earth she would want him, of all people, to run a science college. He could disconnect a sparking car battery and predict the movements of flames within interior walls, but he wouldn't have been able to pick out the difference between Avogadro's number and Newton's Laws if his life depended on it.

"I'm sorry," McKenzie said "I wouldn't have come to you if I had any other choice."

"This is one of your games, isn't it? Another one of your Mensa brain-puzzles? You're always over my head with these things. You have to tell me plainly: what's going on?"

She didn't answer. He held her at arm's length so he could study her face, hoping to find some clue that would help him unravel the riddle or catch the joke. But the only clues he found were the dark circles under her eyes and the worried crease in her brow. Dean felt confused and worried, and the more he tried to figure it out the more he felt like there was a giant hand inside his stomach making fists with his guts.

"Hey, Dean!" The booming voice of the fire chief called to him from the engine. "Were you planning to join us?"

Dean glanced back to see that the rest of his crew had finished loading up and were ready to go. McKenzie took that moment to pull away from him.

"Tomorrow morning, after your shift ends, meet me at that sushi place where you took me the first time I came out here."

"McKenzie, wait." He reached out to her like a blind man trying to find a doorway. "Whatever it is, let me help. I'll get you a doctor or a lawyer—or a hit-man, if that's what it takes."

She gave him a slight smile, her green eyes suddenly sad. "The Institute," she said. "I need your help with that." And then she was gone.

Chapter 3 ~ Soap

"Well, Soap, I talked to your principal," my Dad said as we spread the cloth to conceal my experiment. "She says there will be college professors here today. There's even someone from the admissions office at MIT."

I have to admit, that made this year's New York All-State Science Fair Invitational into a big deal for me. MIT is the most famous school of engineering in the world. Their graduates go on to build robots, space ships, fighter jets, and everything else that's cool. It had pretty much been my dream school since the day my Dad first started pestering me about college planning. But before I could worry about getting into MIT, I needed to worry about winning some science-fair trophies. No awards would mean no scholarships, and no scholarships would mean the only higher education I'd be able to afford would be the Burger Emporium's training video titled "Do You Want Fries With That?"

As usual, most of the science fair was seriously boring. All the students set up their exhibits at little tables that lined the floor of the big gymnasium, and clusters of judges and spectators would move from one competitor to the next, asking for demonstrations and taking notes. Most of the time, there was absolutely nothing to do but sit back and wait for the next group to come by.

I looked over at the kid next to me. He looked South Asian, maybe Indian. He was very good looking, sharply dressed with close-cropped hair and an athletic build you find at these kinds of gatherings more often than you might expect. That made him just about my opposite: I'm short-ish, I wear all black, I keep my dark hair long but tied back in pony-tail, and I'm not really interested in sports. I'm also not really interested in English or history or Spanish, either, which is why my GPA was pretty much garbage. I always thought it was unfair that colleges cared so much about grade averages. I mean, why do they want me to be good at everything when I only want to study one thing? Can't I just be good at the thing I'm passionate about and forget the rest? You just have to add that to the list of life's injustices, I guess.

"I hear there's a judge from MIT here today," I said to the good-looking boy. I'm not too good with talking to people, so the minute I opened my mouth I knew I would regret it. To get my mind off the conversation I had just started, I fidgeted with the cloth covering my invention. That left a grimy feeling on my fingers, so I took three quick pumps of hand sanitizer because I'm kind of a germaphobe. I swear, sometimes I think I'm such a mess I should just be kept in a padded cell.

"Of course there's a judge from MIT," he said. "There's always a judge from MIT. This year, he's the one wearing a green tie." He watched me rub the sanitizer on my hands and gave me a smile like the one you give a homeless person you're tired of arguing with. But his smile looked nice and his lips were thin and strong-looking. My lips are big and fat, which some people call "movie-star lips" but I don't like them because I think it makes my mouth look too wide. For just a moment I imagined what it would be like to kiss him. Then I started to worry that it meant I was a creeper, but I couldn't help it. Besides, I didn't see how it was going to hurt, since it was all just in my imagination. Outside of my imagination, I hadn't ever kissed anyone, which meant that at least I was only a mental creeper and not a real-life creeper.

"What's your project?" I asked. My brain was still screaming at me to shut up before I made a fool of myself.

"I designed blueprints for an antimatter power plant," the boy said.

"Whoa, great idea," and I could feel myself getting jealous. Antimatter fuel would be a thousand times more powerful than a nuclear reaction using uranium, and the only real waste product would be gamma-rays, which could be soaked up with thick shielding. If he had invented that, it would mean the end of the energy crisis on this planet.

"So, how do you make the antimatter?" I asked him.

He shrugged his shoulders. "I don't know. I only designed the plant to burn the stuff in."

I blinked a few times while I waited for him to finish, but apparently that's all he had. Apparently, he hadn't considered that producing antimatter would cost something like 20 billion dollars an ounce—no exaggeration—so it seemed to me like he might as well have been talking about squeezing milk out of dinosaurs.

"Is that seriously all you've got?" I said. "That's pretty lame."

Not for the first time I wished I had an "undo" button for what I said.

The boy just looked at me for a moment. Then he went back to setting up his poster and ignoring me.

"Why do you have to say things like that, Soap?" My Dad was sitting in a folding chair by my project. He put his Popular Mechanics magazine under his arm and gazed up at me with dark, tired eyes. He seemed like a shrunken version of his former self, like one of those ancient Egyptian mummies. It was my fault he looked that way. It costs a bundle for a single father to raise a child in New York, even out where we lived in Flatbush, and I'm way worse than a normal child because of all the expensive electronics I disassembled on the dining room table. And the fires I started in my bedroom whenever I overload a transformer. And the time I designed a robot that could make other robots out of whatever materials were at hand, which was great except that it mistook the neighbor's Honda for scrap metal.

Actually, I've been worried about my Dad a lot lately. Even after my mom divorced him and moved to Chicago five years ago, he still got really excited about two things: electronic gizmos and basketball. But last time there was a game on TV, he just sat on the couch without even shouting at the refs like he usually does. And when we were shopping for the servos and circuit boards I needed for this science fair project, he just didn't seem into it, and his face got really pale when it came time to pay for the order.

I sat down quietly and studied my hands for a while. I felt terrible because once again I had said something stupid and disappointed my Dad. There was nothing I could have done to make it better. The only option I had was to make it up to my Dad was to amaze the judges, get a scholarship, and move out after graduating high school in two years. To be honest, if the rest of the competition consisted of fantasies like antimatter reactors, I knew I had a decent chance of pulling it off.

After a very awkward hour of sitting between my disappointed father and my pissed-off neighbor, the judges showed up for their demonstration. The MIT professor was in that group, and he was kind of pudgy with wispy blonde hair. There were about ten other judges in boring suits that looked really uncomfortable in the heat of the lingering summer. There were a few spectators as well, mostly the parents of other exhibiters who followed the judges like pilot fish following sharks, probably hoping to pick up tidbits that indicate the current rankings. There was also one cute little girl with blond pig-tails playing with a Raggedy Ann doll who was tagging along after her mother.

The judges seemed really interested in the antimatter reactor blueprints. Even the guy from MIT asked a lot of questions, and they all took tons of notes, which meant that they were going to give it lots of points.

Then it was my turn. My palms got really sweaty and I started to feel a bit dizzy. The things I hate the most in the world are germs, followed by bugs and rodents, which carry a lot of germs. But public speaking is a close third. I have a hard enough time talking to people one-on-one, but when there's a crowd I end up doing really stupid things. I think my IQ is inversely proportional to the number of strangers who are listening to me. The bigger the group, the dumber I feel. And this was a big group.

"So, what have you got for us?" said the judge from MIT, and now every eye in the crowd was on me.

"A robot," I answered. I could see that this statement didn't make much of an impact. Half of everyone in the building had come equipped with some little gizmo that could walk or roll or change directions when it bumped into a wall.

"What makes my robot special is two things," I went on. "The first is that Rusty—that's my robot's name—can recognize its master and follow him or her around a room. The second thing is that Rusty can broadcast wireless electricity. That means when Rusty is around, you can run small appliances without having to plug them in."

That got a few of the judges to scribble some notes on their clipboards, but they weren't writing a lot. They needed a demonstration.

"Ladies and gentleman," I said as I gripped the corners of the cloth. "I give you... Rusty!"

The crowd gasped when I pulled back the cover to reveal my Rottweiler-sized metallic monstrosity. I had modeled the robot after a crab, but it came out looking more like a clockwork scorpion, with its eight piston-driven spider legs tensed at its side and its pincer-arms poised in front. Rusty's back was flat and segmented, mounted at the rear by a turret that terminated in a curved radar dish with a long spike protruding from the center. I had tried to make Rusty's head more friendly-looking by making it long and somewhat dog-like in appearance. I had even given him big, round, friendly eyes, but I think it may have turned out more menacing and predatory than I wanted, especially because those big eyes flickered red as they received LIDAR range-finding feedback from their surroundings.

Now I had everyone's rapt attention, but maybe not in a good way. Several of the judges were shaking their heads, perhaps thinking I had been too theatrical in my presentation. The little girl with pig-tails hid behind her mother's legs, her Raggedy Ann doll forgotten on the floor as she stared at the mechanical monster only a dozen steps away from her.

"Question," said the MIT judge. "Can you explain what you mean by 'wireless electricity' and why you would equip your robot with this feature?"

"Sure," I said, twisting the power knob at the control station. Rusty hummed to life, his limbs twisting and clicking through their initiation sequence. "It's based on an electromagnetic pulse—EMP for short. This electricity broadcasting is based on the work of Nikola Tesla, who invented the alternating current which runs every plug-in appliance in your home. Tesla was this amazing genius who wanted to broadcast wireless power all over the world, but he never could get funding because nobody could see how it would make money. Anyway, I'm doing it on a small scale and I figured it could be an energy savings if Rusty followed you around in your home. You know, so the lights would come on whenever the two of you entered a room and they'd turn off when you left. No more forgetting to flick the switch."

One of the other judges raised his hand. "You really think people would want that... that thing following them around in their houses?"

I'm not good with sarcasm or rhetorical questions, but I think that question was really meant to say that Rusty was ugly. That kind of hurt. I'd been working on this robot for years. If you noticed, I even call him a "him" instead of an "it," because to me he was a family pet. Whether you have a cat, a parakeet, or a robotic scorpion-dog, you still love your pet no matter what. You just can't help it.

I cleared my throat and moved on, hoping to get back to the important parts of my demonstration. "Rusty can navigate just about any terrain on his own, even climb trees and ladders. If you wear this tracking bracelet," I held up a black plastic strip about the size of a wristwatch. "Rusty will always follow you obediently wherever you go. Just watch."

For some seriously stupid reason, I picked the little girl for my demonstration. I don't know what I was thinking, except maybe I thought if that little girl could see Rusty as I saw him—a reliable and helpful companion—then maybe everyone else would see him that way, too.

I don't think the girl's mother realized what I was doing when I asked if I could put the bracelet on her daughter's wrist, but she said it was okay. The little girl didn't protest when I clicked it into place.

I returned to the controls and inched the power knob up to ten percent. Rusty hissed as his pistons drew his body up to standing, and the spiked turret on his back twitched. One clanking, growling step was all it took and that little girl screamed and ran. Rusty, following his programming, ran after her.

Rusty wasn't trying to catch her; he was only trying to stay two steps behind her wherever she went. The problem was that nobody, especially not the little girl, could see the difference. The girl and her mechanical pursuer careened through the aisles, first bowling through the crowd and then through the tables. Test tubes, telescopes, circuit boards, and all kinds of other expensive experiments smashed to the floor. One of the dads in the crowd lunged for my robot, but he only managed to knock over someone else, who fell against another person. Before I knew what was happening, half the crowd went down in a tangle of arms and legs.

Everybody was screaming. The girl started shrieking "Help! Mommy, Help!" but that only made things worse because Rusty is programmed to respond to verbal commands, and "help" means you need a hand up. When she said it, those two pincer-arms deployed, reaching out for her and snapping as they came.

The MIT judge was right in my ear, yelling at me to turn it off, but before I could reach for the power knob, another judge shouldered me out of the way and cranked the knob as far as it would go... in the wrong direction.

The thing about broadcasting electricity is that the electromagnetic pulse, the EMP, is the same thing that causes blackouts within a hundred miles of a nuclear bomb explosion. At lower power and at just the right frequencies, Rusty's EMP could run small electronics for short periods of time. Maybe it was a mistake to have fit Rusty with the most powerful Tesla coil I could make, because at maximum power it made the magnifying transmitter dangerous to anything with circuits or wires.

The moment the judge accidentally cranked the power to maximum, there was a bright flash overhead as the light bulbs in the ceiling burned out. On the tables all around us, dozens of experiments with electrical components burst into flame, and everyone within twenty feet of Rusty yelped in almost perfect unison as the cell phones in their pockets overheated. At the same instant, Rusty collapsed in place, a pathetic trail of smoke rising from his back, his battery fried by his own sudden output.

Most of the rest of the day passed in a blur. Thankfully, no one was hurt beyond a few minor burns and bruises. All the same, I got some mean looks from the students whose experiments I had ruined. The judges wouldn't talk to me, either, and the guy from MIT wouldn't even look at me—although I did see him talking with the antimatter kid for a long time.

I felt lower than the scavenging worms at the bottom of the Marianas Trench. Even for me, this was an unprecedented disaster. My experiment had even burned out some of the wiring in the gymnasium. My Dad, being an electrician, had negotiated to repair the gym himself, but it would probably take him days to do it, and that didn't cover the cost of all the cell phones and other electronic devices that were wrecked by the EMP. Here we were, so poor we couldn't afford anything but the crummiest of cell-phones, and now somehow we were going to have to pay to replace everybody else's high-end devices. I couldn't even look at my Dad all the way home.

The weird thing, the amazing thing, was that it turned out the science fair fiasco wasn't the most important thing to happen that day. When we got home there was a letter from the Mechanical Science Institute waiting for me.

I recognized the name of the Institute because about a month ago a professor named Denise McKenzie had sent me a get-to-know-you letter saying she wanted to look into scholarships for me. It seems my cousin Dean had told her about me, but I don't know what he said because I hardly knew him and the last time I saw him I think I was ten, back in the days when the whole family would get together for holidays sometimes. (I remember Dean because he stomped out the fire I accidentally started on the rug after rewiring the Christmas lights.) I guess he and my Dad must stay in touch a little, and my Dad must have bragged (or complained) about my inventions, and that's how word got out to Professor McKenzie.

Anyway, I didn't think much of the Mechanical Science Institute at the time. The letter said it was a special program at some school called Langdon University, which was located in the weirdly-named town of Bugswallow, Minnesota. I had never heard of it before, but I figured it couldn't hurt to look into it as one of my safety schools, so I sent Professor McKenzie the paperwork and copies of a few of my blueprints. Now I finally had her reply.

With a sigh, I decided my day couldn't get any worse, so I opened the official-looking envelope and pulled out the letter.

Dear Sophia Lazarchek,

I have reviewed your transcript, your personal statement, and, most importantly, your schematics. I am particularly impressed with your knowledge and implementation of Tesla's work with wireless electricity broadcasting. I regret that I will not be able to see your demonstration at the science fair, but I trust all will go well.

I am pleased to offer you enrollment in the Mechanical Science Institute with a full scholarship, including expenses for tuition, room, board, and books. Our classes begin on September 13th. I apologize for the short notice, but I hope you will join us this very year, as we are in need of a student with your skill set.

Sincerely,

Denise McKenzie

Professor Denise McKenzie
Dean of Students, Mechanical Science Institute

Chapter 4 ~ Dean

From his parked pickup, Dean took a moment to study the front door of the Ichiban Sushi Buffet while he wondered if he might be going crazy. McKenzie always had that effect on him. That fact, along with his desire not to spend the rest of his life twiddling his thumbs in some little cow-town as a professor's husband, was probably the reason why they had never been able to stay together. The trouble was, he was even worse off without her, and he knew it. There had been plenty of women in his life, but McKenzie was different. She was like a drug addiction, and withdrawal always left him empty and confused.

The first time she had dumped him, he had transferred from UCLA to the fire academy just to get away. The next time it was his turn to break it off, but that hadn't stopped him from needing to escape the pain again, so he joined the army and shipped out to the Middle East. When he returned, they got back together, but the long distance between their lives was too much to overcome. When they split up again, Dean crawled so far into a bottle that the chief had to give him a choice between the psychologist's office or the unemployment line. The thing that hurt Dean the most was that he knew each of these breakups wounded McKenzie just as deeply. Even when he got angry, he couldn't stand to see her in pain: anything that injured her felt like it hit him twice as hard. Over the years, their romantic collisions had left a lot of debris on the road behind them.

When he had seen her on the street yesterday, he had realized that he never wanted to lose her again. Still, he feared something was terribly wrong. She had seemed so distracted and worn down, and her request that he take over her job was both bizarre and worrisome. He didn't know what was happening, but he knew he wanted to be the guy who would save her from it.

After work, he had swung by the bank to open his safe-deposit box to retrieve his great-grandparents' wedding rings. *Damn the consequences,* Dean thought. McKenzie was the woman he would spend the rest of his life with.

The sushi buffet had just opened for lunch, but when he walked in he found that McKenzie was already seated in a booth with a good view of the parking lot so she could see him coming. They exchanged a deep, warm hug, and then sat down as she slid a plate of sushi across the table at him.

"You have to tell me what's going on," he said.

He watched as the conflict played out across her face. "You can't help with it. It's best you don't know."

"Dammit, why?" There was silence between the two of them. She looked like she wanted to answer, but when it became clear that she wouldn't, Dean went on. "This idea of yours," he said. "Me running your school? It's crazy."

"May I ask why you think so?" Now she was using her professor voice. It made her sound detached and objective, and Dean knew it would get him off track, just like always. He wanted to skip to his counter-proposal, but he decided he might as well show why her idea was a bad one before he brought up his own plan.

"Okay, for starters: why would you want me to take care of a bunch of college kids? I don't know anything about teaching or colleges or whatever it is you need me to do. Can't you find somebody else to pack their lunches and wipe their noses?"

"They need someone prepared for emergencies," she looked at the L.A.F.D. emblem on his blue t-shirt. "This group doesn't need someone with an advanced degree, they need someone to keep them from causing disasters. Don't sell yourself short: you're smart, and with your military and firefighting background you've got an honorary Ph.D. in disaster control as far as I'm concerned. Besides, it should only be for a few weeks. I didn't know I would need your help when I sent the offer to your cousin, but I thought with her there now, you might..."

He popped a salmon roll into his mouth and studied her while he chewed. "A few weeks?" he asked. "Where will you be during that time?"

"I have to take care of some business. There's a... professor. He wants something only I can find. But—never mind. I just need a few weeks to take care of it, and in the mean time I need you to watch over my students. Please."

"No dice," Dean said. "I'm going wherever you go. Besides, what do you expect me to do—lie on my résumé? In case you forgot, I don't have a lot of experience teaching biology or whatever it is you need me to teach."

"Don't worry about that," she shook her head. "It isn't necessarily a teaching position. I get sole discretion in naming my replacement. It's in our school charter. Here," McKenzie rummaged around in her handbag and produced a pen and an old pad of yellow sticky-notes. "I hereby name Dean Lazarchek as my replacement at the Mechanical Science Institute. Signed: Prof. Denise McKenzie," she wrote the words as she spoke them. "I'd prefer to write you a proper letter when we get some real paper, but this is all you really need."

"I'm still not taking the job," he said, handing the note back to her without even glancing at it. She folded his fingers closed around it and gestured that he should keep it anyway.

"You still haven't given me a good reason why not," she said.

"Because I've got a better idea," Dean looked right into her green eyes. "Let's get married."

"What?" She almost choked in surprise. "Are you crazy?"

"I'm serious. As long as you're running away, let's run together."

He looked at her hopefully as he produced the worn little box containing his great-grandmother's ring. The matching groom's band was in his pocket. He had hoped that they might wear them out of the restaurant.

"Do you want me to get down on one knee?" He realized her hands were shaking. And so were his.

"You know I can't," she said. "Especially not right now."

"I know you can. Especially right now."

She opened her mouth to say something but her words were cut off by the roar of an engine in the parking lot. Dean watched McKenzie's eyes as they widened first with recognition, then with fear.

Dean spun in his chair to see a huge motorcycle weaving its way through the lines of parked cars outside. The bike was glossy black and adorned with airbrushed skulls; its handlebars, muffler, and other chrome fixtures were lined with jagged spikes. The rear wheel had been modified to ride on two wheels instead of one, giving the machine a distinctive wedge-shape. On the enormous gas tank was stamped a huge, white swastika.

As big and as evil as this bike seemed, its rider was even bigger and meaner. He wore black, studded leather from head to foot, but wore no helmet to cover his scalp. It looked as though an avalanche of fat and muscle had started on top of his head and tumbled down his body, piling up around the ledge of his shoulders before spilling over to land in a heap at his midsection.

The biker was moving slowly through the parking lot, turning his head side to side to look at each car he passed. He paused by a silver

Lexus with Minnesota plates—McKenzie's car. Revving his engine twice, he put on a burst of speed and roared away.

McKenzie stood up so fast that she bumped the table, sloshing water out of her glass and onto their shared plate of sushi.

"What?" Dean said, also standing. "You know that guy? Is that—is that the guy you're running from?"

"I have to go."

He grabbed her by the wrist and held her until she looked into his eyes. "We go together from now on."

She shook her head. "First we need to get somewhere safe."

"My house." Dean said. It wasn't a suggestion, it was a statement.

"Okay, but... give me your keys. We're switching cars. You drive around for a while to throw them off. If they catch up to you, they'll see it isn't me and they'll leave you alone."

"They?" Dean repeated.

"I'll meet you back at your place. Hurry—before they come back."

Dean felt light-headed as he fumbled his fat key-ring out of his pocket while she shoved her electronic key-fob into his hand.

"Wait! What about this?" he lifted the box with the ring off the table and placed it in her hand.

"I—I'll think about it. Let's just get home first, okay?" She slid her hand around his neck and pulled him close for a hard, urgent kiss.

"One more thing," she whispered in his ear. "What they want is in our founder's head."

"...The founder's head? What're you talking about—"

She was already out the door. He followed her, each ducking into the other's car. They pulled out onto the three-lane arterial, she heading straight and he pulling a u-turn at the intersection.

Dean wanted to believe that the whole thing was crazy, but it wasn't like McKenzie to act irrationally. Why would she be running from that big biker? For that matter, why would she want him, of all people, to cover for her job? And what was that business about the founder's head?

He felt distracted and uncertain of what to do—until he glanced into his rear-view mirror and saw the huge man on the black motorcycle behind him. The danger, he could now see, was very real. He may not have understood why someone would be chasing McKenzie, but now all his worry and confusion fell away and in their place remained only clarity of purpose. He had to keep her safe, which meant he had to lead them away.

Dean slouched down in the seat to prevent his pursuer from recognizing that it was not McKenzie driving the car, and then he took a circuitous drive through the city streets. Before long, the big man peeled off and another black-clad biker picked up the pursuit in his place. The bikers, whoever they were, were taking turns shadowing him. They were pretty good at the tag-team pursuit, too. In other circumstances, Dean might not have noticed they were following him, even though they were not exactly inconspicuous individuals. He considered leading them to the police station, but he would have nothing to report—other than the big man's lack of a helmet, they weren't breaking any laws. As long as he had her car, he could make sure they didn't find her, so he kept luring them on, making sure they didn't lose him and yet not letting them get close enough to see his face.

Dean led his pursuers through the downtown streets for more than an hour. He had counted five different bikers by then, and the latest one was the most aggressive. Like the others, this biker rode a heavily customized but older-model motorcycle, but this one wore no shirt. He frequently navigated between cars at red lights to get closer and closer, until he was so near that Dean could see the large swastika tattoo over the left side of his chest.

Dean decided it was time to get a little more elusive. He made a sudden turn through a red light and then veered into a parking garage that he knew had an exit on the other side of the block. After he pulled through to the far street, he saw no more bikers behind him.

His impulse was to drive directly home to be with McKenzie, but he didn't want to risk it. Instead, he headed out towards the coastal highway, where the long narrow roads would expose any pursuers. Only after he was satisfied that he had lost his tail did he return home.

It was early evening by the time he pulled into his driveway, and he was relieved to see his big red truck awaiting him. Dean hopped out of the car and rushed to the front door, intending to throw it open and announce his victory. But when his hand touched the doorknob, his excitement evaporated. The door frame had broken away from the lock. Someone had kicked it in.

In a flash, Dean was inside. The house was dark and silent. When he flipped the switch, the lights didn't come on.

"McKenzie," he called. There was no answer. He called louder, but still there was no answer. He moved through the dining room hallway and found that the lights didn't work here, either. In the kitchen, the microwave and stove clocks were blank. *Power outage,* he thought, but when he looked out the window he saw that the neighbors had their back porch light on.

At the small kitchen table, he found one of the chairs had been overturned. A black suitcase was stashed neatly beside the other chair, and a laptop set up on the table. He concluded that these must be her things, which meant McKenzie had definitely been here. The question was: where had she gone?

He righted the chair and put it back in its spot and jabbed a few of the laptop's keys. The screen remained as dead as the lights, but he noticed a white pad of paper tucked underneath the computer. He pulled it out to find a note in her handwriting:

Dean,

They're coming. They're here. Whatever happens, I want you to know something.

My answer is yes. With all my heart, yes. I should have said it years ago.

McKenzie

Dean suddenly felt frantic. He must have failed to draw them away. They figured it out, and then they found her here, kicked in the front door, and cut the power somehow. But maybe it wasn't too late—if McKenzie had gotten away, then he could still find her before they do.

He looked around, desperate to find some clue as to where she might have gone. Then he saw something black and shiny on the second step of his staircase. It was one of her shoes. He ran past it, up the stairway to find her there, on the landing, halfway to the second floor. She was laying face down, one hand underneath her and the other resting limply beside her.

Desperately, he searched for a pulse and found none. He rolled her over and brushed her hair from her face to find her eyes open and staring.

Even as he began CPR, he knew, with the full weight of his professional experience, that it was too late. His futile rescue breaths would amount to nothing more than a goodbye kiss.

September 4th
(Doomsday minus 14 days)

CHAPTER 5 ~ SOAP

"I think you should reconsider that scholarship," my Dad said as he sat at the kitchen table paying bills. He was resting his forehead on his left palm like he always did when he balanced his checkbook.

I was zig zagging through the apartment with a hand-held version of the EMP broadcasting device. With one hand I adjusted the power level while with the other I kept the focusing dish aimed up at a miniature autogyro helicopter I had constructed from balsa wood pieces salvaged from a model airplane and the motor from an RC car. It flew pretty well, but whenever the autogyro got too high, it would lose its energy and begin to float down where it would come closer to my broadcaster. Then it would get its motor energized by the electromagnetic field I was broadcasting and would go zipping back up to the ceiling. Up and down, up and down in our tiny apartment. The challenge was that it would veer off in all sorts of directions, so I had to move constantly in order to keep the broadcaster directly beneath it. It was kind of like that old game with the rubber ball on the string that you're supposed to get in the cup, except here the rubber ball flies away on its own.

"I know it's short notice," my Dad went on. "But I think it would be a really good experience for you to go to that college."

"Seriously?" I asked, hopping to my right to stay beneath the autogyro. "I'm only sixteen. I'd never fit in at college. Plus, it doesn't seem fair that the only reason I got the scholarship is because my cousin was all smoochy-smoochy with the Dean of Students there."

"That's not why you got this scholarship," he said. "Soap, you have a gift—"

I couldn't hear what he said next because the autogyro veered off and I had to lunge to keep up with it, which made me knock over a floor lamp. The lamp fell with a cymbal-crash, and it made both of my Dad's autographed basketballs fall off their shelf and bounce to the other side of the room.

"Soap," I think my Dad tried to yell at me, but it came out more like a sigh of defeat.

"Sorry, Dad!" I said. "I just have to calibrate the amplifier and then I'll be done."

"I just feel like you might be happier there," he said. "This city is just too small for you."

"Dad," I scolded. "New York is as big as cities can get."

"That's not what I mean. This place is too confining. Too... closed-in. You need open air and empty fields where you can run around and play Frisbee and launch your rockets without raining fire back down on densely populated areas."

I smacked my shoulder into a wall trying to keep up with the autogyro. Aside from knocking the wind out of me, it took away any argument I might have made about not needing more space.

But I did have my reasons for not wanting to go. First, who ever heard of the Mechanical Science Institute? I was still hoping to get into some really well-known science program like MIT or Stanford or Georgia Tech, even though I had no idea how I could afford one of those big-name places. But the real reason I didn't want to go came down to this: I just didn't want to leave my Dad.

For five years now, it had been just him and me and the occasional cockroach living happily in this little apartment. Sure, I was planning on leaving after I graduated high school, but that gave me two more years to adjust to the idea. And now this woman from this crazy school wanted me to pack up and leave my entire life to travel a third of the way across the country with less than two week's notice. It sounded seriously mental. Thinking about it made me lose concentration on what I was doing and I accidentally cranked the power a bit too high. The autogyro's motor emitted a loud POP as it erupted into orange flames and zinged upwards in one last burst of speed. Trailing a line of black smoke, it ricocheted off the ceiling and streaked down onto the stack of bills my Dad was trying to pay. What can I say—my experiments always explode.

My Dad knocked his chair over as he jumped up in surprise. I was already on top of the mess, smothering the flames before they could spread too much. The only problem was that I pushed the papers off the table and they fluttered all over the place.

"Sorry, sorry!" I yelled, stooping to gather up the bills.

"Don't worry about that," he said a bit shakily. "Better shuffled than burned, I suppose."

I started reading the papers as I handed them to him. Water bill: first notice of overdue payment. Electricity: second notice. Rent: warning of eviction.

I unfolded the last one and started reading it.

"Soap, don't—don't read that," he said, but it was too late. I had seen enough.

"We're being evicted?"

My Dad was quiet a really long time. "Not until next month," he finally said. "Then we have 30 days to move out. Don't worry, we'll work out something."

"We're getting evicted and you tell me not to worry? What part of working out 'something' is supposed to make me feel better?"

He put his hands up in a gesture that told me to calm down, but we both knew the electrician job market was in the toilet right then, plus there was the matter of repairing the gym and replacing all those cell phones. All because of me.

I let him take the eviction warning out of my hands. He folded it up neatly and placed it on the stack, then absent-mindedly picked at the spot of charcoal where my autogyro had burned through the table's finish. I sat with my back against the wall and wrapped my arms around my knees.

"This seems like a good time for me to take the scholarship and move out," I said slowly. "Then you wouldn't have to keep paying for me and all my disasters."

"Don't go unless you want to," he said, sliding down to sit next to me, then putting his arm around my shoulders and drawing me in close. "Believe me when I say I don't want you to go if you're not ready. Actually, I don't want you to go ever. I've been dreading the day when you move out, you know. But, well, education is worth any sacrifice."

It wasn't until then that I realized my leaving would be as hard on him as it was on me. Then I imagined him having to live in his van for the rest of his life, which is what would happen if he had to keep paying for my housing, food, and collateral damage. It was only fair that I accept my exile to make up for my mistakes.

Look out, college—here I come.

Chapter 6 ~ Dean

When the knock came on his broken door, Dean was laying on the couch in the darkened front room, his left hand clutching the two slips of paper that McKenzie had left him. He wasn't sure if he had been asleep or awake, which was how he had felt throughout the past two days as the police had crawled all over his house and grilled him with questions. When he had arrived for his next shift, the station chief took one look at him and sent him home on sick leave. That was probably best, because Dean was having trouble concentrating. He kept remembering McKenzie's face at the moment he found her, with her wide-open eyes and the orange hair against her blue cheeks. The memory was tearing him up.

"Whatever you're selling," Dean called to whoever was on his porch. "I'm not buying any."

"Mr. Lazarchek," said his one of his visitors. "We're with the FBI. I'm Agent Brian Nash and my partner is Agent O'Grady. May we come in? I'd like to ask you a few questions about Professor McKenzie."

Dean rubbed his eyes and stood up. His limbs felt stiff and heavy as he went to let them in. One was a short black man with close-cropped hair, a pleasant smile, and a tired look in his eyes. The other was older, maybe in his fifties, with gray-white hair combed straight back and a hard, trim physique that made him look as if his body had been stamped from boiler-plate steel. Both wore matching black suits.

"Your door is broken," Nash said.

Dean just nodded. Right then, he didn't care if it ever got fixed, but he wasn't ready to admit that to a stranger.

"And the room is dark," Nash observed.

"Everything's dark." Dean meant it metaphorically, but it was also literally true of his house. Every light bulb, appliance, and electrical socket had burned out.

The older agent stood by the door while Nash pulled up a seat across from Dean.

"Mr. Lazarchek, I'm sorry for what happened to your girlfriend."

"She was my fiancé," Dean muttered. Somehow, calling her a girlfriend seemed to undervalue his history with McKenzie. A girlfriend might have been someone he knew for a day, but she had been so much more than that. He wanted to argue the point, but decided he didn't have the strength. Besides, the note McKenzie had left wouldn't prove anything to anyone other than himself.

Nash cleared his throat and began again. "According to the autopsy, the cause of Professor McKenzie's death was her pacemaker. It shorted out."

Dean just nodded. Considering the state of his household electronics, he had guessed that the same thing had happened to her. But medical implants like her pacemaker would never simply short out on their own. They were too carefully designed and too rigorously tested. What had happened to McKenzie had not been an accident. Someone had shorted out her heart along with his entire house and then kicked open his front door to make sure the job was complete.

"I'd like to ask you a question, if you don't mind," Agent Nash slid a series of photos out of a brown envelope. "Do any of these men look familiar to you?"

One by one, Agent Nash showed him mug shots of men with facial tattoos, missing teeth, and long, unkempt beards. Dean studied each one and shook his head—until the last photo. His hand froze as he held the image of a man who filled the picture in front of him.

"This one," Dean said. "I saw him the day McKenzie came to find me. She looked at him... it was like she recognized him and she was afraid."

The two agents exchanged a meaningful glance.

"We believe that the man you saw is Morton Hendrix, better known by any of a dozen aliases, including 'Brick.' He is a member of a gang known as the Blitzkrieg Legion, AKA the Blitzkriegers. He is also a person of interest in a series of armed bank robberies."

"A 'person of interest,'" Dean repeated. "You mean he's a suspect?"

"He is a person of interest," Nash said flatly. "His associates are also of interest in the same crimes. Did Professor McKenzie ever speak of Brick? Or did she mention anything that might relate to the Blitzkriegers?"

Dean shook his head. None of it made sense. Why would she have had anything to do with a biker gang? And yet, she must have. For whatever reason, she had been running from that giant of a man and his friends. And it seemed she hadn't run fast enough.

Still, a man as big as Brick could have just snapped McKenzie's neck. Why go to the trouble of burning out electrical circuits? Then again, the courts might convict a man of inflicting a broken neck, but not for inflicting a heart attack. It meant there might not be justice for McKenzie. As he thought about it, Dean's hands tightened into fists.

The FBI agents thanked Dean, collected their photos, and departed. He was free to return to his numbness, but now he found himself unable to do so. McKenzie had been murdered, he was certain of it. What was more, he had seen the face of her killer, or at least the face of someone involved in the killing.

Dean had no answers for who killed McKenzie but at least he was beginning to get an idea of what he needed to do. He took out the two pieces of paper she had left him, the note accepting his proposal and the sticky-note that indicated he could have her job.

He hated himself for failing to save her, but he still had a chance to do something to help the woman he had loved. Her last wish had been for him to protect her students. Maybe, while he was at this institute of hers, he could find out who did this to her and settle the score.

September 10th
(Doomsday minus 7 days)

CHAPTER 7 ~ SOAP

We couldn't afford a plane ticket, so I had to travel to Minnesota by train. That meant while people my age had already been in school for half a week back home, I was on a long, lazy trip aboard the oldest mode of mass transportation still available in this country. It promised to be seriously boring.

My problem was that I was going a little crazy without anything to work on. I wanted to tinker with Rusty, but he had to be locked away with all my tools in the baggage car. My Dad insisted that shipping him in a sealed trunk was the only way we could afford to get him out there. My Dad was probably just worried that if I had access to my tools and my robot then we would end up terrorizing the other passengers. I have to admit, he was probably right.

I had nothing to do but sit there and stew about what my life would be like when I got to the university. I had received a letter that the Dean of Students had died unexpectedly and a selection committee had been established to find a replacement. I was sad to hear about the death even though I didn't know Professor McKenzie. It also made me paranoid that whoever took over might come to their senses and revoke my acceptance letter. But the thing I was most scared of was how I would get along with the other students.

To get my mind off it, I tried passing the time by drawing up blueprints for an improved railway system. After all, we'd been using the same basic locomotive design for a century and a half, so I figured there was room for improvement. I wanted to do some research, but the conductor wouldn't let me see the engine, and he didn't really seem interested in my ideas to upgrade the power source from diesel fuel to a nuclear reactor, let alone to consider my proposal for using supercon-ducting tracks to levitate the train via magnetic repulsion.

My Dad had said that train travel is unique in today's world because you have a chance to get to know your fellow travelers and form a sort of community-in-motion. I'm pretty sure he was just saying that to make me feel better, because the community aboard the train really didn't give me much to work with. For starters, all the passengers were old people, except when they were little children travelling with old people. Also, the only thing I ever heard them talk about was how much they felt safer in trains than in planes, as if they had to justify their choice of travel out loud at least once per mile-post. It made me wonder if airplanes were full of people who started conversations by announcing that they preferred not to be on rails.

After I got bored watching the unending miles of green pas-tures clickety-clacking past my window, I finally decided to try making friends with someone. In the crowded dining car, the waiter sat me next to this old lady who asked me where I was going then told me how wonderful it was for a young woman such as myself to be getting an education so that I could attract a better quality husband. I tried to tell her that I wanted to go to college to study robotics rather than hus-bands, but didn't think she would understand. Then she started telling me how trains were safer than airplanes.

"Trains are also dangerous," I said. "Statistics say that air-planes have fewer accidents." I wasn't trying to be rude, but I hadn't said much in the conversation and I was worried she might start to think I wasn't paying attention.

"Well, they may have fewer accidents, dear," she said with a grandmotherly smile. "But if anything goes wrong in a plane, you fall right out of the sky."

"If something goes wrong on a train," I said. "You're still trapped in a hurtling steel tube charged with enough momentum to disintegrate all the bones in your body at the instant of impact."

Her face kind of turned white and she stopped talking after that. I immediately hated myself for saying such horrible things to her. It also made me even more afraid of how I would get along with college kids, because they might not be as nice to begin with.

I slunk back to my seat in the regular car, got down my backpack, and dug out one of my black hoodies. It wasn't my favorite hoodie, but it was warm and let me pull something over my eyes. If I could concentrate on my designs for long-distance magnetic levitation trains, then I wouldn't have to think about people. People were far too complicated and confusing.

I woke up when we came to a stop in a tiny town somewhere west of Fort Wayne, Indiana. The hood was still over my eyes, but I could hear a few passengers moving around. Then a scent of body odor assaulted my nose. I pulled back my hood to see the worst creeper I have ever laid eyes on, even including all the times I rode the 2 train back to Flatbush after dark.

This guy had a scruffy beard, but only a thin layer of stubble to mark the hairline on his scalp. He wore dirty jeans and scuffed motorcycle boots, but his thin torso and sinewy arms were completely bare except for a few lank chest hairs and some fading blue tattoos of mean-looking wolves and buzzards. On the left side of his chest, right over his heart, was a big swastika tattoo that looked darker and bolder than the rest.

The other passengers seated in my car looked away as the shirtless guy passed by. He studied each of them before moving on. Then his eyes fixed on me, and his mouth opened in a leering smile.

Two of his yellow teeth were missing, but it didn't really matter because he was already at maximum ugliness.

I pressed back as far as I could go in my seat, but there was no getting away from him.

"I got a present for ya," he said in a raspy voice as he slid his hand down his naked belly towards his pants.

I wanted to scream but no noise came out of my throat. Then his hand completed its disgusting journey into his pants and he pulled out... a cell phone.

"A gift from the P'fessor," he said as he dropped the phone in my lap. To my relief, three conductors entered the car and told the shirtless guy to get lost. As he disembarked, he noisily accused the conductors of being tools of an oppressive government.

"Are you all right, Miss?" the oldest of the three conductors asked me. It was the same guy who hadn't let me into the engine room, but suddenly I liked him a whole lot better than I did before.

I nodded that I was okay, but I didn't feel alright. I was shaky and light-headed, and my stomach was queasy. It was such a weird incident and it had happened so fast that I couldn't figure it out. It sure looked like he had come on the train just to find me. But why me?

I looked down at the phone in my hand. It was a really top-of-the-line one, the kind me and my Dad would never be able to afford. It was sleek, black, and didn't have any physical buttons because its entire face was a touch screen. Just when I was starting to figure out how to take off the cover to get a look inside, the phone buzzed.

I froze for a moment, not sure if I wanted to answer it. I really didn't want to hear the shirtless guy's rasping voice ever again, but it didn't seem like the kind of phone that would belong to him. Maybe he had stolen it and its owner was calling to get it back. Maybe there was some other reason I couldn't think of, and I would never find out if I didn't pick up. Curiosity once again overpowered my better judgment as I clicked the "answer" button and lifted it to my ear.

"Hello, Sophia," said a man's voice.

I just about dropped the phone when I heard my name. "Who... who is this?"

"You may call me the Professor," the voice answered. He sounded really mellow, like a radio announcer for a classical music station.

"What's the deal with this phone?" I asked. "Why are you calling me?"

"I wanted to congratulate you on your scholarship."

"Are you a teacher at the Institute?" I asked. "What was your last name again?"

"I am no longer with the Institute," he said. "I do, however, have a vested interest in helping your school as well as its students. I thought I might offer you an extra scholarship package on top of the one you have already received. If you're interested."

"Extra scholarship?" I echoed. "I'm already getting a full ride plus room, board, and books. How much extra could there be?"

"Let's say, ten thousand dollars. Cash."

My jaw went numb and kind of just sagged open for a moment.

"Sophia?" he said. "Sophia, are you there?"

Finally, my brain started working again. "I'm not camwhoring or anything," I stated. "I don't care how much you offer."

"No, no, nothing like that," the Professor laughed. "All I need you to do is some extra research for me. Think of it as a work-study program. Is that acceptable?"

"For ten thousand dollars?" I said. "What kind of thing do you want me to research?"

"This research can only be conducted with Institute resources," he said. "I will let you know the exact details when you get there. Well, what do you say, Sophia? Will you take on this little project?"

My mind was racing, but I couldn't see any harm in some extra work-study research. If it turned out to be something like designing bio-weapons or engineering flying monkeys, I would just quit.

"Okay, sure," I said. "But only under one condition. Don't give the money to me. I want you to give it to my Dad. In New York."

"Easily done. I'll proceed with the arrangements to pay him in advance while I pull together the details about what I want you to do for me. In the mean time, enjoy your new phone. I look forward to working with you, Sophia."

I hung up, hardly able to believe my luck. Inside of ten minutes, I had been given a new phone and a student job that paid better than some people's careers. I could save my Dad's apartment and repay all the damages I'd caused over the years.

I called my Dad and told him that I was having a present sent to him but that it would be a surprise. I only wished I could be there to see his face when he got the money. Then I settled into my seat and started downloading apps onto my phone. It turned out that the train had a really strong Wi-Fi connection, which suddenly made it my favorite mode of transportation in the world.

September 12th
(Doomsday minus 5 days)

CHAPTER 8 ~ DEAN

Everybody told Dean he was being an idiot to walk away from the station house in Los Angeles to go play school teacher in Minnesota. He agreed, but he couldn't stop himself. Something was broken inside him, and he knew that it would never be fixed until he carried through.

Now, Dean sat outside the president's office at Langdon University. It seemed like all he had done for the past week was sit. Sitting in his car as he drove the long highways from California to Minnesota. Sitting in diners and motel rooms, all the while thinking that McKenzie asking him to work here was really a secret code for something else, but he couldn't work out what. Sitting in this office, waiting for his application to be laughed at.

Coming here and following through was the only thing he had, so he had applied for the position. The only thing he hoped to achieve was... what? He wasn't sure he knew any more. It constantly nagged at him that there was nothing to show that she and he had shared any meaningful connection. Aside from a few police reports, there was nothing on paper to link the two: no marriage license, no common address, not even a joint magazine subscription. He hadn't even been invited to the funeral. At this point, if just one person acknowledged his commitment to McKenzie then he might have been able to give up this whole crazy idea, go back to Los Angeles, and take the "for sale" sign off his house.

So far, reality had not been so kind: they took him seriously.

His application, such as it was, had been rubber-stamped by the Langdon University president in record time, and here he was, wearing his old interview suit and sitting in the foyer of the president's office, clutching McKenzie's handwriting sticky-note instead of a résumé.

Dean fiddled with the engagement rings he had hung from a chain around his neck while he waited for the receptionist to give him permission to enter the big office. It never came. Instead, Langdon University's president came out to greet Dean where he sat. President Hart was a tall, thin man whose receding hairline revealed an angular head reminiscent of a breadbox. He extended a bony hand towards Dean as two students bearing oversized cameras snapped pictures with blinding flashes.

"I hope you don't mind the photos," he said as he pulled Dean in close for a well practiced pose. "These students are here on behalf of the yearbook. You know—a day in the life of the president, that sort of thing. You don't mind, do you, Doctor Lazarchek? Oh—I'm sorry—it's just *Mister* Lazarchek, isn't it?" He re-positioned Dean for another picture, this time with the president pointing at some of the plaques on the wall as though he were explaining their long and storied history to a fascinated guest. Dean just blinked and tried to see through the lightning-bright camera flashes.

"I can see the caption now," Hart said as he settled a hand on Dean's shoulder and cycled through a few more poses. "It will say: 'President Hart and the new Dean of Students of the Mechanical Science Institute.' That will play nicely, don't you think?"

Before Dean's eyes cleared of the flashes, President Hart dismissed the photographers and led Dean into the office, deposited him on a leather sofa in the corner, and shut the heavy oak door behind him.

"Of course, this was no accidental double-booking with you and the photo shoot," Hart said as he took a seat behind his broad desk.

"I needed some evidence that I supported you in every reasonable way so that I'll be in the clear when this scheme of yours falls apart."

Dean stared blankly. "I don't think I follow you, sir."

"It's all about appearances, Mr. Lazarchek. Politics to appease the board of directors and give our lawyers some ammunition when I move to close the Institute."

"What?" Dean felt as if he'd been sucker-punched.

"Mr. Lazarchek," Hart laced his fingers together and leaning forward on his desk. A framed photo of him in the same pose hung on the wall behind him. "Let me be frank: You do not belong here. You flunked out of college and now you think you can run one?"

"Well, sir, technically I didn't flunk out. I transferred to the fire academy."

"Laughable. Perfectly laughable. Logically, the only reason you are here right now is because you want money."

Dean's fist balled up. "Look, Mr. Hart—"

"President Hart," he said, smiling as if they were discussing baseball scores over Sunday brunch. "I will also accept Doctor Hart, if you prefer."

"Look, Doctor: you're wrong. This job pays half what I got as a firefighter. I assure you, it isn't about the money."

"I'm not talking about your salary, Mr. Lazarchek. I'm talking about the Institute's endowment. You will be controlling a budget of millions of dollars, but I'm sure you already knew that."

Dean could feel his own eyes bug out of his head. "Millions?" He said stupidly. He was supposed to be a glorified baby-sitter here. Nobody said anything about managing a seven figure budget.

"Let me warn you that even as we speak, the professor who served as Dean of Students prior to Dr. McKenzie is rotting in jail for attempted embezzlement. If you try anything, if you misappropriate so much as a single Bunsen burner, I'll have you behind bars so fast you won't have time to zip up your orange jumpsuit. Do I make myself clear?"

"Look, Mr—Dr. Hart, I understand your concern. A million is a lot of money—"

"Not a million. Millions. Plural. Tens of them, maybe even a hundred, but I wouldn't know because, according to the agreement we made when Langdon University absorbed the Institute, we don't get to audit your budget in any way. That's a pretty tempting situation for crooks like you. Don't deny it and don't play dumb with me—you aren't smart enough to play dumb."

Dean stood up abruptly. "However much is there, it doesn't matter. I'm here because it was the last thing McKenzie—Professor McKenzie—asked me to do. If you don't believe me now, I don't give a damn, because, sir, I'm doing this for her and not for you."

Dr. Hart leaned back in his broad, brown leather chair and thrummed his fingers on his broad, brown wooden desk. He watched Dean for a long minute of appraisal. Then the thin skin around his mouth tightened into a sly smirk.

"Have I misjudged you, Mr. Lazarchek?" he said in a neutral tone.

"I think you have, sir."

"If so, I hope you will forgive me. I am trying to do what is best for this university. I need to consider all the political ramifications. That is my job. You can understand that, can't you?"

Dean nodded cautiously and slowly sank back into his chair.

"You have a big job, and not much help," Hart's tone had changed now. A moment ago it had been icy and cutting. Now he sounded patronizing and slick. "Yes, indeed, you have a lot of responsibility. One misstep and you could end up damaging the lives of a great many young people. You don't want that, do you? Many eyes will be watching you, Mr. Lazarchek. I won't always be able to protect you. On the other hand, you could sign the endowment over to me for safe keeping. Then you would ensure that the prosperity of the university is entrusted in the hands of a dedicated educator."

"President Hart," Dean leaned forward. "I'm no con man, but I can still smell a con job when I step in it."

Hart frowned, then sighed. "Mr. Lazarchek, come join me at the window."

They moved to the panoramic window. Back in L.A., the views Dean had seen overlooked nothing but concrete and asphalt. Here, human-made constructs seemed to be an afterthought nestled in a continent of tranquil glades and flat green fields. Last night's rain left everything sparkling, as though the leaves of the trees and the eaves of the buildings were dotted with glinting diamonds. The sky above was scintillatingly bright and fresh, and with a jolt Dean realized that it was completely unfiltered by smog. Though it boggled his Californian mind, cars were allowed only as far as the parking lots on the outskirts of campus, while all the paths inside were carefully preserved for pedestrians and cyclists.

As he looked out at the green grass and red bricks of the campus, Dean began to connect real-life buildings with the positions on the little map he had picked up at the student union building. He spotted the library, built at the edge of a small valley so that students entered on the top floor. Then he recognized the psychology building with its 1960s avant-garde architecture and the monstrous and languid Humanities building, made out of chalky red bricks and wrought-iron embellishments, all liberally strewn with bright green ivy. To the west, the flags of the field house and football stadium winked at him through the trees.

"Do you see the Institute, Mr. Lazarchek?" Hart asked. "It's located at Topsy House, off behind that grove, there."

Dean knew that Topsy was the one and only building belonging to the Mechanical Science Institute, but he had not yet laid eyes on it. Even with Hart pointing it out, he had to search for it in the distance. First, he found the north parking lot, which students used least often because it was the farthest away from other classrooms. Just beyond that point, there rested a flat building with white columns and a set of steps wide enough to do justice to any courthouse in the country. The trees screened most of the building, and from ground level it would have been difficult to find were it not for the clock tower that projected sixty or seventy feet into the air.

"Your Institute consists of that one building," Dr. Hart said. "In itself, Topsy is certainly not intrusive. It is meant to hold thirty-three students and three professors—those are the numbers spelled out in the Institute's charter endowment. Thirty-three and three. But right now it consists of three students and you. A very small academy wouldn't you agree?"

"If you say so."

"Think of all that money going to support such a small handful of students. What I propose to do, Mr. Lazarchek, is to bring the two schools together. Merge them. We can use the Mechanical Science Institute endowment to expand the sciences for our other students. We could build new classrooms to serve three hundred young minds instead of your thirty-three. The board of directors would be very appreciative of such an arrangement."

"And you would be the man who got it for them."

"That's right. You and I together."

"How is that different from embezzling? Seems to me like you're still trying to steal Institute money for personal gain."

President Hart's face went so tight that it looked as if his cheekbones were about to cut through his translucent skin.

"This is a political situation, Mr. Lazarchek. You need to know that I am empowered to absorb your school if you don't increase student enrollment."

"Sure, no problem," Dean said. "How many students do we need to add?"

"Three. Each quarter you must add three students until you are at your full complement. You must also find professors for all the positions by the end of the year. Do you understand?"

"Sure. Got it. I just need to go find some students and some teachers."

"No, I don't think you understand. Your institute already has a bad reputation. You won't be able to get the caliber of students you want, which means you must decide between losing your enrollment and offering admission to every meathead who wants a ride in college. If you pick the latter, your institute will lose its essence. Professor McKenzie saw that—she was ready to gamble the existence of the school rather than flood Topsy with students who don't belong."

"Don't you worry," Dean said. "I'll make McKenzie proud."

"Oh, I'm not worried. I'm delighted. You don't think I could have challenged your little post-it note? You think that would have held up in court? If I had pressed the issue, your claim would have been tossed out with a laugh. Just like you. I could have picked whomever I wanted to sit as Dean of Students, but I could never have found anyone so perfectly unqualified as you. You will be the death of the Institute. As far as I'm concerned, your girlfriend couldn't have selected a better candidate."

"She wasn't just my girlfriend," Dean's voice was low. "She was my fiancé."

"I don't care if she was your circus clown," Hart said. "Think about my offer: turn over the Institute to me and I'll take better care of your students than you could possibly manage."

Dean let it hang in the air like a storm cloud. His fingers rose to his neck to grip the engagement rings until they dug into his palm. Dr. Hart, he had decided, was a sleazebag, but that didn't mean he was wrong. Dean couldn't disagree: he really was unqualified, and he stood every chance of wrecking the school that McKenzie had cared so much about.

Hart disappeared into the outer office, leaving Dean alone with his thoughts. He stared out the window at Topsy. It seemed like he had to pick between giving in and relinquishing the Institute, or muscling through and probably destroying it. While thinking this over, he saw, away in the distance, that someone was arriving at Topsy's broad white steps. Three figures. And they were all riding motorcycles.

From what Dean had heard, the members of the Institute were a bunch of mild-mannered science nerds. Low-rider choppers seemed a little out of character for them. And the lead figure, even from this distance, looked like he dwarfed the other two.

Dean snatched the telescope that was propped in front of the window. Through the eye piece, the world seemed to swim crazily from blurry greens to blurry blues until he could focus it and find the white steps of Topsy House. Panning down and to the left, he could see the three men, all with shorn scalps and black leathers. Then the big guy turned around, and Dean recognized the face of the man called Brick.

Dean uttered a word that had probably never been spoken in the president's office and rushed out the door.

Chapter 9 ~ Soap

The cab took me from the train station to the airport, where there was a freshmen-only shuttle waiting to take new arrivals to Bugswallow. I wore my best hoodie for the occasion, the one with silver, thorny rose vines entwining a steel-plated skull. My hope was that it would make me look a little older to the other students. Two years might not seem like a big deal on paper, but in real life a sixteen-year-old and an eighteen-year-old might as well have been aliens from different planets. They could vote and I couldn't. They had driver's licenses and I didn't. They had even graduated from high-school and I had technically dropped out to come here. Everybody's supposed to be nervous when they go off on their own for the first time, but I felt like I had a better reason than most.

They came in groups of twos and threes, chattering away with each other. I could always recognize the Bugswallow students because each of them clutched a goldenrod sheet of paper sent from the college to explain where to go once they got to campus. I held my paper at my side, not because I needed it but because I thought the others might see it and come talk to me. They didn't.

Once we got underway, a girl named Hannah started going around talking to every single person on the bus. She was tall and skinny and wore a blue and white Langdon University sweater, a blue skirt, and white tennis shoes. Her hair was a rich, coppery-blond that was done up in blue and white ribbons, and she looked like she was one pair of pom-poms away from running down to the football field to cheer on our team. I knew her name was Hannah because she introduced herself to everyone there, starting with the bus driver and working her way back, seat by seat. She was really good at breaking the ice: she might say "I like your hair" to one person, and "What are you listening to? Oh, you have great taste in music" to the next person. It made everybody like her. It made me wish I could be her.

I was sitting at the very back of the bus, so before she got to me I had time to think about the pattern she used to strike up these conversations. I decided that if I could figure out how she did it, then maybe I could do the same thing. If I had a system for speaking to people, an algorithm for making friends, then my life might suddenly get a lot better. I took out a notepad and continued to eavesdrop.

Hannah would always begin with a compliment and then move on to ask what dorm room the person had been assigned. She would nod enthusiastically as her subject responded, and sometimes she would pull out her goldenrod paper and the two of them would find it on the map together. The final stage of the conversation confused me until I realized it broke down along gender lines. When talking to girls, Hannah would ask if they knew of any upcoming parties. When talking to boys, she would ask them what sports they played. Finally, regardless of gender, she suggested a joint activity to be done in the future, such as "we should go to a party together some time," or "we should go shopping together some time." For the boys, it was usually "you should invite me to a game some time." I also noticed that she spent the longest time with the boys who expressed interest in football, wrestling, or baseball, but I decided that might have been her personal preference and not a necessary factor in the algorithm.

I thought it was such a good system that I made a flowchart, just in case I met more new people later. I titled it the "conversation matrix."

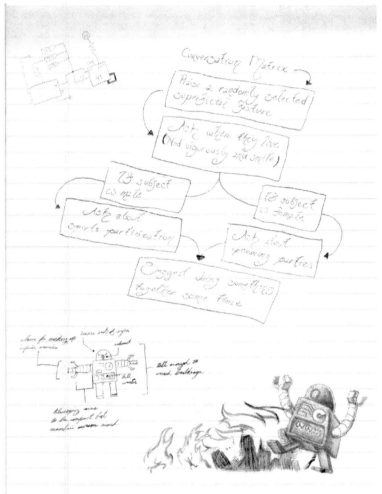

"Hi, I'm Hannah," she said as she swung into the empty seat next to me. "Hey, that's a really nice..." she had to pause for a half a second. It was enough time for me to get worried. Was I the only person on the entire bus she couldn't find a compliment for?

"That's a nice sweatshirt," she finally said. "I like all the roses. I've never seen them go so well with... skulls."

She smiled and showed off teeth that looked professionally whitened, which made her look even more like a plastic Barbie doll than ever.

"I'm Soap," I said, returning her smile as best I could. Then I got nervous and had the sudden urge to show her that I'd been paying attention, so I blurted out the rest of the flow-chart in one go: "You have nice teeth; I'm living in Smiley Dorm; where are you living?; I'm not really interested in parties; we should go find some parties together some time."

I think I went too fast. Hannah just kind of blinked at me for a few seconds while she processed what I had said. But she kept smiling.

"That's...Nice?" She finally uttered. "Wait—did you say you'll be living in Smiley?"

"Leonidis Smiley Dormitory, Room 414," I nodded. "And I already know where it is, but you can show me on the map if you want."

Her smile disappeared for just a second when I said that. "Oh, my goodness. I'm in Smiley 414, too. That makes us... roommates." Then she looked me over really closely, like I was a research grant proposal. "What are you going to be studying?"

I wanted to tell her she was straying from her own conversational pattern, but I decided to trust that she knew what she was doing. Perhaps this was a special question reserved for roommates.

"I'm studying Physics," I said.

"Physics?" she curled up her tiny little nose when she said it, as if the word smelled like dead worms. "Like with math and stuff?"

"Almost always," For some reason, her question really annoyed me.

"That's interesting," she said, but she excused herself pretty quickly after that and went back to the front of the bus to sit in the middle of a group of guys wearing t-shirts with sports team logos.

That was fine with me, because it gave me time to think. Here was another conversation I had messed up, and with my own roommate, no less. That brought my success rate up to a whopping zero percent. Not a good start.

Since I obviously wasn't going to have any luck with the people on the bus, I turned to look out the window. It was a different world out there from what I was used to. Here, the landscape was completely flat, like someone had run a razor over it and scraped away everything except for smooth, green patches with the occasional tufts of trees or clumps of houses. And then there were the lakes. No wonder they called this state the "land of ten thousand lakes." I timed it on my watch and found that, on average, we passed 3.2 lakes every ten minutes, which means about one lake every three miles or so. They weren't big, deep bodies of water, though. These lakes were little divots in the landscape, as if some titan had bounced all over the countryside on a gigantic pogo stick, poking irregular holes wherever he landed and the holes later filled up with rainwater. I've noticed that wealthy people always like to build houses as close to water as they can, but out in Minnesota there was enough water that every family could afford a natural swimming pool in their backyard. It started me thinking that if lakes raised property values, then it might be very profitable to design a lake-building device. I started picturing a sort of drilling machine that would grind up dirt at its front, spit it out the side, and lay concrete behind it as it moved.

I didn't get too deep into this design before my attention was captured by an amusement park only a few miles off the freeway. I could see the brightly colored Ferris wheel and the tops of other rides protruding above the decorated walls. In the very center of the park was some kind of huge tower built with thick railings leading up to a hemispherical dome at the top. It looked kind of like a radio tower crossed with a Van de Graaff generator, which are those things at science museums that make peoples' hair stand on end. As I looked at the park a little while longer I realized that something else was weird: nothing was moving. All the rides were still, all the lights were off, and the big black parking lot out front was deserted.

"Awesome," I heard a boy in the seat ahead of me say. "Check it out: an amusement park."

"Nah," said his friend. "That's Happy Fun Land. I Googled it: they closed, like, two years ago. They dumped all their money into some big ride and then went bankrupt."

I was a bit disappointed to hear that, because I thought it might be fun to have a whole amusement park so close to school. It looked like the kind of place that had cotton candy and skee ball, and that sounded a lot better than the only other form of entertainment in the region, which I was ready to bet involved watching cows graze. Just to confirm what the kid in front of me had said, I dug around in my backpack and found my goggles.

Next to Rusty, my goggles are my favorite invention. They look a little too weird to wear in public because they have external sensors, antennas, and rotating lens packs, but they're all kinds of useful because they can detect transmissions from outside the visible spectrum. For now, I only wanted the zoom feature, so I slipped them on, dialed in maximum magnification, and cupped my hands around the side of my face, as much to hide my goggles from everyone else as to cut down on the glare.

I could see that the big tower in the center must have been the ride that had bankrupted the park. Judging from my rangefinder, it was about 200 feet tall, and it had a big sign on it that said "The Doomsday Machine." It must have been one of those rides that brought its passengers—or should they be called victims?—up to the very top and then dropped them like lead weights. Too extreme for my tastes, but some people love that kind of stuff.

I panned down to get a look at the rest of the park. Sure enough, there were no people anywhere. A chain-link fence ran the full length of the park just outside the decorated wall. Here and there along the fence were red signs that I couldn't read (the zoom doesn't give me great resolution), but it was pretty clear they said something to the effect of: GO AWAY. NO SKEE BALL FOR YOU.

I put away my goggles just in time for everyone to suddenly start murmuring about a road sign out the bus's right window. I was on the left side of the bus, so I had to get out of my seat to see it. In blue, old-fashion letters like the kind you might have painted above an old-west saloon, the sign said: WELCOME TO BUGSWALLOW. POPULATION 16,147. It looked exactly as classy as it possibly could while depicting a big, fat housefly buzzing in circles over a swamp.

The sign was a good thing because it meant we were almost there. Still, I was a bit disappointed. I wanted there to be some explanation of the town's name. I mean, who comes up with a name like that? This sign was the best chance the residents had to justify themselves with a catchy town slogan like "With a name like ours, we've got to be good" or "we already swallowed all the bugs, so you don't have to." I was at least hoping for an explanation of whether it was supposed to be Bug-Swallow or Bugs-Wallow.

Twenty minutes later, the bus crunched its way along the gravel road into the college's east parking lot. People started getting off, finding their luggage, and heading out to look for their dorms. My plan was a little different. I would drop my stuff off in my room in Smiley, but there was something else I had to do before I could get settled in. I pulled out a card that had been mailed separately from the university's registration information. All it said was:

Welcome to the Mad Science Institute

Please join us September 12th, 5pm at

Topsy House.

Pizza Provided.

CHAPTER 10 ~ DEAN

In his rush to exit the administration building, Dean bowled through the heavy wood and glass doors with such force that he almost knocked over a student who was chaining his bicycle to the rack.

Here on ground level, Topsy was almost totally screened by the trees and intervening buildings. Dean was only just getting a feel for the layout of campus, but he figured it was half a mile away, probably more. It would take him at least four minutes to get there at a run, and that was too long.

"Let me borrow your bike," Dean said to the student. The kid, a skinny little mole of a teenager with soda-bottle glasses, froze in place. He looked like he had been born with a "Steal My Lunch Money" sign on his chest.

"I'm not trying to rob you, I just want to borrow it," Dean tried to sound soothing, but the kid quailed, his hand frozen on the unclasped kryptonite lock.

"I haven't got time for this. Here, just... take this," Dean pulled out his wallet and tossed it to the kid, who instinctively flinched instead of trying to catch it. Dean whipped the bike off the rack and pedaled away so hard he left a trench in the freshly watered grass.

"Stop! Thief!" The kid's voice faded into the distance behind him, but Dean wasn't about to turn around. He veered onto the sidewalk where the tires got better traction and thumbed the gearshift to the highest setting. He weaved around buildings and between the small groups of students who were arriving for freshman orientation day. Sixty seconds later, he was veering off the main walkway and approaching Topsy at a speed that could earn him a moving violation on most suburban arterials.

Ahead of him, the big mountain of a man and his two leather-clad friends were still on the greenway outside Topsy, evidently discussing their options. Dean blazed down on them with such speed that they hardly had time to turn to see him coming. He squeezed his fists closed on the brakes, causing the bike to skid and tear up great gouts of wet grass and black dirt. The bike frame wobbled and tilted, and he jumped clear of it just as it smacked onto its side and buried itself in the sod like a deformed javelin. Somehow, Dean managed to land on his feet and skid to a halt.

"You!" Dean marched forward with the roaring inescapability of a tsunami, pointing at the big guy, the one who went by the name Brick. "You were there the day she died."

"Oh, I know you," Brick's voice was hard and cold, like gravel crunching under a boot. "You're the boyfriend. You should have told her to get us the egg when we asked."

"What egg?" Dean demanded. Even as he spoke, the other two bikers spread out slightly, ready to take up flanking positions. "Are you saying you killed her for an egg?"

"Brick," said one of the others, a pot-bellied man with a weasel-face. "Brick, we ain't got time for this. The Professor says we gotta—"

"What professor?" Dean turned on the weasel-faced guy. "Is that your boss? Take me to that murdering son of a—"

"Watch yer mouth," Brick stepped in and placed his enormous, meaty hand on Dean's chest, then shoved him backwards. "You ain't got any business with the Professor. If your girlfriend had cooperated, the dumb skank might still be alive today."

Brick shoved him again. Dean tried to hold his ground, but it was like getting hit by an avalanche, and he had to move so he wouldn't fall. Brick's two friends closed in around him, and it was clear that one of them would throw the first blow as soon as they had fully surrounded their prey.

"What did you say about her?" Dean said, his voice brimming with rage.

"I said, if your girlfriend—"

"Fiancé," Dean said. This time, when the push came in, he sidestepped it and slammed a left hook into Brick's jaw. Dean was gambling that he could knock him cold with a hard blow to what boxers called the "button" at the back of the jaw. If his aim was good, it would flatten almost anyone.

But Dean's aim wasn't that good. Maybe he was blinded by his own rage, or maybe he miscalculated how high he would have to reach to hit the giant's jaw. It caught the big man by surprise, making his eyes lose focus for a second, but that was it. Brick pulled himself up to his full enormity, smiling.

Dean leapt after him, putting his full weight behind a flying knee to the behemoth's side, but all he got for his effort was a grunt. Before he could regain his footing, he felt hands at his back, and then he was on the ground. As they closed in on him, he spun on his back lashed out with a kick. His foot connected solidly with a knee and he felt another body join him on the ground. Instantly, he rolled away and almost got back to his feet, but the grass was too slick to give him traction enough to fend off the rain of blows. He threw his arms over his head, but his world became a flashing gallery of bright red pain and heavy boots. Boots in his ribs. Boots in his arms and thighs. That big boot came down at his head and he wrenched himself to the side so that it mostly missed, but even a glancing blow from those steel-toed size sixteens flattened his nose and caused the world to spin around him like it was going down a whirlpool. His face splattered with blood, he tried to roll away again, but the boots seemed to come at him from all sides.

"The cops!" one of his attackers shouted. The kicks stopped. "The cops! C'mon, Brick, we gotta go!"

Dean struggled to clear his vision. He lifted his head, unable even to come up on his elbows, and watched the three bikers beat a hasty retreat. The weasel-faced man was limping severely, and Brick held his side and wheezed as he ran.

A mass of blinking red and white lights filled Dean's vision. He squeezed his eyes shut, then opened them again, and the blurred colors resolved themselves into lights on top of a police car. It was the campus police, but the real cops wouldn't be far behind. There was a slamming of car doors and Dean was surrounded by three men again. This time it was two campus patrol officers and the university president.

"Arrest this man," President Hart said to his security team. Then he stood over Dean, hands on his hips. "Well, Mr. Lazarchek, it looks like I'll have even less trouble getting rid of you than I had surmised. I'm sure Professor McKenzie would be deeply saddened."

Somehow, those words hurt more than the boots.

Chapter 11 ~ Soap

I wanted to take Rusty along because I thought the other students might want to see some proof that I was smart enough to fit in, but there was no time because it was already almost five by the time I dumped my stuff in my dorm room. Afraid of being late, I rushed out the door, but my haste didn't end up making a difference because Topsy was way out on the far side of campus and I got seriously lost trying to find it.

When I took out my new phone to use the GPS, I found I had accidentally turned the ringer off so I hadn't heard my Dad call. He had left a voice mail from me that he had received two bags full of cash from some guy in a motorcycle jacket, which kind of freaked him out. I decided I didn't have time to call him back right then, but that I would tell him that he should go ahead and pay his bills and then buy himself some Knicks tickets.

Topsy wasn't displayed on the GPS map, but I finally found it by visually homing in on the really tall clock tower that I could see above the trees. When I got there, it looked like some hot-shot had been spinning donuts in his car on the lawn out front. I kept walking towards the big white steps as fast as my feet could carry me. I was already out of breath, had a pain in my side, and was getting a bit sweaty and gross, but I was just hoping they wouldn't kick me out of the Institute for being late on the first day.

Even though I was running so far behind schedule, I had to pause to take in what I was seeing. Topsy looked like a Victorian-era haunted house, only it was in good repair, with all the trim painted gleaming white and the ivy and roses manicured all tidy and nice around the cornerstones. Two stories above me, a spiked, wrought-iron fence ran the circumference of the flat roof, indicating that you could go stand up there in the shadow of the big brick obelisk of the clock tower. At each corner of the roof was a large, snarling black gargoyle.

On ground level, the huge front stairway was flanked by a pair of stone lions, but the building's doors were more frightening still. For a long time all I could do was stare at those doors and try to get control of my breathing. They were each at least four feet wide, and their outer surface was armored with a braid of foot-wide strips of metal, alternating iron and steel. The hinges were carved to look like fists, only each fist was the size of my head. There were even spikes on the doors, pointing out, as if threatening to impale anyone who tried to get in.

Finally, I got up the courage to knock, but found that I couldn't even budge the knockers because they were so heavy. Instead, I tapped at the door with my knuckles. It couldn't possibly have been loud enough to be heard from the other side, but my tapping was immediately answered by the heavy clanking of a titanic lock. The doors, thick as those on bank vaults, began to silently glide open just far enough for someone to step through. Gory scenarios from a thousand horror movies replaying in my mind, I took a trembling step inside. For some reason, I held my breath as I went.

"Welcome," said a voice. "You must be our new student."

The voice startled me so badly that I jumped and collided with a picture on the wall. Recovering, I saw that we were in a short hallway with a crimson carpet, blue-flowered wallpaper, and row upon row of painted portraits. There was a pair of smaller doors at the far end just past a white marble bust on a pedestal, and a big statue in the center of the hallway.

"Sorry!" a woman said with a stifled laugh as she stepped forward. "I didn't mean to spook you. My name's Nikki."

Nikki was young, not too much older than me. Her skin was the color of chocolate and her long, straight, ebony-black hair was dyed platinum blond at the tips, but everything else about her was pink. A pink skirt hugged her round hips, pink platform shoes boosted her an extra two inches, and a long pink coat hung from her shoulders. She was beautiful, but not like a runway model; she was curvier, like Marilyn Monroe.

I recovered myself enough to extend my hand to shake hers. BTW: she had pink nail polish, too.

"My name's Soap," I said. "Um, hey," I said. "I think there was a typo on the invitation. It says 'Mad Science Institute' instead of 'Mechanical Science Institute.'"

She tipped her head back and laughed, and when she spoke I could detect a mild Southern accent. "Well, bless your heart. That's no typo. You might say it's our school's nickname."

"Oh," I said, not liking the nickname at all.

When she turned to lead me down the hall, I saw black embroidery on the back of her pink lab coat that said IT IS BETTER TO BE FEARED THAN LOVED. Below that was a skull-and-crossbones symbol inside a triangle.

"Whoa," I said, studying the skull-and-crossbones. "Are you a pirate or something?"

"Pardon? Oh—no, that's the hazard symbol for poison. Take the warning to heart," she said sweetly. "I've got a mean streak a mile wide for people who cross me."

"Oh," I said again, making a mental note not to make her mad.

Then, as if it just occurred to her, she asked: "Soap, how old are you?"

I froze. Had I given myself away somehow? Did she know I was too young to be there? The silence stretched out awkwardly as I considered my answer. I didn't think I could get away with a lie, so I finally admitted that I was sixteen.

"Cool," Nikki turned and led me down the hall. "I was seventeen when I started last year. Victor was fourteen when he started two years before that. You fit right in."

I tried to wrap my head around that information but it was almost too much to handle. It felt like someone had just popped the balloon of all my fears. Maybe this place really would work out for me.

Nikki had to take me by the hand to get me moving again. She guided me over to the big statue in the middle of the hallway as if to introduce me to an old friend. It was carved from white marble, slightly larger than life, and placed right in the center of everything so you had to walk around it as you made your way towards the inner doors. Its shape was that of a lanky, thoughtful-looking man sitting in a chair, his head tilted against his hand while he gazed off into space. This man had a narrow mustache, hair parted down the middle, and a deeply thoughtful look in his eyes. With a burst of excitement I realized who it was.

"Nikola Tesla!" I exclaimed. "Inventor of alternating current—not to mention radio, x-rays, robotics, and about a million other things."

"You recognize him," Nikki nodded with approval. "Hardly anybody knows about him these days, even though we all still use his inventions every single day. Soap, this here is our school's founder."

"F—founder?" I looked up at her to see if she was messing with me, but she looked serious. "I didn't know he founded any schools."

"It was founded in secret," Nikki walked over to a wall to stand next to the only two pictures in the room that were not portraits of people. One was a photograph of a pigeon. The other was a picture of a tall broadcasting tower with a weird, bumpy cap at its top.

"Do you know what this is?" she asked, pointing to the tower.

"That's Wardenclyffe Tower," I said. Any Tesla fan (and there are a few of us out there) would recognize it as the inventor's attempt to achieve his dream of broadcasting electricity everywhere in the world without using wires. "That tower is kind of what inspired my science experiment with Rusty, even though Wardenclyffe kind of ended in financial disaster... come to think of it, so did my experiment."

Nikki nodded. "Tesla went broke trying to get that tower a-workin'. He spent the rest of his life in deep, deep debt. To be fair, he always had been terrible with money, even before that. But he could envision and design incredible machines all in his head, so all he needed was a laboratory with talented engineers to bring his designs into reality. Only problem was, they had to keep it secret so that Tesla's creditors wouldn't foreclose on it."

"And that's this place?" I asked, feeling suddenly light headed. "The Mechanical Science Institute got started as Tesla's secret lab? Seriously?"

"Can you think of a more out-of-the-way place to go and hide a super-secret private research facility than Bugswallow, Minnesota?" Nikki winked at me before moving on to stand by the far door.

"But if he was broke and all, how did he get the money to build this place?"

"Ah, that's where this gentleman comes in," Nikki patted the white marble bust by the doorway. At first I thought it was Einstein because it depicted a man with bushy hair, a thick mustache, and a sly look in his eye. But when I read the name tag, I saw that it was someone else entirely.

"That's Mark Twain?" I asked. "As in, the famous writer?"

"You bet," Nikki said. "Twain loved new technology and he was a good friend of Tesla. Twain also spent his life either flat broke or filthy rich, and in one of his wealthy moments he donated the money to set up this school. Actually, he financed the whole town, way back in 1907 when there was nothing here but pine trees and swampland. He was also the one who came up with the name 'Bugswallow.'"

Bugswallow. It did sound like the kind of thing Twain would think up. But the rest of what Nikki had told me was ricocheting around inside my skull. Nikola Tesla, my science idol. A secret school. Untold inventions. Tesla had lived almost forty years—nearly half his life—after the Wardenclyffe failure, and he often claimed to have developed amazing new tools, discoveries, and even weapons, but no one wanted to fund his work and so none of it came to light. A lot of people just decided he was a crazy old man, but was it really possible that he actually invented all the stuff he claimed, working like a real-life mad scientist and sending all his designs here, to a tiny school with a lame name in the middle of nowhere?

If it was true, the possibilities were staggering. While he was alive, Tesla was a hundred years ahead of the technology of his day. How far could his inventions have progressed since then if he'd had a group of scientists secretly working on them ever since?

Thinking about it made my head spin. Nikki had to lead me by the hand again through the inner door into a large warehouse filled with books, Bunsen burners, fume hoods, and cabinets of glassware. Off by the far wall was a spiral staircase that led up to the roof, but the rest was wide open, with the enormous wooden rafters clearly visible twenty feet overhead.

After stubbing my toe on a table leg, I brought my attention back down to ground level to study the shelves of equipment and supplies that ran in neat, orderly rows to sub-divide the huge space. There was a high-powered laser array, a six-foot tall model of a spiraling DNA strand, and computer stations every five feet. Still, something felt missing. It was too orderly and sedate, lacking the controlled chaos of an actual lab. Science should be messy, or at least cluttered, but this place was pristine.

"You guys don't use this lab much, do you?" I asked, running my hand over one of the experimentation chambers and coming away with dust on my finger tips. I immediately dug hand sanitizer out of my pocket.

Nikki ignored my question. "There's pizza over there," she pointed to a side table with five pizza boxes and a rack of two-liter bottles of cola. "Victor didn't know what you like, so he ordered one of everything."

"That was nice of him."

Nikki shrugged. "He can afford it. He inherited a ton of money from his parents—sad story. I'll tell you some other time. Anyway, he's always happy to spend the money if it means he can get more time with his special research project. He's like that, you know."

"What's he researching?"

"Don't know," Nikki shrugged. "He never tells anyone."

She led me deeper into the building, around a few pillars and cabinets, to where a young man was hunched over a set of x-ray pictures that he held under a desk-lamp. He looked like he was my age, but he was so serious as he stared at those prints that it made him seem like an adult. His body was lean, like a runner's, as was his face, with high, handsome cheekbones, a strong jaw, and a chin that was just a little bit cleft. His sandy-blond hair was trimmed close on the side but was long enough on top to be gelled up a fraction of an inch in front. He grunted a hello at me when Nikki introduced us, and when he glanced up I caught a flash of ice-blue eyes.

Maybe it was the fact that he was ignoring me that made me a little more comfortable around him. Or maybe I was still reeling from what Nikki had told me in the entrance hall. Whatever it was, I decided I would give Hannah's conversation matrix one more try, so I hopped up on a stool next to him and leaned in to see the printouts.

"You have a nice..." I almost told him that I liked his face. It would have been true, but I didn't want to come off as too much of a creeper on my first day.

"You have a nice set of x-rays," I managed. "What are you studying?"

He looked at me for a second as if he had to remember how to speak. He seemed a little awkward, actually, which had the weird effect of making me feel more comfortable. Maybe if we were both awkward in the same way we would cancel each other out. Maybe this counted as something we had in common.

"I'm working on accelerating dendrite regeneration in damaged nerve tissue," he finally answered.

"Is that your secret research project?" I asked.

"No," Victor said, giving Nikki a dirty look. "This is only somewhat related to my project."

"Why did you go with x-rays?" I asked. "You know, synchrotrons can give you a much more accurate picture of small-scale structures like this."

Yup, there it was. I had just done what I always do: say something stupid or patronizing that gets people annoyed.

Victor just looked at me for a minute with those gorgeous blue eyes, and then he shook his head. "C'mon, Nikki," he said flatly. "I need to show you the video of what happened out on the front lawn earlier."

Without a word of goodbye, he collected his printouts and walked off. As he went, I saw that his white lab coat was adorned with a warning triangle, just like Nikki's. Except the one on the back of Victor's coat had a biohazard symbol. Was everyone around here so dangerous they had to be labeled?

"Don't worry about Victor," Nikki said. "He's like that with everyone who isn't actively helping with his special research. Oh, and here, you'll need this. It's the key to the front door."

Nikki tossed me a big, old-fashioned brass key. I fumbled it but finally managed to slap it to my chest before it dropped to the floor. It was heavy and cold in my hands, and it looked like it was an honest-to-goodness antique.

"I don't remember a keyhole out there," I said.

"There isn't one," she said over her shoulder as she followed Victor up the stairs. "The door will detect the key's special radio frequency. Bring it close, and the gate will automatically open for you."

The two of them ascended the spiral staircase and disappeared through the door.

I explored the lab for what must have been an hour, charting out the locations of the wires and welding torches to build some interesting things, but I couldn't find any scrap metal and I wanted to ask if they had any available. The two of them had gone up the stairs a long time ago, and I was beginning to wonder what was taking so long. After another fifteen minutes of me waiting, I gave in to impatience and went up the spiral staircase to find them.

The door exited into a short hallway with two more doors. The first one opened up into a large shower room, like the kind you would find in a locker room. That seemed out of place to me, but Nikki and Victor were not in there, so I didn't spend long inside. The second door had a little plaque that said it was the 'Dean's Residence,' but no one answered when I knocked. The door wasn't locked, so I went in.

The dean's residence was an apartment, way bigger than the one my Dad and I had in New York but set up for a single occupant, judging from the fact that there was only one bedroom. With Professor McKenzie deceased, I guessed that it was awaiting whoever would become the next Dean of Students. At the back of the apartment was a glass door that looked out on the roof of Topsy, which held an amazing garden, complete with fruit trees and rose bushes. But still no Nikki or Victor.

I backtracked and searched again, but it was simply impossible that anyone was up here. It was also impossible that they had come down earlier, because the spiral staircase is clearly visible from anywhere in the lab below and I would have seen them come down. It was equally impossible that they could have disappeared into thin air, but they seemed to have done just that.

I returned to the top of the stairway and leaned over the railing to look out at the laboratory below. I pouted, as much because they had ditched me as because I couldn't figure out how they had done it. Unfortunately for me, my sulking was cut short by the phone buzzing in my pocket.

"This is the Professor," said the smooth voice on the other end of the line. "Are you inside Topsy?"

"Yeah," I said, trying not to sound too upset about my vanishing classmates.

"Good," he said. "Now, are you alone?"

That seemed like a strange question. What did it matter if I was alone? Still, I couldn't see the harm in telling him I was.

"Excellent," he said. "It is time for you to begin your research."

Chapter 12 ~ Dean

Sheriff Kidd had scowled throughout the booking process. He was a tall man with a black handlebar mustache and a bow-legged swagger.

"I don't like your kind of trouble-makers in my town," he said as he pushed Dean's inky fingers onto the finger-print page.

"Sounds clichéd," Dean responded. He was too tired to play cowboys-and-robbers. After all, he stood accused of stealing a bike, not rustling horses.

Evidently, the sheriff didn't like to be reminded that sleepy little Bugswallow was not the Wild West, because Dean never got a new ice pack for his nose. Instead, he was taken to the hospital for a mandatory medical evaluation. Three hours and three x-rays later, the doctor told Dean what he already knew: he had a broken nose and a small crack in his rib, so he should try to get some rest. For that, the doctor charged one thousand nine hundred dollars. Back in his cell, he put his head down to rest just in time for the Sheriff to clang open the cell door once more.

"C'mon," Sheriff Kidd grunted. "You got a call on the computer."

Dean didn't know why anyone would be calling him, but he was sure the sheriff wouldn't give him an answer, so he just struggled back to his feet and limped down the hall to the office desk, where a rolling chair was stationed in front of a computer. The sheriff's deputy, a husky, middle-aged woman with a Viking-esque braid running down her back, leaned over the monitor, plugging in a web-cam.

"Ain't you got it working yet?" Kidd said as he handcuffed Dean to the rolling chair.

Dean caught the deputy's eye and gave her a sympathetic look, which she returned in full. Evidently, working for Kidd wasn't much more fun than being arrested by him.

The deputy clicked a few buttons, and after a moment the blank screen came to life with the video feed of Brian Nash, the FBI agent who had questioned Dean back in Los Angeles. Agent Nash was in a car seat, evidently connecting via the webcam in his phone. His face was lit only by the dome light which allowed most of his features to fade into the darkness of an interstate highway at night. The picture bounced around as Nash's car went over some pot-holes and Dean caught a glimpse of Agent O'Grady at the wheel, his steely gaze aimed out at the road ahead of him.

"The FBI is calling me?" Dean said. "How much trouble am I in for one little fist-fight?"

Nash ignored the quip. "Mr. Lazarchek, I understand you had an encounter with one or more of the men we discussed at our last meeting."

"Yeah," Dean said. "It was that big guy, Brick. Him and a couple of friends."

"These are dangerous criminals," Nash said earnestly. "I ask that you leave them to trained law-enforcement professionals."

"I wasn't looking for trouble," Dean lied. "The thing is, they showed up on the front lawn of a school building. I was just going to ask them what they were doing there."

"Any idea what these men were doing at the school?"

"I don't know," Dean said. "But they did say something about an egg. Apparently that's why they were following McKenzie."

"An egg? What sort of egg?" Nash reached past his camera to find a pen and make a note.

Dean shrugged. "I don't know, but I don't think they were try-ing to make an omelet. They also said something about working for a professor. Any idea who that might be?"

"I will let you know what we find when the case goes to trial," Nash said, but did not make a note about the professor the way he had noted the egg. This, Dean realized, meant he already knew about the professor.

"In the mean time, Mr. Lazarchek, I would caution you again to stay away from these men."

Dean knew that Nash was right, but he couldn't leave it alone. Besides, if Brick and his Blitzkriegers were here in Bugswallow, that meant they still didn't have what they wanted and they might still threaten the school and the students, including Sophia. For the first time, he realized why McKenzie had asked him to cover for her. She didn't need someone to run the school: she needed someone to protect it from these men, whoever they were. McKenzie hadn't asked him for a small favor; she had trusted him with a task that was both crucial and dangerous. All he needed to do now was carry out her last wishes.

In order to properly defend the Mechanical Science Institute he would need more information. If Nash wouldn't answer direct ques-tions then Dean would need to resort to other means.

"I don't get what's so dangerous about these guys," Dean said, rolling his neck to casually work out the kinks. "I mean, I just beat up three of them and sent them running."

It was complete bluster, and Dean knew it. But Nash fell right into the trap.

"These men are suspects in dozens of armed bank robberies," Nash said. "They are also suspected of assault, murder, and a dozen other felonies."

"Really?" Dean pretended to be more interested in picking a tuft of padding out of the chair's armrest.

Nash rose to the bait. "You may be interested to know that each of the banks they robbed experienced catastrophic electrical failure at the moment of the crime. Alarms and phones didn't work. Cameras burned out. Lights went dead. Does any of this sound familiar, Mr. Lazarchek?"

Now Dean could no longer fake indifference. "Just like what happened at my house," he said slowly, remembering the dead appliances and the damage to the wiring. And McKenzie's pacemaker.

Nash nodded. "Whatever they are doing to cause this, I hope you see now that this is a very serious situation indeed."

Dean certainly did. He also now saw what he had to do: find the bikers and find the Professor. He had no idea where to look, but he knew they were after some kind of egg. If he could find that egg, he could get them to come to him.

CHAPTER 13 ~ SOAP

Maybe I misunderstood the Professor about how much research he needed me to do, because what he asked for was ridiculously
simple. All he wanted was for me to look into RFID—Radio Frequency
Identification—which is the kind of thing that businesses do with key
cards that open locked doors. It's also how the doors of Topsy recognize
the key Nikki gave me. It's basically an electronic lock-and-key system:
if the key frequency fits the lock just right, the doors open. If not, they
stay shut. The Professor was especially interested in how the key to
Topsy worked, so I copied its frequency and included that with the other data. He said he wanted it by tomorrow evening, but it only took me
an hour to prepare the report. I uploaded everything to my phone and
was ready to send it, but I thought I would wait until the next morning
because I didn't want it to look too easy. If he was paying me ten thousand dollars for this research, I at least wanted him to think I had put
in the hours.

It was dark outside by the time I left Topsy. I had missed my
chance to register for my meal card that day, so I had to use the last of
my pocket cash to buy food at one of the campus cafeterias. Even
though it was way past the main dinner hour, there were plenty of other
kids there. I still ended up sitting alone, though. Some things never
change, I guess.

Back at Smiley, I saw that Hannah had already decorated her
side of the room with posters of pop singers and celebrity athletes. Her
book shelves were now lined with makeup containers and organic, diet
snack foods, and the open door to her closet revealed that it was brimming with crisply folded clothes, most of which were in the school colors of white and blue. Then there was my side, which currently con-

tained the standard-issue dorm furniture, plus my single foot locker and my backpack.

First I unpacked Rusty, who was now fully refurbished following the science fair disaster. I had him use his long pincer arms to hand me the clothes that had travelled with him in the footlocker across the country. I didn't own much. Including what I was wearing, I had three black hoodies, three pairs of black jeans, and nine each of t-shirts, underwear, and socks—all black. Some people think I'm depressed because I always wear black, but the truth is when I wear other colors I get too distracted with dots of grease from whatever I'm working on. Also, black is great because it goes with everything so I can spend my time thinking about robots instead of picking outfits. I got the idea from Einstein, who had a dozen copies of the same suit and never wore anything else. He was pretty smart, if you ask me. Still, when I was done unpacking, my collection of clothes hangers looked like a ghost town compared to all the things crammed into Hannah's closet. It made me feel kind of plain.

I was just pushing my black backpack under my bed when I heard a burst of giggling out in the hallway. A moment after that, Hannah and three of her girl friends crashed through the door with huge smiles on their face. All of them wore short skirts and had long, wavy hair that bounced on their shoulders.

"Oh, you're back," Hannah said. Then she saw Rusty and somehow managed to frown while still showing off her perfectly white teeth. "What is that?" she demanded.

"That's Rusty, my personal assistant," I said proudly. "Say hello, Rusty."

My robot recognized the verbal cue and responded by spreading his arms, ducking his head, and leaning forward in a kind of bow. I thought it was a cute trick, but Hannah wasn't impressed.

"That thing's disgusting," one of her friends said.

"Can you please hide it somewhere?" Hannah said. "Quickly? I have a really cute guy coming and—oh, hi, Brett. Everybody, this is Brett Jenson, our school's new varsity quarterback."

The girls parted reverently to allow a very tall young man entered the room. He wore one of those jackets that athletes wear and he had the physique to go with it. He was broad shouldered, dark eyed, and dark haired. Back in Flatbush there were some good-looking guys in my high school, but they all seemed small by comparison. I don't mean they were shorter than he was, just that if I gathered them all together on a stage, the other guys would fade into the background while Brett would shine so bright you could see him from the back row.

"Whoa," he said when he spotted Rusty. "That looks cool. What is it?"

I told Rusty to give another bow, and Brett's face lit up.

Hannah sneered. "This is my roommate, Soap. She's really into math and physics."

"That's cool," Brett said, as if it might not be. "Where did you get the robot?"

"Built it," I shrugged.

This seemed to knock Brett for a loop. "That's totally awesome," he said. "What else can it do? Does it shoot missiles or anything?"

The other girls were giving me dirty looks because I had Brett's attention. Still, he had asked for a demonstration, so I showed how Rusty could retrieve my backpack, carry it with him, and hand me a screwdriver or a voltmeter when I asked for one.

"You've got to be the smartest person I've ever met," Brett concluded. "I can't believe you built this thing."

"Hey, Brett," Hannah cooed. "Here's that popcorn maker I was telling you about. It's way better than microwave popcorn. I can make it fresh right here any time you want it."

She plugged in her air popper and it started to whirr, but Brett was still focused on Rusty. Seeing this, she crossed over to him and pretended to pick some lint off his jacket.

"So, Brett, what are you studying?" Hannah asked. It was a question I heard a lot of students asking each other, so maybe it was part of a different conversation matrix.

"I don't know yet," Brett said. "Maybe pre-law. Or economics. I haven't decided. I think Freshman year is too early to decide."

Hannah said she was thinking about those exact same majors. But then Brett turned to me. "What are *you* studying, Soap? Robot-building?"

I nodded. "Physics. With the Mechanical Science Institute."

Usually, I can figure out why I offend people after I've done it. This time, however, I couldn't imagine what made my answer erase the smile off Brett's face quicker than you can drop a wrench. He just stood there, looking at me.

"What?" asked Hannah. "What's the matter?"

"The Institute," he said to me. "Don't."

"Don't what?" I asked

"Don't study with them. Just stay away. They're dangerous." He looked really serious, but I still couldn't understand why.

"What do you mean?" I asked. "Is it because Professor McKenzie died?"

"It goes way back before that," Brett said. "But, listen, I gotta go. Just remember that I warned you." Brett exited the room really quickly. The girls, including Hannah, followed him out, talking about how they should go get ice cream. BTW: Hannah never unplugged her popcorn machine, so I had Rusty do it for her after she left.

I sat down on the uncovered mattress of my bed, deeply confused for about the four hundredth time that day. I replayed it over and over in my head, but I couldn't see what I had said that offended Brett so badly. I had to go with the theory that, for once, it wasn't me. It must be something about the Institute, something bad.

College was turning out to be a confusing place. In less than a day I had already stumbled upon the secret laboratory of one of the greatest inventors in history, misplaced two of my classmates, and then scared off a football player just by mentioning the name of my college program.

At least I had been able to complete my assignment for the Professor. Just to give myself a feeling of accomplishment for the day, I decided to go ahead and send off my data, including the frequency used by my key. I didn't see that it could be a problem.

September 13th
(Doomsday minus 4 days)

CHAPTER 14 ~ SOAP

My first class started at 8am, a time slot that most college students considered cruel and unusual. I left Hannah gently snoring into her pillow while I headed over to the Grangerford building for Chinese Language 101. To my surprise, Brett was also registered for the same class.

I was a little early because I wanted to get a seat in the back. The problem here, as I soon discovered, was that unlike in high school where the desks are all self-contained units, in small college classes everybody sits around tables with actual, free-standing chairs. The tables in this room were arranged in a big square, which meant that there was no back row.

The professor was already there, a balding guy with suede patches on the elbows of his tweed jacket and the roundest nose I have ever seen on anyone of Chinese descent. Since I was the first person there, he kept asking me why I was interested in Chinese and if I had any questions before we started the course. I didn't want to tell him that I had picked Chinese because back home my favorite place to eat, besides DiFaro's Pizza, was the China New Star restaurant. I was really relieved when some other students came in and he started talking to them instead.

Then Brett walked in, followed by two other guys. He looked around the room and when he saw me he smiled and sat down in the seat to my right. One of the other guys sat on the other side of me, which made me feel like I was in the middle of a herd of buffalo. Brett acted like nothing unusual had happened last night. At least he was nice to me and seemed glad to see me, and when I paused because I had forgotten the words in our brand new Chinese dialogue script he helped me through the phony conversation. Like I would ever ask about the weather: if I needed to know, I would check my phone for local conditions.

There were no bells or PA announcements. The class ended just the same way it began, with the professor looking at the clock and deciding it was about time.

"Ni hao ma?" Brett said to me as I stuffed my spiral notebook into my backpack. I just looked at him blankly—he was picking this up so fast and I couldn't even remember the basic words I had learned half an hour ago. So much for me being the smartest person he had ever met.

"What I meant to ask," Brett explained, "is if you're okay. You're kind of scowling."

I hadn't realized I was scowling, but he was right. "I can already tell I'm going to have trouble in this class. I feel kind of stupid."

"Any girl who builds awesome robot monsters isn't stupid," he said. Then he paused, and after that he added in kind of a rush: "Do you want to form a study group?"

I didn't know what to say. I just stood there working my mouth like a fish's, but no sound came out. In high school, when a boy and a girl "formed a study group," it actually meant they were going over to each other's apartments to make out while their parents watched TV in the front room. Maybe it meant something different in college, because I was pretty sure the sun would burn up all its atomic fuel before a guy like Brett would ask a girl like me out for a date.

"I mean," Brett said. "Me and the guys were going to the library. You know, to practice Chinese and stuff. Would you be interested in that?"

"Um, okay," I said. I was getting that light-headed feeling I get when I'm nervous. It felt like all the hairs on my scalp had picked up a static electrical charge. "When?"

"I dunno," he looked at his two friends who stared blankly back at him. "How about tonight? Seven o'clock?"

"Sure, I guess," I said, brushing some hair out of my eye.

We went our separate ways and I was so distracted that I didn't realize until half way back to my dorm that I hadn't asked Brett about why he had freaked out at the mention of the Mechanical Science Institute. Maybe I could ask him at our study group.

When I got back to my room, Hannah was getting ready to leave.

"I hate 10am classes, don't you?" she said as she set out a row of makeup vials and tubes in front of her illuminated desk mirror. "It's only three days a week, but it's *sooo* early. We're in college now. Why do we have to get up so early?"

"Hey, Hannah," I said. "Can I ask you a question? What does it mean if a boy asks you to a study group?"

"It's a date," she said while applying a silky black line of eyeliner. I kept watching the reflection of her eyeball which looked as big as a grapefruit in her special mirror. "Or maybe a pre-date," she went on. "He wants to get to know you better, but not have the pressure of actually going out. That's what's so cool about the study group, because you can pretend like it doesn't mean anything even though it really does. Why—did someone ask you out?"

"Well, that's the thing," I flopped on my bed and looked at the ceiling. "Brett's in my Chinese class and—"

"Brett *Jenson*?" she just about dropped her eyeliner and turned to study me. Those blue eyes of hers seemed even bigger now than they were in the mirror. "Are you sure you heard him right, Soap?

You don't think he might have been talking to the girl sitting behind you or something?"

I was a bit insulted by that suggestion, but I couldn't blame her for being surprised. I was surprised, too.

"Yeah, that's the thing," I said. "It doesn't make sense, right? Maybe I misunderstood what he wanted."

"That's probably it," Hannah carefully capped the eyeliner and set it down with an audible click on the desk. "When is your...*study session*?"

"Tonight," I said. "I was having trouble with Chinese and getting seriously psyched out, so maybe he was just being nice."

"Are you going?" she asked.

I just stared up at the ceiling. I had told him yes, but now I wasn't so sure. I mean, who was I kidding? Sixteen-year-olds and eighteen-year-olds date in high school, but college was different. How could it end in any way other than disaster?

Hannah held me in her gaze until I felt like a mouse that had been spotted by a hawk. Her smile suddenly came on as if she had flicked a switch.

"Don't stress yourself about it," she said, turning with a little too much casualness back towards her mirror. "What time did he say?"

"Seven," I said.

"Seven pm," repeated Hannah, sliding on a fresh coat of red lipstick. "That's good to know."

I was still so confused by the situation that I couldn't concentrate in my next class, which was History 152: British Colonial Era. My lack of attention wasn't helped because the class was taught by a professor with really bad posture who rambled on and on about how the industrial age paved the way for conquest. I tuned out after about five minutes and started reading the syllabus. In high school there had always been one big, fat text book we spent the whole year working our way through, but here there was a whole list of smaller books we needed to buy and the first one was due in one week. I assumed that was a typo: no one would assign an entire book in a week. Would they?

After class, I jetted over to Topsy. Maybe I wasn't equipped to figure out Brett Jenson, but I was determined to unravel the mystery of how Nikki and Victor had vanished. When I got there, the place was abandoned, just like it had been when I left it the day before. For a couple of super science people, Nikki and Victor didn't seem to spend much time in the lab. For all I knew, I would never see them again.

I went back upstairs and searched the dean's residence again. This time I flipped couch cushions looking for clues, stomped on the floors in search of trapdoors, and fiddled with books on the shelves in hopes of triggering a Scooby-Doo style secret passage. Nothing. I even went outside and searched the garden and the base of the clock tower. Still nothing.

I sat down on the stairway to glower. If college was going to be this complicated, maybe I wasn't ready for it yet. I would have caught a train home that very minute if there had been one. I missed my Dad. I missed my apartment. I missed the big city, even with all its noises and smells. At least back home there were people I could ask for advice.

Then I remembered the phone in my pocket. I pulled it out and dialed the number for the Professor. His name meant he was a teacher, so maybe he could teach me something. Besides, I couldn't think of anyone else to ask, and I didn't see how it could hurt.

"Sophia," he answered the phone. "I didn't expect you to call. I got the data for the key combination. Thank you."

"Glad to hear it, but I have a question about something else."

"I'm afraid I'm frightfully busy at the moment," he said. "Make it quick?"

"You used to go here, right? I mean, you used to be in the Mechanical Science Institute, right? You said you were."

"Yes, that's right. Is that your question?"

"No. My question is: where's the secret room? I know there must be one because the others are never around in the main part of Topsy."

"Oh, you mean they haven't told you yet?" the Professor said as though I had asked for nothing more serious than the location of the cookie jar. "Unless things have changed considerably since my day, all you have to do is go to the shower room at the top of the stairs. Go to the far corner and then count nine tiles over and nine tiles up from the far wall and you'll find a hatch that slides back to reveal the elevator controls."

I was stunned that it was that easy to get the answer. "Seriously?" was all I could say.

"Seriously," said the Professor. "I must go now. I have much to prepare for tonight. I'll see you soon."

Chapter 15 ~ Dean

The kid with the bike had dropped the charges, so Sheriff Kidd had no choice but to let Dean go. After a mere 23 hour stay in the holding cell of the building that doubled as Bugswallow's police station and city hall, Dean was a free man.

The whole town couldn't have been more than four blocks long, bookended on one side by the college campus and at the other end by the local grocery store. Most of the buildings in between had the scenic, turn-of-the-century brick architecture style with businesses on the ground floor and apartments or private offices on the second. There were no franchise restaurants or big-box retailers here, just local shops owned by local people, many handed down from generation to generation.

The ice-pack he had been using to fight the swelling in his nose had long since melted, so he dropped it into a trashcan about a block up from the police-station-slash-city-hall. Even the trashcans in Bugswallow were beautiful, encased in decorative stone sconces topped with cigarette sand-trays that were so smooth that there must have been a secret team of Zen monks working full-time to keep them perfectly raked. When he leaned over to spit a clot of blood into the trashcan, an old lady passing by on the street shook her head accusingly.

After cleaning himself up, Dean made it back to the university just in time to get his orientation packet before they closed up for the day. The fat manila envelope handed to him by the human resources director contained a stack of employment paperwork, and, more importantly, a big brass key that was supposed to give him full access to Topsy.

Dean slid the key deep into his pocket where he kept the letters from McKenzie. Now he could begin his investigation in earnest. Maybe, if he was lucky, he could find the mysterious egg that the Blitzkriegers were after. Had that been what McKenzie had meant when she said "what they want is in our founder's head?" Her parting statement still haunted and confused him.

Twenty minutes later, Dean parked his big red pickup in between the only other cars in the Topsy lot, a jet-black BMW and a beat-up blue Volkswagen. For all he knew, one of those cars belonged to Soap. Then it hit him that he had never called his cousin or her father to let them know he was coming out to Bugswallow. She had no idea he would be her Dean of Students. In hindsight, he thought it was a stupid oversight, but he had been so wrapped up in his grief and his confusion during the last week that it hadn't occurred to him to call. *No point now,* he thought. *It'll just have to be a fun surprise.*

His duffel bag slung over his shoulder, the ex-firefighter followed the path out of the parking lot and up the broad stairs to some very melodramatic doors. He had his key out looking for a lock when the doors, as if sensing his presence, opened with a clang and swung slowly outwards under their own power.

After a brief hesitation, he entered into a hallway full of old portraits and one big statue of a little guy sitting in a big chair. Judging from the man's mustache and center-parted hair, Dean guessed it was a statue of Edgar Allen Poe. At the far end of the hall, he saw the marble bust of a man with bushy hair and a thick mustache.

"Hello, Einstein," he said, patting the bust as he passed.

The next room contained the most advanced science lab Dean had ever imagined. It was a large space filled with hundreds of drawers, cabinets, and cubby-holes, any one of which could have contained the mysterious egg. Still, Dean was willing to bet that what he was looking for was not out here in the open. Instead, he found the spiral staircase and ascended to the Dean of Student's residence, where he found the door unlocked.

His new residence consisted of a spacious apartment that occupied an area of the roof at the base of the clock tower. Dean set his brass key on the kitchen table and showed himself around. The carpet and the walls were all cream colored, and the furnishings and decorations had that art deco look that made everything seem grandiose and imposing. A group of hand-carved African masks were the only ornaments on the walls of the living room. In the dining room there were some weird paintings that looked to Dean like tentacles, but when he read the little tag of paper in the lower corner he discovered that they were electron microscope scans of flower petals. Not exactly Dean's preferred kind of art, and not what he would have expected from McKenzie, either.

McKenzie was supposed to have lived here, but he couldn't see her anywhere in this place. Actually, it lacked the feeling of being lived-in by anyone. All the drawers and closets were empty, and the only thing in the refrigerator was a neat stack of pizza boxes.

Dean slumped on the well-padded couch. His cracked rib stung like crazy and suddenly he felt tired. The physical injuries didn't worry him—he had recovered from all manner of cuts, sprains, and breaks in the past, and he had faith in his body's physical process. It was the emotional wounds that left him drained.

He had known it would be a long-shot to find the egg in the apartment, especially since he didn't even know exactly what he was looking for. Was it a big ostrich-sized thing that would hatch a dinosaur? Or a tiny bead that contained some generically enhanced insect? He didn't know and, as he sat on the couch, he realized he didn't care.

What he had really hoped to find in that apartment was some trace of McKenzie.

Dean decided some fresh air might help. He winced as got up and pulled open the door at the back of the apartment.

The entire roof was carpeted in grass. Real, living grass, the kind that invited picnics and barefoot running. There were trees, too: mostly thin-trunked fruit trees but some were as big around as Dean's thigh, and all of them were planted in gargantuan ceramic or wooden pots. And there were also raised beds of neat, orderly flowers and vegetables that crawled up lattices or carpeted the ground with color. The air smelled of jasmine and honeysuckle, scents he couldn't name but which he had learned to love. It smelled of McKenzie.

Dean sat down and ran his fingers through grass. McKenzie had lived out here, and still did in every one of these trees and bushes and thorny vines.

"Hello, again," he whispered, finally seeing her spirit all around him.

What he didn't see was the scaly thing perched on the first terrace of the clock tower. It slipped out from behind a gargoyle statue that might have been its twin, but it was no stone carving. It crept forward on long, sinewy limbs and flexed the barbs that ran down its back as it tracked Dean's movements with red eyes.

Chapter 16 ~ Soap

The elevator took me down, down, down, and when the doors finally slid back I found myself in a mad scientist's wonderland. This laboratory was almost as large as the one on the ground floor of Topsy, but its low ceiling and windowless walls wouldn't let me forget that we were deep underground. While everything upstairs was polished and shining, here it was rusty, gritty, and real. It looked like someone had vivisected a hundred cars, vacuum cleaners, and computers and spread all the pieces over dozens of metal tables. In another spot, strange vapors rose out of flasks and flowed through elaborate tracks of glass pipes and latex hoses. One wall was covered in hundreds of shelves, each lined with jars of bleached white specimens, including a centipede the size of a garden hose and a whole bunch of other stuff I couldn't even recognize. Everything was illuminated by the full spectrum lighting in the ceiling, but there was so much stuff that long shadows connected every workbench and shelf. These shadows shifted and danced in time with the pulsing blue electrical discharges from an enormous Tesla Coil that was sealed off by a chain-link fence in a corner of the room.

There were no inner walls here, but the density of the shelves, gizmos, and tools made the place seem like there were. The first area appeared to be storage, with boxes lining the shelves. I peeked under a lid and pulled out a big pistol with six shiny silver rotating barrels and a trailing cord that looked like it supplied both ammunition and electrical power. It was surprisingly light in my hands, and when I unscrewed it I saw that it was a rail gun—a weapon that uses magnetic pulses to accelerate its projectiles to amazing speeds. The only thing I couldn't figure out was why it had those six rotating barrels. Big machineguns sometimes need multiple barrels to prevent overheating due to friction, but a rail gun had no friction and so it simply wouldn't heat up that way.

"Soap?!" the exclamation was paired with a metallic clatter off to my right. I turned to see a very surprised Victor staring at me, his ice-blue eyes wide in astonishment, a tray of surgical implements on the floor at his feet.

"Oh, hi," I said. "Hey, do you know why this rail gun has so many barrels?"

"What are you *doing* here?"

"I wanted to see the real lab," I said. "I was feeling kind of left out."

Nikki entered the aisle, and when she saw me she laughed. "Oh, sugar, I figured it wouldn't take you long to find out, but this has got to be a record."

"Hi, Nikki. Do you know why this gun has six barrels?" I held up the pieces to show her what I meant.

"No idea," she said. "Maybe it's just to look cool."

I looked down at the weapon in my hands. All those barrels did look snazzy in a Star Wars kind of way, but no engineer worth his paycheck would add so much complication to an experimental device just for the sake of appearance.

"You can't be down here," Victor said. "You're not ready to see this place. You have to leave."

"Oh, relax, Vic," Nikki said, sweeping past him to gently take the rail gun from my hand and replace it on the shelf. "She already knows about the place, and you can't un-know a thing."

Victor went off grumbling about getting back to his research while Nikki gave me a brief guided tour. We didn't get very far before my curiosity overwhelmed my listening skills.

"What's that?" I asked about a vat of liquid that bubbled and changed colors like a kaleidoscope.

"That there's my chameleon dye," Nikki said. "I'm trying to get it so you can change the color of your clothes or your hair with the press of a button. Still workin' out the bugs, I'm afraid."

"Oh. And what's that?" I pointed to a steel cylinder about the size of a can of soda.

"Resonating oscillator," Nikki told me. "We call 'em earthquake grenades because they can crumble buildings."

"Oh. And what's that?" I pointed to what appeared to be a metal box sprouting nozzles and tubes in all directions.

"That's our espresso machine," Nikki smirked. "Why don't you come over here and take a look at our computer pavilion."

She led me into an elevated area that contained dozens of computers on two long tables. Most of the machines were standard desktop PCs, but others were customized and assembled from what must have been experimental pieces. One of them had a clear case that allowed me to see that the motherboard was submerged in a bath of what looked like vegetable oil. Another one sprouted fiber-optic cables that lit up like little rainbows.

Nikki showed me that I could use my regular school log-in and password to access the system. Once logged on, I could control the security cameras placed all over Topsy or even access the records in the sheriff's department, but for starters she just told me how to call up a catalogue of the inventions housed down in this secret lab. I scrolled through the list for a while and was pretty impressed by what I saw. If even half of this stuff actually worked, then the Mechanical Science Institute was decades ahead of the rest of the world.

"There's something I don't get," I said to Nikki, who was busy fiddling with the security camera feedback. "Everything here is really power-intensive. Like that rail gun back there—it would need a battery big enough to run a car."

Nikki swiveled slowly in her chair towards me. She studied me for a moment as if deciding whether to trust me.

"The Institute has a pair of secrets," she finally said.

"Only a pair? I would have thought digging machines and insect-mounted cameras and all this other stuff counts as more than two secrets."

"Oh, those things are nifty, all right" she said. "But none of it would be possible without our two secret ingredients. The first of which is a room-temperature superconductor."

My mouth dropped open. Superconductors were amazing materials that could store and transfer electricity much more efficiently than typical batteries and wires. The problem was that the best recorded superconductors only work at temperatures less than 150 below zero degrees Fahrenheit. With a room-temperature superconductor, it wouldn't be too difficult to do all kinds of amazing things, like make a belt that would let you fly around like Superman. No wonder the Institute had invented such cool toys.

"If you can make a room-temperature superconductor," I said. "Why don't you patent it and get rich?"

"Well, there's the problem," Nikki leaned back in her chair and made a steeple with her fingers. "We have some of it, but we don't know how to make more of it."

Victor joined us in the computer pavilion where he began checking up on some kind of analytical software he'd been running. He obviously heard what we were talking about, though, because he joined in the conversation.

"For lack of a better name, we call the superconductor teslanium after its inventor. It's not clear whether Tesla actually created it or just found it somewhere, but if he knew how to make more, he took the secret to his grave. Hey—did you know there's somebody at the door?"

Victor leaned over and tapped the monitor with the video feed from the front gate. I could see that there was a crowd of people gathering on Topsy's front steps, but I couldn't see much more in the thumbnail image.

"That's just the new dean," Nikki said without looking. "He got here about ten minutes ago and went up to the residence."

"No, that's not the new dean," Victor rose and clicked some keys that made the video feed full screen. Now I could see that the people at the front door were a mean-looking bunch. Many had shaven heads or grizzly beards. A lot of them had black leather jackets, and one of them was shirtless. I shuddered as I thought back to the creeper who had sought me out on the train. It was hard to tell from the video, but it looked like the same guy.

Nikki was out of her seat and at the monitor to get a better look. "They look like the same bunch who stomped on our new dean yesterday. What do they want with us?"

"I don't know," said Victor. "But I'm betting it has something to do with Professor McKenzie."

I leaned to the right and the left, but the two of them blocked off my line of sight to the screen. "Are they going to break in or something?" I asked. "You don't think they can find us down here, do you?"

"Doesn't matter," Nikki said. "This place is tougher than it looks. All those old-looking bricks are actually carbon nanotubes, built for toughness. We're a fortress. A bunker. Even the glass is better than bullet proof. So don't worry, the only way to get in here is to have a key with the right frequency—"

The screen showed the shirtless guy step forward and hold up a box—and the doors opened.

Immediately both Nikki and Victor exploded into a flurry of panicked activity.

"Where'd they get a key? Where'd they get a key?" Nikki said repeatedly, her voice high pitched with fear.

"Defenses!" Victor yelled. "Start the defenses!" He lunged for a keyboard, but so did Nikki, and they bumped each other out of the way.

I backed away, feeling numb as I watched my fellow students panic while the bikers poured in through the front doors. Right then, my phone buzzed.

"Sophia," said the Professor's smooth voice. "I need you to do some more research. Right now."

"I'm kind of having an emergency at the moment," I said. "Can I call you back?"

"No," he said, and he sounded really determined. "Are you at a computer? Log in now, right now. Find the application titled Topsy Security."

I looked back at Nikki and Victor, who were still swarming around the computers on the other table. It really didn't look like there was any way for me to help them, and the bikers were already inside the ground-floor lab, smashing everything in their path. Most of them had baseball bats, and one guy was throwing firebombs made out of wine bottles.

I turned back to my computer. Maybe the Professor would give me some way to help. After all, he was the guy who told me about the elevator. I was already logged on so it didn't take me more than a second to open the Topsy Security application.

"I'm in," I said, pinning the phone to my shoulder with the side of my head while I typed.

"Good," said the Professor, his voice sticky-sweet. "Now: turn it off."

My fingers froze on the keyboard. I had no idea what the security system could do, but I knew if I shut it off, even for only a few seconds, there would be nothing to stop the mob upstairs. And if the Professor had told me about the secret elevator, then he must have told the creepers as well.

"Sophia," hissed the Professor. "This is the moment of truth. If you turn it off and let my men get what they came for, I promise I won't let them harm you. If you don't, I will punish you. And I will punish your father. Do you understand?"

Chapter 17 ~ Dean

When Dean heard raised voices at the entrance below, he went to the edge of the roof to see what was happening. The Blitzkriegers must have arrived while he was inside, because the parking lot was crowded with at least two dozen motorcycles, and their owners were down below, charging through the open front doors of Topsy as if they had an invitation. Brick was among them. The giant tilted his head back to look up at the roof, saw Dean, and extended a single finger upwards. Then he disappeared into the building.

Dean spun and raced back across the roof garden, but stopped short. There, on the ledge in front of him over the door, was a gargoyle that hadn't been there before. And it was moving.

It skittered along like an insect, belly to the wall. Suddenly, it stopped and reared up on its hind legs. It was the size of a mountain lion, but it looked like a giant lizard with gray, pebbled skin and hooked barbs projecting from its spine and protruding from its elbows and knees. Dean didn't know much about the Minnesota wildlife, but he knew this was nothing that belonged here.

Dean hesitated. If he ran inside, all it had to do was jump down on him, and he wasn't eager to find out what those claws could do.

Suddenly, the creature opened its mouth and hissed at him.

"You must be the new Dean of Students," a voice came from nowhere.

Dean took a step back in surprise. It sounded as if the voice had come from the monster.

"Who are you?" Dean spoke because he was unsure of what else to do.

"I'm the Professor." The voice was tinny and slightly distorted, sounding as if it were coming through a speakerphone.

"*You're* the Professor? You're a lot uglier than I was expecting."

"And you're a lot stupider than I was expecting," the Professor said. "I control this animal, but I am speaking to you through a remote relay. I can see you, but I prefer that you not see me."

Without taking his eyes off the creature, Dean inched towards the residence. From his new angle, he could see that it wore a thick, black collar that blinked a single green LED light with each syllable that the voice uttered.

"Is this how you killed McKenzie?" Dean called. "Did you send your little gecko here to take care of your dirty work?"

"We wanted to take Professor McKenzie alive," the Professor said. "I was unaware of her heart condition. When my men kicked open your door to find her there, it was... a regrettable accident."

"An accident you caused," Dean inched closer. From where the creature was perched, it could easily grab him if he tried to dash through. There was, however, a small tool shed on the side wall that might contain something to help even the odds against those vicious claws.

"I want you to help me find something," the Professor said. "I'll make a deal with you."

"Deal with this!" Dean lunged sideways, plowing his right shoulder hard into the tool shed. Wood snapped and nails tore free, and Dean fell into the midst of an assortment of spades, weed whackers, and hedge trimmers. He grabbed a shovel and pulled it back, ready to hurl it at the creature.

"Get him," the Professor commanded his creature.

There was a crackling sound as the creature's neck was ringed in skeletal fingers of blue lightning. The electrical discharge caused it to tense its body in sudden pain, but it did not attack. A second and a third shock jolted its neck. Disoriented, the thing stumbled, lost its grip, and fell off the roof to land directly in front of the open door.

This was clearly not the reaction the Professor had hoped to induce in his creature, but Dean wasn't about to miss his advantage. He charged in, but the creature was quicker. It darted backwards, through the doorway to the apartment. When it turned to face him, one of the spines on its tail snagged the door, swinging it closed with a small but audible click.

Intending to break the door's casement window and drive the shards towards the creature like a storm of razor blades, Dean slammed his shovel into the glass. The blow didn't leave even a scratch. He struck another blow, and another, each one harder than the last. His hands ached from the impact and his rib burned from the exertion, but the glass remained. In all his years of firefighting, he had broken out plenty of windows but he had never seen anything like this.

The creature glanced back over its shoulder as he pounded, but then scuttled away into the dark interior of the apartment. Dean pulled in vain at the locked door handle and then cupped his hands to the glass so that he could watch the creature as it tracked a scent up the wall to a large ventilation grate. In a single flash of claws, it pried the grate away, and then it slithered into the hole, kicking its back feet behind it as it disappeared down the ventilation shaft.

All Dean could do was to watch it go.

Chapter 18 ~ Soap

"Make up your mind, Sophia," the Professor's voice hissed in my ear, urging me to shut down the security system. No, not urging— threatening.

Victor and Nikki were setting up some kind of surprise for the bikers storming through the upstairs lab and I was one click of a mouse away from stopping it. If I did, maybe the creepers upstairs would take whatever it was they came to get, break a few things on the way, and then they would leave us alone. On the other hand, if I didn't, then my Dad would become a target for the Professor's anger. I didn't know who he was, but I knew he could deliver ten thousand dollars on two day's notice, which suggested that he was serious.

I glanced over at Victor and Nikki again, who were working intently. They had been so nice to me. I enjoyed how Nikki always called me "sugar" and Victor—well, Victor had been a bit rude at first, but I would be a hypocrite if I complained about someone else's lack of social graces. The Professor had promised that the bikers wouldn't hurt me if I let them in, but he never said anything about what would happen to my fellow students.

I left the security system running and hung up the phone without another word.

"Soap, honey, come look at this," Nikki said with a smile. "We've set up a little game of hotfoot for our guests."

She stepped aside so I could join them at the monitor. The video feed from upstairs showed the shirtless guy leading a charge up the spiral staircase when something flashed under his feet. There was no audio, but I could tell from the way his mouth opened wide that he yelped really loud. He fell backwards, knocking two other guys down

like they were bowling pins. One second later, there was another sparking flash under the next guy's foot, and he dropped to his knees and
rolled away.

"We electrified an expandin' area of the floor," Nikki said.
"With each pulse, the shocks will drive them farther and farther back."

"It's classic behaviorism," Victor said, folding his arms and
surveying his work. "They're being punished for going in any direction
except out the door."

I watched as the electrified area spread like the incoming tide
across the floor of the lab. The bikers were thrown into confusion, trying to run in different directions but getting zapped for going the wrong
way. A few turned and bolted out the door, and then more followed.
There was one guy who stood head-and-shoulders above the rest, and it
seemed that the shocks didn't hurt him quite as much as they hurt the
others due to his colossal size. Still, he winced with each flash under his
feet, and as his companions fled past him he decided to turn and leave
with them. One biker hurled a firebomb over his shoulder as a parting
shot, but the walls and tables of the lab were so perfectly fireproof that
all he achieved was a little blackening around the edges.

In the computer pavilion, the three of us cheered at our victory. My cheer, though, was shorter than theirs, because I was wondering
if the Professor would punish me for this humiliation. I felt betrayed
that he had lied to me, but mostly I was getting frightened.

"Hold up," Victor said, his voice serious. "We're not out of the
woods yet. Look at this—we have an intruder in the ventilation system."

Victor shifted the display to show a darkened, square tunnel.
It was shadowy in there, and all I could see was something, maybe a
tail, disappearing around a corner. He shifted to another camera feed
and then another in an attempt to get a good view of the thing, but the
best image he could capture was a flash of what looked like lizard eyes.

"Looks like a giant iguana," I said. "Except uglier."

"We don't have great video coverage inside those airways," Victor said. "But it looks like the Professor has sent us a chupacabra."

"A what?" Nikki asked, and it made me glad that I wasn't the only one who didn't know what he meant.

"A chupacabra," Victor repeated. "At least, that's what Professor McKenzie called it. Before she pulled her disappearing act this summer, she told me she had spotted it spying on her a few times. Maybe that's why she left, I don't know, but now it looks like the Professor designed a two-pronged attack to increase his chances of getting in."

I spun around to look at him. I'd never heard either of them mention the Professor before, but it was obvious they knew him.

"Where'd the Professor get that thing?" Nikki asked.

"Who knows," Victor shrugged. "Genetically engineered it? Got it from outer space? There's no telling, but every mad scientist creates a monster sooner or later."

I shuddered at the sight of the shadowy creature slinking around through the vents.

"Where is it right now?" I asked. "Where's it going?"

To answer my question, Victor pulled up a schematic of the air ducts. This was the first time I had seen the full extent of Topsy House. I could see that the lab in which we stood was ten feet below ground. The maze of air ducts, however, went way, way deep, twisting and branching off like tunnels inside an ant hill.

"Who designed these ducts, M. C. Escher?" I asked. "And why did they make them just perfectly big enough for a lizard monster to travel around inside the walls?"

"The ducts need to be that big to get air down to the reactor room," Nikki said.

I shot her a glance. "Reactor room?" I said cautiously. Nikki had mentioned that the Institute had two secret ingredients for their inventions. One was the superconductor. This reactor must've been the second one.

"It's nuclear, isn't it," I concluded. "No wonder Brett was afraid of you guys!"

Nikki and Victor gave each other a long look, as though they were having a silent conversation about whether they could trust me.

"It isn't nuclear," Victor finally said.

"A fusion reactor, then?" I asked. Fusion was as far beyond nuclear as nuclear was beyond gasoline, but all the other inventions here were a few decades ahead of the rest of the world, so it stood to reason that their power source might be, too.

Victor looked me in the eye and mouthed a single word: "antimatter."

Ridiculous, I wanted to say. Preposterous. Laughable. But when I looked into their faces they both looked so serious that I couldn't say anything.

"Another secret invention," Nikki explained. "Just like with the teslanium, we don't quite know how it works. But our engineering students—like you—have found it pretty easy to copy the reactor design. It also scales down really well, so you could power your house with something that fits into your pocket."

Superconductors and antimatter. This wasn't decades ahead of the rest of the world, this was centuries ahead. These were the kinds of things that could change the course of human history in every conceivable way. With that kind of power, I could turn my wildest dreams into functioning inventions. I could create giant robots, make cars that fly, and send rockets to distant planets... heck, with that kind of power, I could bring distant planets to us!

I had a million questions, but Victor brought me back to the immediate reality of the lizard-beast running loose inside our building.

"The chupacabra is pretty obviously heading down to the reactor," he said. "It must be either really well trained or have some kind of guidance system, because it knows right where it's going. My guess is, the Professor wants to knock out our power supply so we're defenseless."

"So what do we do about it?" I asked.

To answer my question, Victor went to a locker on a nearby wall and pulled out a heavy-duty rack of big, bulky brown suits with rounded helmets. They looked like space suits, except they were flat and featureless, without even any openings for eyes, mouth, or nose. From the way he had to heave and strain to move the rack, I could tell the suits must have weighed about a hundred pounds apiece.

"Radiation suits," Victor announced. "We're going to have to wear them down in the reactor room while we're looking for that creature."

"Wow," I said. "Do they come in black?"

Chapter 19 ~ Dean

Hot rage pumped through Dean's veins. He pounded on the unbreakable glass, but it did no good. The creature was in there. The gang of angry bike-thugs was in there. His key was in there—he could see it on the dining room table, right where he left it. And here he was, trapped outside like an idiot.

He attacked the glass with other tools he found in the shed: a hammer, a pick, an ax. None of them worked. Finally, he flipped open his cell phone. All he had to press was 911, the three little numbers that had summoned him to so many disasters.

Before he brought his finger down on the 9, he heard another commotion at the front door. Dean ran to the edge and saw, to his amazement, the Blitzkriegers running out of the building. Hidden loudspeakers around Topsy simulated the sound of approaching police sirens, and inside of sixty seconds they had made it to the parking lot, mounted their bikes, and roared away. Their departure was as sudden and inexplicable as their arrival, but Dean decided he would need to figure it out later because the lizard-thing was still in there, crawling around in the walls.

If he called 911 now, the local emergency services would need to get into the building, maybe deep into the building in order to find it. McKenzie had always said the Institute held some important secrets, and part of Dean's new job was to protect those secrets. Having a platoon of emergency responders searching through Topsy House didn't seem like something he wanted to bring about. Besides, he, too, was a trained emergency responder. What could they do that he couldn't?

He flipped the phone shut and put it back into his pocket.

Dean then rummaged through the tool shed. Before, he had grabbed whatever had come to hand most quickly, but now he actually had time to find what he was looking for: an ax. Not a fire ax, as he was most accustomed to wielding, but a sturdy wood-chopping tool, with a heavy, chiseled head and a long, wooden handle.

Ax slung through his belt, he gathered up a length of garden hose, tied one end to the heaviest tree he could find, and lowered the other end down the side of the building. He swung his leg over the wrought-iron fence and began his descent. His rib protested all the way down, but otherwise it wasn't a difficult climb, and the thick, rubbery hose afforded a secure grip while his feet moved from window sill down to brick ledge down to gutter brace.

The doors of Topsy House were still wide open. There was a black plastic box about the size of a small laptop next to the door, and it didn't take a rocket scientist to figure out that this was what they had used to trigger the entrance to open. He scooped up the plastic gizmo, carried it past the threshold, and stomped on it once he was inside. When he did, the big doors slid shut behind him and sealed with a satisfying clang.

It looked like the bikers hadn't been very interested in the entry hall because it was pretty well unscathed, save for a few portraits that had been knocked off the wall. Still, there was no telling what they had left behind, so Dean readied his ax and proceeded cautiously. Three steps later, all the lights went out.

"Stupid lizard must be chewing on the wires," he muttered to himself, digging in his pocket for the keychain flashlight. If he was lucky, maybe the creature electrocuted itself when it caused the blackout. Somehow, Dean knew he wouldn't be that lucky.

His tiny flashlight was designed to shed enough light to see a door lock on a dark night, but here in the high-ceilinged entrance hall it could hardly illuminate the floor in front of him. He needed to do a fair amount of groping to make sure he didn't collide with the statue of the person Dean had assumed was Edgar Allen Poe. As he passed, his flashlight beam reflected off the brass plaque at the statue's foot. The word "founder" caught his eye. Dean took two more steps, stopped, and went back to get a closer look.

It wasn't a statue of Edgar Allen Poe after all, but some guy named Nikola Tesla. Dean had never heard of him, but the important thing was that he was the founder of the Institute.

What they want is in our founder's head.

Dean rose to take a close look at the head of the statue, leaning in to study the details. The sculpture was so lifelike it almost felt rude to invade its personal space. With the flashlight at point blank range, Dean could see the individual lines representing the hairs on the man's mustache, the delicate texturing on his lips, and the intricate curves of his alabaster ears. It also allowed him to see the seam that ran along the back of the statue's head.

In full light, the seam would have been invisible, washed clean of its visible depth by the lack of contrasting shadows. Here in the dark, the little flashlight revealed a perfect little door. The sight of it hit Dean like a slap in the face. This was what McKenzie had tried to tell him on that fateful day. "Inside our founder's head" wasn't figurative language for an idea or a piece of information. It wasn't a riddle pointing him to a secret invention. She had been saying, flat out, that Dean should look inside the head of the statue of Nikola Tesla, founder of the Mechanical Science Institute.

With shaking fingers he used the blade of his pocket knife to pry the compartment open. There was no egg inside, but it did contain a single piece of paper. Dean drew it out and squinted at it in the glow of the flashlight.

Chapter 20 ~ Soap

Luckily, the power didn't cut out until after we had reached our destination, a narrow, overheated underground cavern nearly five hundred feet below Topsy. It seemed like a ridiculous depth, but Victor said it predated the Institute, and it was convenient because it ensured that no gamma rays escaped from the reactor to the surface.

To protect us from the radiation, our suits didn't have gaps for eyeholes, but instead used fiber-optic video feeds to little screens placed on the inside of our helmets. When I turned my head the video also moved, so I was seeing the world around me, but at the same time the image was distorted because it had to display three dimensional objects on a flat screen. It's okay to watch something like that on television, but when you're trying to navigate the real world by video relay it can seriously mess up your depth perception. I walked smack into a wall almost as soon as I was out of the elevator car, and it took us a while to get me standing again because the suit was so heavy. Cadmium-plated depleted uranium clothing blocks gamma rays pretty well, but it weighs a ton.

All of us moved slowly in those heavy suits, and I began to wonder how well we would be able to defend ourselves if we could barely lift our arms. Nikki wanted to use the rail gun I had been fiddling with upstairs, so I had reassembled it as best I could. I still had a pair of screws left over after I put it back together, but that always happens. Victor said he wanted to take the creature alive if he could, so he had a rifle loaded with special tranquilizer darts he'd designed. The fingers of the suits were so heavily insulated that they might as well have been iron mittens, so the two of them needed to tie strings from their triggers to their wrists in order to operate the weapons. I carried a big stun rod that apparently had been designed to fend off great white sharks. We looked pretty funny in those big suits with our little weapons. If we had a photo of us at that moment, the caption would say "Astronauts on Safari."

We set off down a corridor that turned sharply in one direction, proceeded about twenty feet, and then turned sharply again. It went on like this until after the third turn in the corridor, I noticed some etchings in the wall. I stopped and leaned in so my camera could get a better angle.

I was looking at really faded carvings of some creatures dancing around what might have been a big, reptilian face. It was too faded to make out most of the other details, except that the dancing figures came in many shapes and sizes. Some were up on their hind legs with their arms stretched over their heads. Others ran or jumped or fought with each other. Around these carvings was faded writing. It was hard to see in the narrow beam of light from my suit's headlamp, but I was certain the writing didn't even remotely resemble any language I had ever seen because it contained lots of jagged little lines and maddening spirals. I might have dismissed it as a random design, but the patterns were too regular. This was meant to communicate something... but not to me.

"Those were down here long before the Institute," Nikki's voice buzzed in my headset. "In fact, near as we can figure, it dates back to the Triassic period, although we have no idea who carved them."

"The Triassic period?" I echoed. "The Triassic period that had a bunch of dinosaurs in it? Wasn't that, like, a couple hundred million years before human beings existed?"

"That's the only Triassic period I know of," she said.

"Then how could these designs be so old? It isn't like anyone was around back then to carve them."

"We don't know who—or what—built this cavern," Victor said. "But it isn't a natural formation, and those carvings were made when this place was built. That's the fun part about science: there are always mysteries to unravel."

I looked at the reptilian eyes carved on that wall. Those eyes had supposedly been staring out into the darkness for longer than the human species had existed, yet they looked strangely... familiar. Where had I seen them before?

We moved on until we passed under an archway, and the cavern opened up into a vaulted underground dome. Judging from the curve of the walls, I guessed that the room was maybe a hundred feet across and thirty feet high, but I couldn't be sure because the outer reaches were shrouded in darkness. There were more carvings here, all around us. Hundreds—*thousands*—of those creepy stone eyes stared out from the darkness on all sides. But in the middle of the room was something much newer and more demanding of my attention: the antimatter reactor.

The reactor looked like a giant kettle-bell, a half-globe that was as big as an SUV and had a loop of pipe running from one chamber to the next. Its body was marked by a big red radioactive symbol, and it was hooked into a gently curving pipe that ran from its top up through the stone ceiling above, while another pipe ran down from the ceiling and into the dome on the opposite side. I wanted to rush over and pull it apart to see how it worked, but there was a chupacabra loose down here that we needed to deal with first.

"You guys—there it is!" Nikki said urgently. She pointed with her glove off into the far distance. It was the chupacabra, all right. It stood at its full height, its forelegs up against the wall and its face pressed close to the carvings. At its feet was an angular pile of something white and metallic.

"What's he got?" I whispered. "What is that thing down at its feet?"

"You don't have to whisper," Nikki said. "It can't hear our intercom. And that thing at its feet is our reactor core, which explains why the lights went out. That core's pure teslanium—it's incredibly valuable to us."

"That creature must be pretty smart to be trained to find that core," Victor said. "Okay, you guys wait here and turn off your lights. I'll loop around try to get on the other side of it."

"Let's get this over with," Nikki said. "I'm worried this radiation suit is making me look fat."

Nobody laughed at Nikki's joke. I was too busy thinking about what would happen if the creature spotted us before Victor got to it. Suddenly my suit seemed ten times heavier, but that might have been good because its weight was about the only thing keeping me from running away.

Victor shuffled silently around the outside of the cavern and disappeared behind the reactor. With our lights off, I could barely see anything, so I pressed up against the wall and watched the chupacabra, which was outlined in a very faint beam generated by a red light in its collar. The creature looked like it was in some kind of trance, leaning its head in really close to the wall, almost like it was sniffing those carvings. Or reading them. I wondered what the chupacabra was seeing when it looked at those designs.

Then it struck me with a jolt why the carvings had seemed so familiar. The snake eyes, the flared nose, the short, flat mouth—it was a two hundred million year old bas-relief of the same creature that now stood, alive and in the flesh, not far away from us.

"Nikki!" I was panicking. "Nikki! Nikki! It lives here!"

"What?" she reached out and grabbed my arms to hold me still. "What lives here?"

"The chupacabra! The chupacabra made this place! Or maybe his ancestors did, I don't know. All I know is, it's connected to this cavern somehow. Look at the carvings!"

I stepped towards the wall, intending to point out the similarity between the creature and the spooky, eons-old carvings, but I misjudged the distance again due to the flat video screen. I smacked face-first into the wall and bounced backwards, pin-wheeling my arms in a vain attempt to keep my balance. Nikki tried to catch me but the suit was too heavy to hold up and I plopped down onto my butt, dropping my stun-stick with a ringing clatter.

The chupacabra's head snapped around in our direction. Then it charged.

I don't know how fast a human athlete can cover fifty yards, but I found out that a chupacabra can travel that distance in close to zero seconds flat.

Nikki snapped on her helmet lights, raised her rail gun, and pulled the string tied to the trigger. The gun didn't fire. Actually, the gun's slide pulled free and all those shiny barrels bounced uselessly down to the floor.

I tried to rise to my feet, but I was like an upside-down turtle, and I couldn't avoid the incoming chupacabra. When it pounced, I felt the suit buckle around my chest and saw the screen inside my helmet cut to static for just a second. When it came back on, my entire field of vision was filled with red eyes and pointed teeth.

I had no chance of getting up, so I reached blindly for my stun-stick, but I couldn't turn my helmet to look for it. Nikki tried to push the thing off me, but she lost her balance and ended up falling, too.

Suddenly Victor appeared around the reactor. I could see him over the creature's shoulder, coming to my rescue as fast as a person could run while wearing armor that weighed almost as much as he did. He moved in a slow, determined stagger as he struggled in close enough to get a shot. He raised the rifle and yanked the string-trigger... the dart went wide of the target. I could hear the *clink!* as it harmlessly bounced off the stone wall next to me.

The creature turned at the sound of the dart whistling over its head, and that gave me just enough room to roll away. I didn't get far, but I got far enough to feel the handle of my weapon. When the chupacabra jumped on my chest again, I swung the stun-stick and jabbed for the creature's neck. There was a jolt and a flash, and my attacker jumped backwards. It was apparently unharmed. Except that now it no longer wore its collar.

The chupacabra crouched there for a second, just staring at me. It wasn't hurt or frightened as far as I could tell. If anything, it looked... curious. Then it reached up to caress its neck, running those long, clawed fingers from its ear-slits all the way down to its shoulders, as if gently probing its skin in search of the collar that it no longer wore.

My suit was way too heavy to allow me to sit up, so I had to roll to my stomach and push up to my knees from there. When I did, I could see the collar on the stone floor, still smoldering from the charge the stun-stick had released.

By then, Victor had reloaded, and this time his dart found the creature's haunch. The chupacabra spun and slashed the air behind it, but before it could close in on Victor it slumped forward onto the stone floor, its long tongue lolling from between its pointed teeth.

"This tranquilizer won't last long," Victor said. "Soap, do you think you can repair that reactor so we can take the elevator back upstairs before this thing wakes up?"

By the time he spoke the words, I was already standing over the reactor core, puzzling out how it worked.

Chapter 21 ~ Dean

Discovering the location of the egg was important, but Dean wanted to take care of the lizard-creature before he did anything else. He moved systematically through the ground-floor lab, ax at the ready, peering under tables and listening at walls for any sign of movement. His boots crunched over plenty of broken glass left behind by the Blitzkrieger's little rampage, but he discovered nothing else of interest, even after the electric lights came back on.

Next he searched the residence upstairs, tapping on the walls in hopes of eliciting a response from inside the air ducts. Still no luck.

Suddenly, Dean heard a clank through the wall that connected the residence to the oddly-located shower room. It was muffled, but when he pressed his ear to the wall, he heard it again.

In a flash he was at the shower room door. Listening for a moment, he heard more clicks and a scraping noise that he was certain must be the sound of claws on shower-stall tiles. Dean allowed himself one deep breath before bursting in with a roar, ax held high.

He was greeted by the screams of three very startled students.

"Sorry! Sorry!" Dean quickly lowered the ax and held out his hand in a gesture of peace.

The three teenagers before him had to be the three members of the Institute, and he was able to recognize them from the information in his orientation packet. The boy in the white lab coat was Victor von Stommel, the girl in pink was named Nicole Du Bois, and, of course, there was his cousin, Sophia. All three of them looked sweaty and disheveled.

"Dean...?" Soap stared at him with wide eyes. "What are you doing here?"

It was a fair question and one that he had asked himself often in the past few days.

"I work here now," he announced. "Sorry for the surprise. I probably should have called."

She looked blankly at him. She must have been amazed to find him here, but he was almost as amazed to see how she had grown. The last time they had met had been at a family Christmas when she had been no more than ten years old. He remembered how she had re-wired another child's remote control car so that it could go faster, and how she had zoomed it around the house until the motor overheated and the car rolled to a stop, a trail of burning plastic droplets marking its final run across the white carpet. Now, six years later, she still wore all black with her dark hair pulled back into the same shoulder-length pony tail, but she was growing into her long arms and her high cheek-bones. That little girl Dean had once known was becoming quite a beauty.

"He's your *cousin*?" Victor asked. "That's so weird."

"Hang on a second," said Nikki. Dean saw that she had the body of a pinup model and the wardrobe of Science Lab Barbie. "Your name's Dean?" she said. "And you're the Dean of Students? ...That makes you Dean Dean?"

"Just call me Dean."

"Double Dean? Dean Squared?"

"Listen," he raised his voice. "You guys have to go home. There's something dangerous in this place. I can't explain right now, but you have to get out."

"You mean the chupacabra?" asked Victor. "We caught it."

This stopped Dean cold. "You... you what?"

Victor held his hands up to indicate the height and width of the creature. "You're talking about a five-foot tall reptilian thing with sharp claws and red eyes, right? Yeah, we caught it. We've got it in a cage down in the... never mind."

Dean looked at the three of them and they all nodded. They seemed so sure of themselves, as if scaly monsters were a daily occurrence in the lab.

"I have to go," Soap announced suddenly. "I'm late."

Dean looked at his watch and saw that it was almost nine pm.

"Hold it for a second," Dean said. "I need to ask you guys some questions. I want to know everything you can tell me about Professor McKenzie, particularly about why a gang of motorcycling bank robbers was chasing her."

"Beats me. I'm new," Soap said, her voice strained. "Can I go now? Please?"

"No, this is serious," Dean said. She looked like she was about to cry, but he was standing in the doorway so she had no easy escape. "Those guys who came in here earlier—did you see them?—they're dangerous. Hey, speaking of that—do any of you know how they could blow out the power for an entire building? And I don't mean cutting the wires. I mean frying all the electronics in an area, even... even medical devices inside a person."

"Are you talking about my experiment?" Soap asked distractedly. "I keep telling everyone that I didn't mean to blow up all those phones, but now my Dad has money for—oh. Uh oh."

She pulled a phone from her pocket and swiped the face, but the screen remained black.

"I really have to go," she said, and this time she pushed past Dean to get out of the room. He made a half-hearted attempt to stop her, but there were tears in her eyes and she seemed genuinely upset about something, so he let her go.

"What was that about?" Dean asked. The other two just shrugged. "Okay, then," Dean went on. "Do either of you know what she was talking about? With the science experiment, I mean? Nicole?"

"Call me Nikki. And Soap was probably talking about an EMP-bomb, which is a thing that uses an electromagnetic pulse like a weapon to wipe out anything with circuitry."

"You think those bikers could have made one of these EMP-bomb things?" Dean asked.

"No way," Nikki shook her head. "Not without some big-time help. You would need a special power source. If you're just using the standard batteries or wall plugs, the best you could do is create a short-range annoyance. If you want to use it against a whole building, you would need military hardware or—"

She stopped herself and looked over at Victor, who shook his head.

"Why do you think they didn't use it today?" Dean asked. "When they charged in here, they could have fried the school first."

"It wouldn't work on us," Victor said. "This building has some, er, special wiring. They must have known."

"Okay, tell me about Professor McKenzie," Dean propped the ax on his shoulder and paced back and forth beneath the shower heads. "What happened that made her come find me? One of you must have been around to see something."

"I know she started getting threatening emails during the summer," Victor said. "She wouldn't let me see any of them, but she said that some professor-guy wanted something and she was afraid of what he would do with it. She thought she was being spied on, too, so she packed up and left. That was in late August. I think she wanted to make those people chase her so they wouldn't bother us. It's the kind of thing she would do." Victor cleared his throat and wiped his sweaty brow with the back of his white sleeve. "So now it's your turn, Dean—I mean, Dean. Sorry, I don't know what to call you. But can you tell us what those bikers wanted?"

Dean thought about it for a second. He pulled open the door and gestured for them to get out.

"You're safer not knowing," he said. He could read in their faces that this was not a popular answer. "Don't worry about it. I'm going to take care of these guys and then I'll quit so you can get someone with a college degree to run this place again."

"You're not a professor?" Nikki said as if Dean had just confessed to tax evasion. "Then what are you doing workin' here?"

Instead of answering, he just jerked his thumb at the open door again. Nikki led the way, but as Victor approached the door, Dean dropped his arm to block the exit. Victor looked up at him as Dean leaned in close until the boy was almost entirely enveloped in his broad-shouldered shadow.

"Three sweaty teenagers in a shower," Dean hissed. "I may not be very smart, but I was 18 once. Stay away from my cousin with that stuff. Got it?"

Victor opened his mouth to respond, but Dean tightened his grip on the ax so that his fist made an audible squeaking sound against the handle. Victor nodded and hurried out of the room.

"Kids!" Dean said, shaking his head.

September 14th
(Doomsday minus 3 days)

Chapter 22 ~ Soap

After I left Topsy, I ran to my room to call my Dad. I needed to tell him that something bad might happen if he didn't leave home and hide. Even if he didn't believe me, I might still be able to convince him to take the money and go on vacation. Maybe he could come to Bugswallow and we could keep each other safe.

When I got back to Smiley, I found that my long-distance telephone account hadn't been activated so I couldn't call New York. Hannah wasn't around, so I ran to the library, but Brett was long gone, too, and the library was closing up. I drifted around for a while, desperately trying to figure out what to do. Finally, I ended up at the student union, where I found a group of kids smoking out on the front benches and convinced one of them to loan me her phone. There was no answer at the apartment, and no answer on my Dad's cell. All I could do was leave messages, and I couldn't even give him a call-back number.

I knew I wouldn't be able to sleep, so I headed back to Topsy. It was past midnight, and a cold wind whipped me in the face as I walked, telling me a storm was coming. To make matters worse, when I got to the top step of Topsy and held out my key, the big double doors didn't open for me. I moved the key all around in the air, pressing it against the wall in different places in hopes of tripping the sensor, but the doors didn't budge. I also tried knocking, but nobody answered. Finally I ended up walking around the entire building, peering through windows in hopes of spotting someone, but the building was dark and empty.

I found the Professor's phone in my pocket. It was still dead and blank, so I threw it as far as I could and I heard it smack into a tree somewhere in the darkness. But that didn't help my situation. I still couldn't get in touch with my Dad and I couldn't find any of my friends. I felt so isolated that I might as well have been at the bottom of a well in Outer Mongolia.

Then I heard the clang of Topsy's door behind me. Someone was coming out, which meant I was saved.

I pelted back up the path to the base of the stairs to see Nikki, her pink lab coat draped over her arm as she stood above me.

"Nikki!" I said. "I'm so glad to see you. I really need your help—"

"Shut up," she said. Her face twisted in a snarl as she spoke and her eyes sliced into me like lasers.

I stopped cold, not knowing what to say or do.

"I checked the security logs for the break-in," Nikki said. "They used your key code. *Your* key code let them in. I don't know if you knowingly betrayed us or if you're just so stupid that they tricked you, but it doesn't matter."

"But I—"

"No," she cut me off. "There is no excuse. I told Victor about it. As far as I'm concerned, you don't belong here anymore."

She pushed past me and strode to the parking lot without looking back.

I stood there for a long time, just staring up at Topsy House. Soon, the rain came. It soaked my clothes and drenched my hair, and I didn't even care.

Chapter 23 ~ Dean

Dean slid his fingers across his scalp, made a fist, and tried to yank his hair out by the roots. No good: his black hair was not nearly as close-cropped as it had been two weeks ago, but it was still too short to pull out in his moment of frustration. He would just need to find a more productive way to torture himself while he wrestled with the most difficult aspect of the new job that he had encountered so far: logging on to his email.

On his first day as Dean of Students, he had been thrown into jail. On his second day, he allowed a giant lizard into the building, and then, after failing to find it, he discovered his cousin frolicking in a shower with two other students. Dean had been so tormented by thoughts of murderous professors and bikers with EMP-bombs that he had been unable to sleep, so he arose early on his third day in the hopes of actually getting something done. Maybe in the grand scheme of things, email wasn't as important as the other stuff, but it was proving to him that he was way, way out of his depth here.

He had the instructions that the nice lady in human resources had given him, but none of it covered the very first question the computer asked him when he logged on, which was whether he wanted access to the local directory or to the server. Dean wouldn't have known the difference between a local directory and a server if they had both been handed to him on a silver platter with a side of French fries, so he had clicked a button at random. This resulted in a ten-minute wild goose chase of error messages, which only ended when Dean gave up and started over from the beginning. Then he wasn't sure which button he had pressed the first time around, so he ended up repeating the goose-chase. Now, after his third try, the thing said it was loading files, but the little green bar that indicated the progress looked like it hadn't budged as long as he had been watching it.

In the brightly lit study of his apartment, he could see the ghostly reflection of his face superimposed above each and every error message on the computer screen. He looked into his own dark-ringed eyes and wondered how McKenzie could have possibly expected him, a blue-collar meat-head, to run a school for junior techno-geniuses. He found himself longing for the good-old-days when he ran into burning buildings.

"How long do you think you can keep fooling people?" he asked the faint outline of his reflection. The only response he got was a slight tick in the green bar that indicated progress on his mailbox configuration.

He sighed and dug into his pocket for the piece of paper which he had discovered inside the Nikola Tesla statue. Here, at least, he thought he had something good, although it was difficult to know for sure. The paper was a pink invoice form, the not-quite-darkened letters in the boxes indicating that it was a duplicate copy. A decorative logo at the top read "Detroit Museum of Natural History. Detroit, MI." It was dated two years ago and described the donated item as an "Egg-shaped geological specimen of indeterminate origin."

It was now clear that he wasn't hunting an actual egg, just an egg-shaped rock. He could also guess that McKenzie had donated this "geological specimen of indeterminate origin" to the museum long before the Professor came calling. She probably hadn't known it was worth anything, but when he started threatening her she must have figured it was safer where it was, so she put the invoice in a secure spot to ensure there would be nothing to lead him to it. It was nice to have an answer to some questions, but too much still remained unknown. For starters, what was this egg-rock-thing and why was the Professor ready to kill for it? And how was Dean supposed to get his hands on it? He doubted he could just walk into the museum with the receipt and get it back. Worse, if the Professor got wind of what he was trying to do, then the Blitzkriegers would just roll into the museum and take the egg while Dean was still filling out paperwork.

Dean looked back up at the mailbox progress. It was almost fifty-percent done now, which was encouraging. In a strange way, this gave him hope that maybe his mad quest would also work out, if he gave it enough time. But time was something he didn't have. Shipping the egg would take too long, not to mention that it could provide the Professor's goons plenty of chances to snatch the package while it was in transit. No, he needed to pick it up personally, but Detroit was a twelve hour drive each way, and Dean was loath to leave the school unguarded for that amount of time. By air, he could be there and back in a single day, but that cost money, and Dean had already maxed out his credit cards to repair the wiring in his house back in Santa Monica. Until he got a paycheck or sold that house, he couldn't afford a movie ticket, much less an airplane ticket.

Suddenly, he had a thought. He might not have any money, but the Institute did, and he was now in possession of an official Mechanical Science Institute credit card. He didn't know how much he could draw, but he knew the school had ample resources. Millions of dollars, President Hart had said. The President had also threatened jail time for misuse of those funds, but this was an emergency.

While the green progress bar crept closer to its destination, Dean surfed over to an airline site to make his travel arrangements. By the time Dean had booked a flight and a rental car, his email finished loading and his inbox came up on screen. He found he already had two messages. The first was from human resources and contained a document with the instructions he could have used when setting up his email account.

"Thanks for that," Dean muttered as he deleted the email.

The second message said "Congratulations, Dean." Considering that he had never used this account before, it seemed a little early to be receiving spam, so he clicked on the message.

> Salutations and congratulations on your new appointment as Dean of Students at the Mechanical Science Institute. Allow me to introduce myself: I am Doctor Bill Helmholtz, and I was the Dean of Students prior to Professor McKenzie.
>
> I would like to offer my services to you. Should you have any questions about the school or your job, or if you simply need a sympathetic ear, please click below to contact me. I seldom have reason to stray far from my computer, so I will await your reply.
>
> Yours, William Helmholtz, Ph.D.

Dean rubbed his chin as he stared at this note. William Helmholtz was the dean prior to McKenzie—the dean who had been convicted of embezzlement. Hadn't President Hart indicated he was still in prison? Maybe that was why the guy said he rarely went far from his computer. Still, Dean couldn't see how it would hurt, so he clicked the link. It opened up another window, this one obviously a video feed from a webcam. It displayed a slightly pudgy, middle-aged gentleman who wore a bright orange prison jumpsuit. The man hummed to himself as he watched his fingers clicking away on his keyboard. Evidently, he had not noticed that the video link had opened

"Hello?" Dean said. "Are you Dr. Helmholtz?"

"Oh!" The man looked up, startled by Dean's voice. "Please forgive my inattentiveness. To whom do I have the pleasure of speaking?"

"I'm Dean Lazarchek. The new Dean of Students of..." Dean trailed off, suddenly unsure of what he was supposed to say. He had been expecting a website or an email link, not a video chat.

"I'm Doctor Helmoltz, but please call me Bill."

"And you can call me Dean. Dean Lazarchek. You can call me by my first name, which is Dean, not my job title... which also happens to be Dean."

Bill's face brightened into a smile. He looked like someone's jovial uncle, not someone serving time for a felony.

"Dean Dean... what a delightful happenstance," he said. "Very well, sir, I shall address you as Dean," he then leaned in to the webcam and lowered his voice as if sharing a secret. "But only I shall know whether I am calling you by your first name or your title."

"Well, Professor—Doctor—"

"Bill,"

"Well, Bill, I'm sorry to interrupt you. I didn't know this was a video link."

"Oh, think nothing of it!" Bill said. "You certainly didn't interrupt me—I have nowhere to go for another ten years, minus parole," he sat up in his chair and pointed to the prisoner's serial number stamped onto his orange jumpsuit. "I hope it causes you no perturbation to consort with an incarcerated man."

"I'm sorry?"

"You cool talking with a guy doing a dime in the joint?" he asked, his pronunciation still crisp and professorial.

"Oh, that. President Hart told me. He practically banged me over the head with it, and then he threatened to put me in the cell next to yours."

Bill nodded sagely, with a slightly mournful look in his eye. "Yes, President Hart hated me. Unfortunately, so did the judge—he was one of those anti-intellectual types, you know. That's why I'm serving time in a maximum security prison for a minimum security crime."

"I'm sorry," Dean said. He wasn't really sure what else to say.

"Oh, I get along okay." he made a swift gesture to someone off camera. It surprised Dean to see a stringy young man with dirty hair arrive obediently at Bill's side, offering a plate of pancakes. Bill pushed them to the side and gestured towards his cup, which the young man promptly filled with coffee.

"It's not so bad here," he said between two quick sips. "The guards treat me well and I have established a certain understanding with the other prisoners. They don't hassle me, out of respect for my great learning. You just have to know how to get along with people, that's all. I'm better off than most of the other Deans of Students in the history of the Institute, you know. Most of them died on the job, like that poor McKenzie girl. What a mind she had. Her loss is a true blow to the Institute."

Dean said nothing.

"Well," Bill said, raising his cup in a kind of salute. "Let the Institute's turbulent and bloody history be a lesson to you, my friend. Watch your back and make sure not to drink anything out of an unmarked beaker."

Before Dean could answer, there was a ping from his computer to announce a new message in his in-box. Dean clicked it open to see that it was from President Hart.

"What's the matter," Bill asked. "You look like a man who's just lost a research grant."

"I just got an email from Hart. He says: 'I just received an automatic notification that you've used your expense card to book a flight...' God lord, the man really is keeping a close watch on me. And he says I need to be 'prepared to justify the nature of the expenses.' Wow," Dean looked at his watch to see that it was only seven am. "That's way too Big Brother for so early in the morning."

"Let me tell you something," Bill said. "Hart will stop at nothing to destroy the Institute and lay claim to our assets. You didn't use the credit card they gave you, did you? Oh, tisk, tisk. That card is too easily traced. The Institute has plenty of other funds that he can't trace—oh, but I'm sure you don't want to take fiscal advice from a convicted felon."

"You know more than I do," Dean said. "I'm open to ideas right now."

"That depends. What did you charge to the card? Gambling? Pornography?"

"No, no, nothing like that. I booked a trip to Detroit."

"And what's in Detroit?" Bill leaned in closer to the screen. "A girlfriend, perhaps?"

"No," Dean said a little too loudly. "I need to find something... special. Something McKenzie needed me to get. I don't want to talk about it, but it's very important."

"Okay, forget I asked," Bill leaned back and waved his hands as if shooing the question out of the air. "But I have an easy way to escape your predicament: recruiting trip."

"I'm sorry?"

"You're down to, what—five students?"

"Three," Dean said.

"Well, that's a bit small by anyone's standards. The school charter calls for 33 students and three professors, so it only makes sense that the dean would have to do some travel to interview and inspect potential candidates. In all honesty, the Institute needs very special students, so you have to be choosey. You can set up a meeting with a potential student or two while you're in the area. Anyone will do: even if they don't work out, no one can blame you for the expense."

Dean looked at Bill smiling away at him, and he kind of warmed up to the man. He might be stuck in jail, but he was infinitely better qualified to run the Institute than Dean had ever been, so he deserved some respect.

"Thanks," Dean said. "That sounds like a good idea."

"You are quite welcome, my boy," Bill beamed with pleasure. "As they say here in D Block: stick it to the man, however you can. By the way, you will find student applications under the directory "prospective students" on the server. I expect there are precious few in there right now because our school is not well known, so you may also wish to search the university admissions board files for candidates. And I meant what I said about being choosey about students. The institute is a very special place. Look for passion—if they don't have passion, this isn't the place for them."

Chapter 24 ~ Soap

The stormy night was transforming into a dark, wet morning where violent winds tore the clouds to shreds and rained the pieces down on the University. I hadn't wanted to go back to my room and I knew I wouldn't be able to sleep anyway, so I just wandered the campus all night, mostly staying in the student union building but not wanting to stick in any one spot too long. Finally, the time approached eight am, so I hunched over in my hoodie and scraped along the walkway towards Grangerford for my Chinese class because I couldn't think of what else to do. I had forgotten all about Brett until I got there.

"Sorry I missed you last night," I said even though he didn't look at me when I sat down. "I can't even tell you how crazy things were for me."

He had his notebook out and was doodling the Chinese characters "bu hao," which meant "not good," over and over again.

"That's fine," he said after too much of a pause. "Hannah said you changed your mind."

"Wait, Hannah was there?" I asked. The realization found its way to my brain like a fast-acting poison. She had known about the so-called study group. She had decided to replace me.

"It was just the two of us, so we ended up going for ice-cream," he said.

Before I could say anything else, I felt a tap on my shoulder and I looked up to see a campus security guard. Not one of the student patrol minions who did security as part of their work-study program, but an actual, full-grown man with a utility belt and a handle-bar mustache. It made me wonder if the mustache was a required part of the uniform, because it seemed like every man in this town who worked in any field even remotely related to law enforcement had one of those mustaches.

"You Sophia Lazarchek?" the guard asked.

I nodded, and he gestured that I should follow him. "You'll want to bring your stuff," he added, which made me nervous. When I asked him why, he just repeated his suggestion to bring the stuff.

On my way out of the room, I looked back at Brett, who was watching me go. This time he didn't pretend to look away when I made eye contact, but I couldn't read his expression.

The security guard led me towards the Thatcher Administrative Building, and the whole way there we got dumped on by a classic Minnesota downpour, the kind that only lasts five minutes but comes at you with raindrops the size of baseballs. Each gargantuan drop made me feel like God himself was slapping me in the face and saying "go ahead and cry, you big baby." By the time I got inside, my hair was plastered to my face and leaking a river down the back of my neck. I started shivering, but no one seemed to notice.

The main floor of the administrative building looked like a sweat-shop for cubicle workers, with everyone crammed in to their little spaces, moving stacks of paper around beneath florescent lights. The storm kept any sunlight from getting in, which made those artificial lights even more depressing.

I didn't have long to wait before I was led into an office that said "President Hart" on the door. Inside, an old guy wearing a Langdon University tie sat behind a big desk. He gestured for me to have a seat, and when he smiled at me his big teeth made me think of the wolf in Little Red Riding Hood.

"Do you know why I called you here, Sophia?" he asked in a voice that was honey and gravel at the same time.

"Is it about my father?"

"Yes," he responded.

A huge wave of relief flooded through me. If the president of the university knew about my predicament, he could help me.

"I regret to inform you," he said slowly, "that I am withdrawing you from your classes. Effective immediately, you are no longer a student of this university."

I sat stunned. Finally, I realized my mouth was hanging open, but I couldn't bring myself to shut it.

"But what did I do?" was all I could think to say.

"Your father was arrested last night," he said. "An anonymous call led the police to find ten thousand dollars in cash in his apartment. I understand that the serial numbers on the bills matched those stolen in a recent bank heist, and that your father now stands accused of armed robbery and criminal conspiracy."

I started shivering again. So this was the Professor's revenge: no monsters or street thugs this time. All he had to do was frame my father for grand larceny with the same money he used to bribe me.

"Naturally, this arrest impacts your standing at Langdon University," Hart said. "Your application forms indicate that your legal guardian—namely, your father—had no money in savings with which he might pay tuition. Now it has come to light that he had thousands of dollars in unreported assets. As stated in the form which you signed, any dishonesty in your application is grounds for expulsion."

I blinked a few more times. I had been wrong—President Hart was no care-giver. He was a vulture, come to pick the meat off my bones.

"But he's innocent—we're innocent," I mumbled, already knowing my words wouldn't make a difference. "What happened to innocent until proven guilty?"

"That only applies in the courts," Hart leaned back in his chair and folded his hands over his stomach. "Whether or not your father acquired the money through illegal means hardly matters to me. You had it and didn't report it to us, which makes you guilty of dishonesty. Now, the student bill of rights allows you seven days to pack up and vacate your dorm. You had better go attend to that. Oh—and say hello to your cousin Dean for me, will you?"

I stumbled out of the office in a daze. I had lost my father, my friends, a potential boyfriend, and now my scholarship and my college enrollment. I had lost my past as well as my future. All because of the Professor.

I was supposed to clean up and get out of my dorm room, but where could I go after that? I couldn't return to my apartment in Flatbush with our eviction about to go into effect. One way or another I was about to end up on the streets, and I didn't even know which streets.

There was one person who might still be able to help: my cousin. He was the Dean of Students; he was in a position of influence. Maybe he could talk some sense into President Hart or tell me how to appeal this decision. At the very least he could look out for me until I figured out what to do.

When I got to Topsy, the door was still locked tight against me and there were no cars in the parking lot.

I leaned back against the wall next to the door, slid to the floor and cried quietly into my hands. I don't know how long I was there, but I think it was a long time. Eventually, I heard a car roll into the parking lot and pretty soon Victor appeared through the trees. I made a vain attempt to wipe the tears away from my eyes. I even considered running away to hide in the bushes before he got to me, but I knew I couldn't get away without being seen.

When he reached the top of the stairs, he froze in place while he looked at me.

"Hi there," he said, his tone soft. I had honestly expected him to snap at me the way Nikki had, but he didn't seem angry.

"Is my cousin in?" I asked, trying to keep my voice from disintegrating.

"You didn't get the email?" Victor asked. "He sent it to all of us this morning to say he was flying to Michigan and we were supposed to stay away from school until he gets back. You can see how well we're following his orders."

So Dean had abandoned me, too. While I tried to keep from crying, Victor came and sat next to me, right there on the ground outside the door, and he put his arm around me.

"I've had a seriously bad day," was all I could say.

Victor just sat with me and I cried a little more. When I was done he reached into his pocket and pulled out a Hershey's bar and broke off a chunk for me. Honestly, I was even more grateful for his presence than for the chocolate. As my experience with Brett proved, I'm pretty stupid when it comes to boys, but I know enough to love a friend who has chocolate when you need it.

"What can I do to help?" he asked. I considered giving him a hug, but I didn't want to make him feel awkward. Instead, I put another square of chocolate in my mouth and wiped my eyes with the back of my right hand.

I thought I was going to cry again, but discovered that my tears were gone. I had emptied out all my sadness, and now the only thing left inside of me was anger. Not a hot, burning anger, but a cold, calculating rage. It was always there, this molten core of fury, but I never knew until that very moment that I could burn the world to ashes if that's what it was going to take.

"I need your help with something," I said.

"What do you need?" he asked

"Revenge," I stated, and my voice was as cold as liquid nitrogen.

September 15th
(Doomsday minus 2 days)

Chapter 25 ~ Dean

Dean hunched over on the museum bench and stared at the display of rocks and crystals behind the glass in front of him. His trip so far had been a continuing accumulation of setbacks. First, he had missed his flight. He booked another seat, but the new route took longer because it went through Chicago. By the time he turned the key in the ignition of his rental car in Detroit, he knew he wouldn't be able to make it to the Museum of Natural History before it closed.

At least he had been able to use the plane ride and the evening at the hotel productively to set up an appointment with a Grosse Point High School counselor. The counselor introduced him to several students, but to Dean they all seemed like carbon copies. Four point GPAs. Virtuosos with the violin/piano/saxophone/whatever. National honors for this, distinguished test scores on that. Dean figured he should probably offer admission to all three, but it just didn't feel right. All these candidates were missing something. Bill Helmholtz may have been behind bars, but his advice about preserving the special culture of the Institute had been good. McKenzie would have wanted students with a passion for learning, so that's what Dean would hold out to find. He would just have to come up with some other way to satisfy President Hart's ultimatum to increase enrollment.

The candidate research meant he could justify his charges for the trip, but Dean dreaded that he had left his current students without protection for too long. With luck, they would be sensible enough to follow his instructions to stay home until he returned. However, after catching them in the shower together, he didn't feel right about letting Victor alone with his young, innocent cousin. *Maybe I'm too overprotective,* he thought. *But she's only 16 years old, for crying out loud.*

Dean was beginning to realize how right McKenzie had been when she had said the students needed someone to look out for them, and it was becoming clear that Soap needed that protection more than the other two.

For all his worries about his cousin and the other students, he had come too far to leave empty-handed. He wandered the museum for an hour, studying the mineralogical displays until he finally found the plaque that read "Bugswallow Egg. Indeterminate Origin. Courtesy of Mechanical Science Institute, Bugswallow, Minnesota" and the accompanying diagram indicated that the so-called egg was a lump of rock not much bigger than a softball, tucked in the back of a display of glittering crystals and mirror-polished volcanic minerals. The egg was wrinkled and pinched so that it might have looked like a disembodied brain except that its surface was black and glassy, shimmering with the same grimy rainbows that appear when motor oil and rainwater mix on asphalt.

He had found the egg, but now came the hard part: figuring out how to ask the curator to hand it over. Most likely, there would be endless paperwork. Or maybe they wouldn't want to give it back at all. Dean had been hoping that the egg had just been in some dusty drawer in the back room, but if they had it out on display, they probably wanted to keep it.

"I know the feeling," said a woman's voice above him.

Dean snapped out of his stupor and looked up to see a tall, slim young woman in a gray business suit. Aside from the suit, she didn't look much like a business woman: she was maybe in her mid twenties, and was lean and toned with an athlete's strong legs, a firm waist-line, and shoulders that didn't need pads to strike the right proportions in the suit. She wore her blond hair in a tight bun, but a few fugitive strands escaped their bonds and raced one another down her cheeks. Her brown eyes darted around the room, burning with a constant spark of amusement at some secret joke.

Instinctively, a list of old pick-up lines scrolled through Dean's mind, and then his gut clenched as his grief for McKenzie recaptured his thoughts.

If he gave any external sign of turmoil, the woman didn't seem to notice. She strolled slowly past the display case, one finger trailing behind her to caress the line where the glass met the metal frame. She ran her finger around the little sticker that said "Please Do Not Touch the Glass," leaving it encircled in a faint smudge.

"I know how you're feeling," she said. "Been up all night, exhausted from the plane ride but unable to sleep."

"How...? I mean, what?" Dean sat back. "How do you know I've been on a plane?"

She pivoted to face him by shifting the weight on the balls of her feet. She wore black running shoes—very practical and sporty, even if they were a little bit out of place with the suit. She also had a sleek, silver day pack, the kind you might buy at a high-end outfitter. The pack's straps hugged her shoulders as snugly as a parachute's harness.

"Of course you took the plane," she said. "This is Detroit. The only people who actually live here are criminals or unemployed factory workers, and you don't look like a factory worker. More importantly, I can see the stub of your plane ticket in your jacket pocket."

Dean self-consciously looked down to see that, yes, the corner of his ticket protruded from his pocket, with the airline's logo visible to the world. He tucked it back out of sight.

The woman leaned back against the exhibit window case. "So if you aren't a criminal or a line worker, would you mind if I ask your line of work?"

"I'm a, um..." he almost said firefighter, but then corrected himself. "I'm in academics."

"Academics," she said with a laugh. "You don't look like an academic. What'd you do to your nose, get it stuck in a text book?"

Dean rubbed his nose instinctively when she said that, and pain shot through his face. The swelling and the black eyes had diminished greatly over the last twenty four hours, but black tracks still filled the skin beneath his eyes and the whole area felt raw and tender.

"It was a... bicycle accident."

Her head dipped back as she let out a light, tinkling laugh. "Looks more like the kind of thing that happens in a fight. Am I right? I'd hate to see what the other guy ended up looking like. Let me guess— he was huge? And bald? And he drove a motorcycle and had two friends with him. Lucky guess, right?"

Dean looked up at her in shock, his fingers frozen in the air an inch above his injured nose.

"Relax," she said, walking over to him and placing a hand under his elbow and guiding him to his feet. "I know who you are, Dean. My name's Angela. I graduated from the Institute last year, and now I'm here to help you."

Dean's mind reeled as he tried to re-categorize Angela from "random hot chick" to "unexpected ally." He groped through his memory for explanations, particularly about how she had found him here. Perhaps McKenzie had asked her to keep an eye on the museum. Dean had also mentioned where he was going in his email to the current students, so one of them could have sent for her. Whatever the case, Angela seemed like she knew what she was doing.

"I'll answer all your questions later," she said, hooking her arm through his. "For right now, just walk with me."

"Walk—where? Why?"

"Shhh. Walk casual." She gestured with her eyes up to the ceiling at a black patch of plastic. "There are security cameras all over the place."

"Why do we care about the cameras?"

"I thought that would be obvious," Angela said. "We're about to rob the museum."

Chapter 26 ~ Soap

Victor let me into Topsy and even got me another key. After that, I worked through the night to improve Rusty. If I was going to get revenge on the Professor, I would need my robot in top condition.

The first thing I did was cannibalize one of the scaled-down antimatter reactors from some big gizmo that was already broken. As far as I could tell—and this was only a guess because I didn't have time for any experimentation—the reactors worked by accelerating the formation of virtual particles on the quantum level. These virtual particles always came in pairs, one part matter and one part antimatter, and the energy came when these particles annihilated each other in the same instant they formed. There were no dangerous materials because the fuel—the virtual particles—were already everywhere in the universe. It's possible they were coming through from a parallel universe or that they were quantum strings changing their vibration frequencies or something, but the bottom line was the same either way: unlimited, weightless fuel that was stable until use. Also, the only waste products were some gamma rays which could be soaked up by some nice, heavy cadmium-plated depleted uranium shielding.

Right then, I didn't care about the operational theories or how the reactors seemed to scoff at the first law of thermodynamics. All I cared about was the power.

Before, Rusty was methodical and slow, so he was hard-pressed to keep up with a person walking briskly. Now, with the antimatter reactor in his core and superconducting servo motors for all his moving parts, he could carry a pair of anvils and still outrun me. I also restored his scorpion tail with the magnifying transmitter, which meant he could blast focused EMPs in different frequencies and with different strengths. I thought about adding some rail guns or flame throwers or something, but I didn't have any of those things handy, and every hour I spent tinkering in the lab was another hour my Dad was rotting in jail.

Aside from robotic backup, I also needed information on where to find the Professor, or at least his men. I remembered that the Topsy House computers connected to the sheriff's station servers, but Victor said that only Nikki had the passwords to get into the police databases. I dreaded seeing Nikki after what she had said to me, but I was ready to beg if that's what it took.

The only problem was that Nikki never showed up.

"Where is she?" I finally said to Victor in exasperation.

Victor was taking a study break to feed the chupacabra. Choop, as we were now calling the creature, seemed very appreciative of the anything we gave him. My guess is that the Professor hadn't been feeding him enough and was probably abusive in other ways, too. Now, the spiny gray reptile (Victor insisted he was a reptile and not a lizard) was all too happy to live in our jail cell. It turned out that Choop was really smart, too, and he even seemed to recognize a wide variety of verbal commands like "sit" and "roll over" and "stop trying to eat your bed cushion." Not for the first time, I wished I knew where this creature had come from.

"Nikki usually isn't gone this long," Victor said. He had a pocket full of Slim Jims and was peeling them open, one at a time, and handing them through the bars of the cage. Choop would grab them eagerly and make a kind of chirping bird-song while he munched away. Then Victor reached through the bars to pet the creature. It seemed like the right way to lose an arm, but the big reptile nuzzled his hand and kept chirping.

"You think Nikki's staying away because of me?" I asked. "I mean, because of the thing with the key?"

"Probably," Victor was never one to candy-coat a situation. "Nikki gets pretty vindictive sometimes. Here," he offered me a Slim Jim. "Help me feed Choop."

It didn't look like he needed any help, but he wouldn't let me off the hook.

"Give it to him. Go on. He's an amazing creature, you know. He reached right into the core of that badly shielded reactor and he never showed the slightest sign of radiation sickness. Don't you think he's earned a snack?"

I slid the stick of processed meat only a little way into the cage because I was afraid to get any closer than that. Those red eyes studied my face for a minute, then they looked over at Victor, then back to me. Finally, Choop grabbed it and retreated to a corner, where he could eat his prize and keep watch on me at the same time.

"Don't feel bad," Victor said. "It takes time to build up trust."

"Do you mean with Choop or with Nikki?"

Victor's lips twitched upwards at the corners. I almost had him smiling.

"If you really want to talk to her, she's going to be at the Pi Delta Pi party tonight. You can find her there."

If she was there, then I was going to a frat party. Hannah would be proud of me.

On my way out of the lab I passed a shiny steel cabinet and jumped when I saw my reflection. Two solid days and one solid night in the lab had left my hair all tangled and messy, plus there were some evil black circles under my eyes. It made me look like an actual mad scientist. It was scary and I didn't like it, but all I had time to do was pull the stray hairs behind my ears and head over to Pi Delta Pi.

Everything I knew about fraternities came from movies and television shows. All that stuff led me to believe that a frat party consisted of a bunch of attractive young women and buff young guys in polo shirts, all dancing with red plastic cups in their hands while pounding music playing in the background. In reality, the lighting was much worse, the music was much louder, the people weren't nearly as good looking, and everybody stood around trying to talk over the music instead of actually dancing. Also, the Pi Delta Pi house radiated the stench of yeast, the result of decades of spilled beer soaking into the carpet.

I searched the main floor for Nikki's face and then pressed my way upstairs to see that people were packed in all the way back to the steam-coated windows in each room. It wasn't easy to find anyone in that crowd, especially since the lighting in one room consisted of blue Christmas lights strung around the ceiling, and in another room it was just a plastic, multi-colored disco ball that rotated around a sixty-watt bulb.

The people at the party were actually much nicer than I expected. Unlike the beautiful, selfish characters on those college television dramas, these people here were just regular students. They wore t-shirts and baseball hats and their main goal for the night seemed to be looking casual while standing near people they wanted to meet. At any given time, no more than three people danced to the deafeningly loud music, while the rest leaned against the walls or stood in tight clusters that made it difficult to get around them. I got polite but indifferent smiles from everyone I bumped into, and when I pushed my way past the keg in the kitchen, somebody slid a sloshing plastic cup into my hands.

"Oh, I'm not old enough to drink," I said. I would have preferred to whisper it, but I had to yell to be heard. I offered the cup back to him but he didn't take it.

"You're in college," he said with a half smile. "The drinking age is lowered for college girls."

I didn't remember reading anything about that addendum to the state liquor laws, but I thanked him for the drink and moved back into the living room.

Sidling through the crowd, I found a run-down beige couch that looked as if it had served as a scratch post for eight generations of tomcats. At first, I only had room to lean against one of the dilapidated sofa arms, but I found it was a great place to see the crowd and search for Nikki. From that couch, I had the front door ahead of me, the staircase that led upstairs on the right, and the kitchen on the left. If Nikki was anywhere at that party, she would pass by one of those places eventually.

The turnover rate of couch-sitters was high enough that I calculated that it would only take about five minutes to get a seat. Five minutes and twelve seconds later, there was still no Nikki, but I had moved down from the arm of the couch to claim a cushion, or at least a part of it. I had to be wedged up against one end of the seat because there was a group of rowdy guys in backwards baseball caps who were all excitedly discussing some sports video game.

I looked down and realized I still had the beer cup in my hand even though I hadn't taken a sip. I sniffed it: it smelled like wet socks. I took a tiny drink and found out that it tasted like wet socks, too. There were no convenient potted plants nearby, so I couldn't pour it out, and I wasn't going to dump it out on the carpet, no matter what the norm in here seemed to be. So I kept holding onto it without drinking. Besides, everyone else seemed to have a cup, so I figured it would help me remain in disguise.

As I watched for Nikki, I tried to eavesdrop on the discussion of the boys next to me and thought about what Hannah would have done to join in. The first step of the Conversation Matrix, as I recalled, was to find something to compliment, but the problem was that I didn't know much about sports. When the boy wedged into the couch next to me mentioned that his pinch hitter (whatever that was) kept flying out, I jumped at the chance to congratulate him.

"What did you say?" he shouted over the music at me. He had green eyes and his dusky-blond hair poked through his baseball cap at odd angles, which probably meant he had chosen the hat as a substitute for combing his hair that morning.

"I said: congratulations on your man flying out," I shouted. "It sounds like he must've been moving really fast. Also: you must be exceptionally good at this game, which suggests talent in other areas as well."

"Hey, no need to get sarcastic," he said. I hadn't meant to be sarcastic. I decided to cut my losses and move on to the second step.

"What sports do you play?" I asked. "Also: you seem to have a very athletic build."

He looked at me for a moment with that blank look that people get when they try to solve differential equations in their heads. Then he smiled.

"What's your name?" he asked.

That was trouble. He wasn't supposed to ask my name yet—Hannah always asked theirs first. Had I missed a cue somewhere? Was he off script, or was I? I wished, not for the first time, that conversations were as predictable as microchips.

"I like to skateboard," I said in a futile attempt to keep the conversation on track. "It's all about vectors and geometry and stuff. Also: you seem to have an athletic build."

I grimaced. I knew I was getting it all out of order even worse than before. I clutched the plastic cup a little too hard and it creased in the middle, just enough to send some of the pale liquid cascading down the side and over my fingers.

"How wasted are you?" he asked with a suddenly-huge smile. Now our knees touched and it made me uncomfortable, so I skipped to the final stage of the conversation.

"Want to go to a party?" I said. Then I wanted to smack myself because I realized we already were at a party.

The guy stretched his arm across my shoulder and said "Sure, baby, let's go party. Where's your room?" His friends were all watching us now, wooting like primates and high-fiving each other.

"I think I better go," I said. If he heard me over the music he ignored me, because he kept his arm tight around my shoulder so I couldn't leave.

Suddenly someone yanked me off of the couch. The boys behind me laughed uproariously and called for me to come back, but I was already being dragged through the crowd by a hand with long, pink-painted fingernails.

"Nikki!" I could hardly believe it. The person I had been trying all night to find had found me instead.

She didn't say anything until she pulled me through the kitchen and into the back yard, which had even more empty plastic cups strewn about it than the inside of the house. It was a lot less crowded out there and the music was only a deep, thumping bass that didn't impede conversation quite as much, even though my ears were still ringing like mad. I wondered how much permanent damage my eardrums had suffered even from the short exposure to that level of noise.

Nikki gestured for me to sit on one of the white plastic lawn chairs that were arranged around a wobbly plastic table on the patio. I took a moist towelette out of my pocket and wiped the beer residue off my hands. Then I used the towelette to start scrubbing the film of green mold off the chair.

"You're still mad at me, huh?" I asked as I worked at the chair.

"I'm still mad at you because you're still an idiot," she said. I felt like someone had slapped me across the face, but she didn't slow down. "You fell right into his trap, didn't you? You almost got us all killed. And then I have to go and rescue you from a bunch of drunken frat boys. Honestly, Soap, you're so naïve that you're a danger to everyone, especially yourself."

I started scrubbing the chair even harder. I was opening up a little clean spot in the middle of the field of mold. With each stroke the spot grew bigger, but it was still tiny in comparison to the rest of the chair, an insignificant dot of purity in the middle of a world of filth.

"I'm the victim..." I said pathetically.

"Victim? Ha!" she stopped her pacing to wave her hand dismissively in my direction. She was frowning and her teeth were clenched. "The Professor, he's dangerous. You hear me? You've seen what he can do. He will kill you if he thinks it will help his cause."

"That's why I need your help," I said. "The Professor's framing my Dad for a crime he didn't commit, but you can work the computer to access the criminal database. I know we have cameras in the parking lot, which means we have license plate numbers for those motorcycles—"

"Are you nuts?" she threw her hands up in the air. "I might as well kill you myself and save them the trouble."

"I promise not to track them down in person. I just want to come up with information I can give to my Dad's lawyer."

It was a bald-faced lie. I wanted to go lay waste to their lives the way the Professor had laid waste to mine.

Nikki stepped in close to me, looking into my eyes. Something fierce burned inside of her, and I was sure she could see the same thing burning in me.

"You swear that's all you're fixin' to do?" she demanded. "Maybe you deserve the chance to play Nancy Drew—so long as you stick to the paper trail only. You promise?"

I nodded the lie again.

"Okay, then, I'll get you into the database. But I need something from you in return," she folded her arms and leaned back on the tall heels of her lavender pumps.

"What?" I said. "Anything."

"I need you to drop out of the Institute. After this, you get gone and you don't come back. You hand in your key and you don't get another one—ever. You hear?"

I felt like my ribcage was closing in on my lungs and I had to struggle for breath. Sure, President Hart had withdrawn me from my classes at Langdon University, but as long as my cousin was the Dean of Students at the Institute there was always a chance I could get into Topsy, where I could learn all kinds of things even if I wasn't officially enrolled. Now, though, Nikki wanted to rip that gift away from me. And if I didn't do it, I would lose my father, the only family I really had outside a mother who left when I was a child and a cousin I hardly knew.

I just stared back at her. I wanted to say something, but I couldn't make any sound come out.

"Think about it," she said. "I think you'll see it's for your own good. If you agree, meet me at Topsy in a half hour."

She turned her back on me and disappeared into the house while my mind struggled to put together the pieces.

"Wait!" I called after her, but it was too late for her to hear me. "Wait, Nikki, I already know my answer—"

I dashed through the door into the kitchen, but instead of finding Nikki I collided with a big, muscular guy. Of course, I bounced off him like a ping-pong ball bouncing off a side of beef, but the collision was still enough to knock his cup of beer into his chest and spill it all over his shirt.

"Oh my God," I said, my hands covering my mouth because I didn't know what else to do with them. "I'm so sorry! I'm so sorry!"

"Soap?" he said to me.

I looked up from the wide, wet stain on his shirt to see his face. It was Brett Jensen.

Chapter 27 ~ Dean

"We're going to do what?" Dean tried to pull away from Angela, but she just clamped her arm down on his and kept him walking towards the Museum exit.

"A heist," she said with a voice that mimicked prohibition-era mobsters. "We're gonna rob this joint, see? You know, knock it over. Clip the goods. Pull a fast one. Capiche?"

"Are you crazy?" Dean said loudly. He checked himself and then spoke more quietly. "I don't want to rob this place. It's a museum, for crying out loud."

She stopped in between a collection of stuffed devil rays arranged artfully along one wall and a replica of a deep-ocean habitat on the opposite wall.

"If we don't take the egg," she said, looking him straight in the eye. "What do you think the Professor will do when he discovers that what he wants is right here, protected by a thin pane of glass? I guarantee we won't get caught and no one will get hurt. If you're willing to bet that the Professor would be so considerate, just walk out the door. Go on—you don't need to be involved in this."

Dean stood for a moment. "Who are you?" he asked.

Although he meant it as a rhetorical question, she turned to him with flashing eyes.

"I'm your guardian angel, sweetie," she said, patting him on the cheek. "Now, let's get down to work. Ever seen one of these?"

Without removing her backpack from her shoulders, Angela twisted her arm behind her to pull out a short piece of metal from a side pouch. She opened it like a telescoping antenna until it was two feet long. At first, Dean thought it was a collapsing baton for self defense, but it was far too thin. She flicked a switch in the pommel and the thing started to buzz like a bee.

"What is that?" Dean asked.

"It's an EMP generator," she said. "I call it my harp, because it makes such heavenly music that electronic equipment stops working to listen to the song."

Angela strode back the way they had come, towards the main entrance that connected the oceanic evolutionary exhibit to the mineralogical wing. As she went, the lights overhead flickered rapidly, as though they were short circuiting. The museum's patrons murmured with concern and a security guard by the entrance reached for his walkie-talkie only to be greeted by an earful of static.

"Whoa, hold up," Dean said, placing a firm hand on her shoulder. "I don't like this. There's a bike gang that knocks over banks using a thing like this."

"You mean the Blitzkriegers? Yeah, I've heard of them," Angela waved her hand dismissively. "What they use is more like a sledgehammer that smashes all the electronics within a city block. My harp is more subtle. It just causes things to go on the fritz for a little while but doesn't actually damage anything. It might burn out your cell phone if you stand too close for too long, but that's about it."

As she said it, Dean realized there was a warm sensation in his pocket that was rapidly growing uncomfortably hot. He pulled out his phone and it burned his fingers. The screen was a riot of colors as the pigments squirmed and swirled in the electromagnetic field.

"Sorry," she said, stifling her laughter. "I probably should have warned you. You'll have to buy a new one later. The important thing is that the cameras can't record us right now."

She held her "harp" on the inside of her arm to make it less conspicuous and led Dean by the hand to the room with the egg.

"Would you reach into my pocket?" she said, turning her back towards him. "The pocket on the backpack, I mean—sorry to disappoint. There's a little steel rod I need in there."

Dean unzipped the pocket and found what looked like a sawed-off piston housed in a thick pipe. It weighed about five pounds and had an LCD screen that showed a flat red line against a green graph. The display looked like a heart monitor that was currently reading a flatline.

"What's this?" Dean asked, handing it to her.

"Earthquake grenade," she said nonchalantly as she stuck the device to the center of the display window.

"Huh-uh, no way," Dean said. "You're not going to start blowing things up."

"No explosions today, cowboy," she said. "It's a vibrational oscillator. It emits the perfect harmonic frequency to shatter whatever it's attached to. In other words, it will rattle anything to pieces."

"I'm going to take your word that whatever you just said means it won't explode. Will it work, though? This glass looks pretty thick. There are diamonds in that display, after all."

"Nikola Tesla once almost leveled an entire building with a device like this," she said. "Of course, I improved the design by adding a circuit that finds and maintains the best possible harmonic frequency."

"Where do you get this stuff?"

"I already told you," she said. "I'm an Institute grad; I invented half these toys."

She flicked the switch and stepped back as the line on the earthquake grenade's screen jumped to life. It coiled erratically for a second until it settled into a steady wave, which then sped up, faster and faster, until it blurred into a haze. As it did, the steel rod vibrated like a paint shaker until the entire window shook in tune with it. In less than three seconds, the glass shattered. It happened so quickly that Dean didn't see any cracks: it was as though the whole thing had suddenly turned into powder and cascaded to the floor. The bomb fell with a heavy thump at their feet.

"See?" Angela said, picking the earthquake bomb up and handing it to Dean. "It's reusable, which is good for the environment. Now, which rock do we want?"

A crash emanated from the neighboring room. The guards, evidently disoriented by the flickering lights, were nevertheless sweeping the exhibits to usher patrons outside. Dean handed the earthquake grenade to Angela and leaned over the precious crystals in the display to snatch the wrinkly black rock at the back. It was oddly cool to the touch, and it now seemed to glow in a way it hadn't before. Even after he closed his hand around it, there was an aura of red, blue, and yellow streaks that projected past his fingers. Weirdly, these colors flashed in time with the lights overhead.

Angela didn't seem to notice the swirling colors, and Dean wasn't about to take time to point them out at the moment. The two of them jogged out of the room and through the emergency exit before the guards entered the area.

They emerged into a narrow alley, alone but near enough to the museum's main entrance to see and hear the crowd of evacuated patrons accumulating outside. Museum employees were attempting to keep everyone calm, and a teacher was counting her elementary students to make sure all of them were safe. A police car arrived and two officers began pushing their way through the crowd towards the door, instructing everyone to disperse.

"Give me the egg," Angela said.

"Why?" Dean moved to put it into his jacket pocket.

"I should take it because we both still need to get out of here and you're more likely to be caught than I am."

"How do you figure?"

"Because you didn't bring a jet pack," she said. With that, she snatched the egg out of his hand, turned, and ripped the outer covering off her backpack. Underneath was a contoured device consisting of two chrome cylinders with a rounded engine in the center. In a flash, she had blasted up to the third-story fire escape of the next building over. By the time the silver cloth that had formed the outer layer of her backpack fluttered down by Dean's feet, she had jumped into the air again and disappeared over a nearby roof.

Chapter 28 ~ Soap

It turned out Brett wasn't actually mad at me. He said he was worried about me when I didn't show up, and then got more worried after I told him about my Dad being in jail. Now he wanted to help—and that was the problem. Somehow he got it into his head that I was going to get myself into trouble, and when I told him I needed to go back to the lab, he insisted on going with me. There didn't seem to be any way to get rid of him, so I let him drive me there.

"I knew it," he said as I held out the key to open Topsy's front door. "This place—the people—they're wrong, Soap. You need to quit while you can."

"And how do you know that?"

He followed me inside and we walked past the statue of Tesla. "I grew up in this town. People talk. The professors who teach here have a tendency to end up dying in strange ways. The students, too. This place is bad news."

I nodded because I honestly couldn't disagree. He was like the big brother I never had, trying to protect me from the world. Trying to protect me from myself. I wanted to trust him with what I planned to do, but how could I explain that I intended to track down a gang of armed robbers and blow up their motorcycles out of revenge? Somehow, I needed to convince him to go home, because he would never let me finish what I set out to do.

"Thank you for worrying about me," I said. "I really mean it: thank you. But you can go ahead and take off now; I'll be okay here."

"I'm not letting you out of my sight."

He stopped in the doorway, eyes darting around the big, empty, ground floor lab as though we were entering a den of grizzly bears.

"Go," I said.

"Never."

"Okay, look, I just need to get something and I'll be right back."

"But—"

"Just wait here. *Please.* We'll talk more in a minute."

I was up the stairs before he could say anything else. I really wanted someone to pull me out of the black pit that had swallowed my life. But even Brett, the big-shot college football star, wasn't strong enough to do that for me. So I wiped the tears out of my eyes, climbed into the shower, and opened the hidden elevator panel. The stall descended into the floor, down towards the underground lab.

Nikki was waiting for me when the elevator door opened.

"Have you made up your mind?" she demanded. She was wearing her pink lab coat again. Somehow it gave her an air of authority.

"I'll do it," I said. "I'll drop out of the Institute. Just like you want." There was no going back with her: she and I wouldn't be able to co-exist in the Institute after this anyway.

Her stance relaxed, but she was still frowning. "I hope you understand," she said. "I want you out for your own protection. Maybe you can come back when things are safer."

I nodded, but I knew perfectly well that things were never going to be safe, at least not unless someone took care of the Professor and his Blitzkrieger stooges. If he hadn't threatened my Dad and cost me everything that was good in my life, then I could have just gone back to the old version of me. But the Professor had left me no choice. All I could do now was nod and keep my secret plan to myself.

Following Nikki through prototype storage, I passed Choop, whose red eyes followed me with curiosity. Then we went by Victor, who was working in the glass sterilization room. He was wearing full surgical gear with cap, mask, and a white apron. He looked up at me as we went, and he watched me with those ice-blue eyes that seemed somehow more sad than usual.

"Is he working on his secret research?" I asked.

"It's none of your concern anymore," Nikki answered.

I let her drag me away, but her words stung my heart. I had hardly had a chance to get to know this place, but I already felt like I belonged here more than anywhere else in the world. That included my apartment back home. And I would have to give it all up when I came back... if I came back. I could feel the tears in my eyes again, but I dug down deep, until I could touch the steady, steel-hard rage at my core. I had a job to do.

Nikki was already scrolling through data in the computer pavilion. Without looking away from her screen, she pointed at another screen which was evenly divided into four grainy photos of motorcycle license plates.

"Most of our cameras are relatively low-rez," Nikki said. "But the parking-lot cameras are HD for just these occasions. We got the whole lot of their license numbers. I'm running them through the local DMV and FBI databases right now."

"You can do that?"

"Funny thing," Nikki said, her fingers flying across the keyboard. "The sheriff's servers are housed in city hall. A few years ago, city hall had its network installed by a student from—guess where?— the Mechanical Science Institute. Luckily, the mayor—bless his heart— hasn't upgraded since then, which means we have ourselves a back door into all the government databases you could want. That means: bingo! Here's your printout."

Nikki snatched a piece of paper out of the high-speed printer and shoved it into my hands. The names of the registered owners of the four bikes were on it, along with their photos, home addresses and occupations, and criminal arrest records for three of the four. I didn't see the shirtless guy in there, but the other photos still looked familiar after their raid on Topsy two nights before. One driver's license picture stood out because his weight was reported at 404 pounds. His name was listed as Cecil Stellenlieter.

"Cecil?" I read out loud as I looked from the printed name to the picture of the bald-headed giant and back. "What kind of biker-mamma names her oversized son 'Cecil?'"

"It's got to be a fake identity," Nikki said. "Notice he's the only one without a criminal record, but the other three all served time for a bank job they did together ten years ago. I'd bet dollars to donuts that the big guy was in on it, too, but he used a different name. If not that, then they must have met in prison. Don't these guys know Facebook is free? You don't have to go to the slammer just to do your social networking."

I knew she was attempting a joke, but I wasn't in a laughing mood.

"There's another reason why our friend Cecil would be using a fake identity," Nikki went on. "He's on the run from the law. Coincidentally, the cops have been looking all over the country for a group of bikers who rob banks by frying their electrical systems with EMPs. You can take that to the cops and maybe they'll forget about your Dad."

"But there's no way these guys could have come up with an EMP-bomb to rob those banks," I said. "Not on their own, anyway. Not to mention that they had a chupacabra trained to steal reactor cores. It's pretty obvious that the Professor has been the one behind all this, but why would he want to team up with a bunch of criminals?"

"Seems clear enough to me," she laced her fingers behind her head and leaned back in her chair. "You're the Professor, an evil genius who wants a bunch of money, but you don't want to get your own hands dirty. So what do you do? You hire a gang of thugs by givin' 'em some special toys to help their robberies. Then you sit back and let them do the heavy lifting."

It made a lot of sense as far as it went, but I still wanted to know who the Professor was and what he really wanted. He'd gone to a lot of trouble to try to break into Topsy, which made me think he was after something more than just bank loot.

"Hmmm..." I said, studying the printout, "All of them have the same employer. It says they all work at Happy Fun Land. Isn't that the amusement park just outside of town?"

Nikki's smile stopped immediately. "I'm sure it's nothing. That place is closed down. It's probably just a cover-up for their parole officers. Just ignore that part."

I looked closely at her and saw that her right eye twitched for just a second. I read on a website that people usually make that kind of expression when they're nervous about something, but I couldn't think of what would make Nikki nervous just then. However, I did think it made sense for a biker gang with a mutant lizard for a pet to hide out in an abandoned fun park. They would have plenty of room to run around and no one would see them. Plus, free skee ball. At least now I knew where to look.

"Hey, remember," Nikki put her hand on the print-out as if she might take it away. "This is just to get your Dad out of jail. You promised not to go do anything stupid, right?"

For me, promising not to do something stupid would be like promising not to breathe, but I lied again and said I wouldn't go anywhere near the bikers or the Happy Fun Land. Then I walked out of the computer pavilion.

Nikki called after me. I didn't turn, but I stopped to show I was listening.

"I meant what I said," she told me. "I only want to keep you from getting hurt. You know that, right?"

I nodded again just to make her happy and then left her there. When I walked past the sterile room, I saw that Victor was concentrating so hard that he didn't even look up to see me. Then I looked over at the medical storage refrigerator, open and unguarded.

I didn't want to take anything that might be missed, and I knew I better be quick if I didn't want to get caught. Victor had his back to me as he worked, so I opened the refrigerator and found a rack of syringes containing the tranquilizer Victor had used on the chupacabra. I grabbed a syringe and stuffed it into my pocket.

"Do you want to kill someone, or just put them to sleep?"

I was so startled that I almost knocked the rest of the syringes off the rack. Turning, I found Victor looking directly at me from behind the sterile-room window. He had spoken through an electronic speaker in the doorway.

"Um, I was... I was just going to put it back," I stammered.

"No, keep it," he said. "But just use half a vial to put someone to sleep. More would be... bad."

"Um... thanks," I said. I just looked into those blue eyes for a while before I asked: "You know what I'm going to do, don't you?"

He nodded, and I think he gave me a sad smile under his surgical mask.

"Are you going to tell me what your research is?" I asked.

"Not unless you let me come with you," he said. "I'll go, Soap— I'll go with you right now if you ask."

"And if I say no?" I already had one guy upstairs who was insisting that he come and that was bad enough. Right then, I didn't want anyone looking after me or standing in my way. This was my mad plan, and mine alone: I wasn't about to drag anyone else I cared about down with me.

"I respect your procedural methodologies," he said. In other words: he trusted me to do what was right. "I think they underestimate you, Soap," he added. "I think you underestimate yourself, too. But I knew, from the moment we first met and you suggested using synchrotrons that you would work out here just fine."

We looked at each other, and then I walked over to the window and spread my hand flat against it. He spread his hand out as though it were touching mine. His glove had some purple goo on it, so I was kind of glad for the glass between the two of us, but I also wished our hands really were touching. It was kind of a weird moment.

Then I left without saying another word. My heart was racing during the entire elevator ride back up, but I didn't have time to figure out why.

"There you are," Brett said as I thundered down the stairs.

I reached up to put my hands on his cheeks, drawing him into a kiss right there in the dimly lit lab. He didn't react at first, so I could tell I caught him by surprise, but after a few seconds his hands slid around my back to pull me in close. It was my first kiss ever. I probably wasn't any good at it, but it felt amazing. His lips were hot against mine, and they felt as smooth as silk. It was so good, I didn't even care about the germs.

I kissed him because I wanted to thank him for his concern, but in a weird way I also hoped it would derail our relationship. He was starting to feel like the older brother I never had, and kissing him would probably mess that up forever. I knew I would probably regret it, but it wouldn't be the biggest mistake I made that night.

I also kissed him because I wanted to keep him from seeing me uncap the syringe.

"Ow," he jumped when the needle pierced his jeans. Then his eyes went unfocused and he kind of wobbled his way down to the ground. I put the cap back on the syringe—still with half the tranquilizer inside—and tucked it into the pocket of my hoodie.

"I'm sorry," I said, hunkering down over him and giving him a short, soft kiss on the lips. It was kind of like the Sleeping Beauty fairy tale in reverse, with the princess knocking prince charming out cold.

I knew Brett would wake up in an hour or two. I was hoping he would forget the details and just assume he'd had too much to drink—from the smell of the beer still on his shirt, that's what anyone else would assume.

"I think I like you, Brett," I whispered in his ear. "But I'm just not sure right now. Still, there is something I need from you." I reached my hand into his pocket and pulled out the keys to his yellow Camaro.

Right then, I didn't need a boyfriend or a brother. I needed wheels.

September 16th
(The Day Before Doomsday)

Chapter 29 ~ Dean

Dean dropped his duffel bag on the bed at the Topsy residence, and then dropped himself into the arm chair next to it. He felt like he had been kicked in the teeth. He had let Angela run off with the egg and as far as Dean knew, Angela was working for the Professor, and was handing it over to her boss at that very moment.

Realizing that the only food in the residence was the three-day-old pizzas in the fridge, Dean headed out for a grocery run. Someone knocked just as he reached the door. He was astonished to see that it was Angela.

"I was beginning to wonder if I'd ever see you again," Dean said. "That was a mighty fancy jet pack you had there."

"Technically, it's a flight pack," she said as she strolled into the room. "It doesn't use jets, just electrogravitic repulsion powered by superconducting coils."

"Whatever," Dean folded his arms. "Did you bring the egg?"

"You didn't think I would run off with your prize, did you?" she shoved the egg into his hands and favored him with her mischievous smirk. "Besides, I haven't been able to figure out what that little rock is supposed to do."

"What do you mean, 'supposed to do?'" Dean turned the wrinkly black stone over in his hands. "It's a rock. It isn't supposed to 'do' anything except sit there."

He moved to the kitchen window and held it up to the early morning sunlight, but there was no change in its appearance.

"You don't know how it works, either, do you?" Angela said with disappointment.

"Maybe there's something inside it," Dean plopped it down on the cutting board. He pulled a chef's knife down from the magnetic rack above the counter, stabilized the egg with his left hand and raised the knife high in preparation for a heavy strike.

"No!" Angela lunged for Dean's wrist. Her fingers seized his, but her right hand slipped and the sharp blade split the skin of her palm. Dark red blood oozed out, and she reflexively jerked her hand in close to her body, unintentionally spattering a few drops onto her black leather jacket.

Dean cradled her hand in his and guided it under the faucet. Angela flinched slightly when the water hit the open cut, but she didn't make a noise.

"It doesn't look too bad," Dean said when enough of the blood had been washed clear to see the wound. "I don't think you'll need stitches, but you might want to see a doctor."

"I'm not worried about it. I've had far worse," she said, watching the red streaks swirl around the stainless steel drain.

Dean opened the pantry cupboard by the refrigerator and drew out a day-glow orange satchel, unzipped it, and readied a packet of gauze and a roll of athletic tape.

"You keep your first aid kit in the kitchen?" she said as he laid the gauze across her palm.

"Most household accidents happen in this room," he said. "The bathroom is second, but if you trip on the tub and break your hip, a bandage probably isn't going to help, so the first aid kit is the first thing I put in a kitchen."

He wound the tape around her palm, expertly criss-crossing it so that it held the gauze firmly against the wound. Then he raised her hand up to the level of his chest and massaged the end of the tape down.

"How does that feel?" he asked. "Not too tight?"

"It feels wonderful," Angela stepped in closer, so that their hands were only an inch away from her heart.

Dean stopped working on the bandage and looked into her flashing brown eyes. He thought he should release her hand now, but he couldn't bring himself to do it.

"I'm really sorry," he said. "About cutting you, I mean. I didn't expect you to grab for the knife."

"I took my chances," she said. Then she leaned forward to bring her lips next to his ear. "You have to take chances if you want to play with fire. But the risks are worth it, though, don't you think?"

Softly, smoothly, she pressed into him, her firm, athletic legs sliding along his muscular thigh while her left hand found its way up to his broad shoulders. She drew him down towards her, and he felt the electric vibration of her hand on his back as acutely as if she were touching his bare skin. He wanted so badly to have someone help him find his way out of the dark cavern that had entrapped him these last two weeks, and now, in a moment of weakness, he allowed his hands to drop away to her sides so that she could bring the full length of her body against his.

Then something jabbed him in the sternum. It felt like an iron finger prodding him awake. Angela felt it, too, because she backed off, rubbing the spot where her chest had touched his.

"Ow," she said. "What was that?"

Dean reached inside the neckline of his shirt and drew forth the chain containing the two engagement rings, the symbol of his commitment to McKenzie.

"So that's what came between us," Angela held the rings at the end of the chain and inspected them briefly. "Gold's a fantastic conductor of electricity, you know."

"I'll have to remember that," Dean said, slipping the chain back under his shirt. The mood was broken, and Dean found himself relieved to be released from Angela's spell.

A knock on the door startled both of them. Dean looked through the peephole to see Victor wearing a somber silk tie and, of course, his white lab coat.

"What do you want," Dean growled when he swung the door open.

Victor had midnight-black circles under his eyes, as though he'd spent the last week cramming for finals. When he stepped in and saw Angela, he froze like a rabbit in headlights.

"Vickey!" Angela said. "Long time no see. Still locked away in your mad pursuit of scientific impossibilities?"

"You two know each other?" Dean asked, looking back and forth between Victor and Angela.

"Unfortunately, yes," Victor said. "She was the physics student here before your cousin joined us."

"Your *cousin* goes here?" Angela clasped her hands beside her cheek like a child treasuring the idea of ice-cream for dinner. "That's so cute! What's a little nepotism among family members?"

"Sophia's better qualified to be here than I am," Dean said. "I'll be the first to admit that."

"She's actually why I came to see you," Victor said. "I need to talk to you about Soap—I mean Sophia."

"I don't want to hear it from you," Dean growled.

Angela cleared her throat noisily as she scooped the egg up off the table.

"Excuse me, you two," she said, tossing the wrinkly black rock up and down in her bandaged hand. "I'd like to remind you that we have a pressing matter here. Are you boys ready to take a shower with me?"

Dean looked back at Angela in astonishment and tried to say something, but the sputtering sounds that came out of his mouth did not count as words.

"You didn't tell him, did you?" Angela wagged her finger at Victor. "Oh, Vickey. You kept the underground lab a secret from your own Dean of Students?"

Chapter 30 ~ Soap

It ended up taking me all night to get to Happy Fun Land. You would think it'd be easy to find an amusement park that featured a two-hundred foot extreme ride sticking up out of the pancake-flat country-side, but I had no map, and I started off heading the exact opposite direction. There were no road signs advertising the park, not many street lights to illuminate the roads, and in rural Minnesota there are no all-night internet cafés where I could use Google Earth to find where I was going. Even the people I asked were fuzzy on the directions, which I thought was weird, but I guessed the park never was all that popular. I didn't want to drive too fast or backtrack too much, because getting pulled over by the police would not end well for an unlicensed teenager in a canary-yellow Camaro that was registered to someone else.

Oh, and I think I trashed the transmission of Brett's car. Of course I had studied the mechanical components of automobile engines, but apparently there's a gap between diagramming blueprints for a clutch and being able to use a real one without making the whole car shake violently and causing horrible grinding noises whenever I shift gears. Sorry, Brett.

As the sky over the western hills was just beginning to lighten with the approaching dawn, I allowed the Camaro to rattle to a stop in the rear parking lot of Happy Fun Land. I unloaded Rusty and we proceeded to the chain link fence that encircled our target. I had all my hand tools in my pockets and my backpack, but Rusty handed me the big bolt cutter I had given him for just this occasion. In under five minutes, I cut a hole just big enough for a girl and her robot to get inside.

The original plan was to walk along between the chain link fence and Happy Fun Land's own outer wall until we came around to the front gate and then slip into the park from there. It turned out that I didn't even have to walk that far, because we came to a maintenance door only about thirty feet from where I had cut our way in. It was locked, but it had an electronic key pad built into the doorknob.

"Rusty," I said, pointing to the lock. "Blast this"

Rusty's flat head swiveled around as he got a visual recognition of my finger. Then his scorpion tail wiggled as though he were a happy dog. Fortunately, happy dogs don't emit focused electromagnetic pulses when they get excited. This was the first time I had tested Rusty's new antimatter-fueled capabilities, and it was a bit stronger than I had anticipated. The green LEDs on the keypad blazed to life, then flashed and sparked. Orange flames crawled out of the pad and I smelled burning plastic. I had only meant to give it enough juice to trigger its circuits, but instead I blew it up. I started to wriggle out of my backpack, intending to smother the fire with my hoodie, but then I checked myself and eased my arm back into my sleeve. What was I worried about? I came to rain burning vengeance upon the heads of those who angered me, and a little fire at the doorway seemed like a good way to kick off the festivities.

I watched the flames for a minute as they blackened and cooked the handle and the surrounding wooden frame. Then I kicked open the door and swept through as if I owned the place. For a second, I wished I had been wearing a lab coat because it would've been a perfect moment to have it fluttering out behind me. Then I remembered that a white coat would just get stained and messy, not to mention get in the way of my pockets. Sometimes drama just has to take a back-seat to easy pocket access.

The door opened into a tiny alley that ran between a ring-toss booth and a bb-gun range. This was only the outskirts of a maze of deserted concession stands and empty rides, mostly the kind that swing people around in cars shaped like airplanes or Viking longboats. I could see why the park went out of business, because people were not going to come from miles around just to ride along a track in a plastic car that looked vaguely like a rocket ship. The place was also really messy, with discarded nacho trays and empty soda cups lining the booths and collecting in the corners of the lanes, and that didn't make the place look any more inviting.

The sidewalks were completely disgusting and grimy, and I only got about fifty feet closer to the center of the park when I felt my foot stick to something. When I pulled my shoe off the sidewalk to see what it was, a ropy green tendril ran from the bottom of my sole to a nasty lump on the ground. Chewing gum. I hate chewing gum. Even under the best of circumstances, it's a sponge for your mouth-germs. To touch someone else's gum, even if it was just with the bottom of my shoe, made me want to vomit. Not only that, gum never comes off cleanly, and no matter how much you try, your shoe will still make a gooey, clicking sound whenever you take a step. Nasty. I had to dig through my pockets to find a screwdriver I didn't particularly like just so I could scrape the gum off my sole.

I found a trash can and disposed of the screwdriver—as far as I was concerned, it was contaminated. I considered throwing out my shoe, too, but that would mean walking around the park in my socks, and a gum-stained sock would be even worse than a gum-stained shoe.

I began to consider how long it would take gum on the sidewalk to dry out, and that thought made me pause. Even with all the rain we'd been having, it would probably only stay sticky for a day or two. If that gum had been waiting for me on the sidewalk for only a day or two, it meant other people had been in the park recently—really recently. As in: maybe they were still here!

I looked at the mess around me and suddenly saw a new story behind the greasy, mustard-splattered wrappers scudding across the pavement in the breeze. This mess almost certainly meant that the bikers were nearby. Considering that I had come looking for them, I probably should have been a little more prepared for that realization, but it still broke my confidence. All the swagger I had felt when I entered the park was gone. I was burgling a secluded park full of biker thugs. I suddenly felt less like the angel of vengeance and more like a big, juicy fly buzzing straight for a spider's web.

This would be my last chance to turn back. I could still run back to Bugswallow and enjoy the last five days of campus life before I had to vacate my dorm. Or I could press on, maybe commit an act of petty sabotage on a few motorcycles, and probably get myself seriously messed-up in the process.

I looked over at Rusty, as if he could give me some advice. He looked back at me with those big, innocent, laser range-finding eyes. Weirdly, I started to feel like I owed it to him to carry through. I know it's stupid to read that kind of emotion into a collection of steel and wires, but it gave me what I needed to keep myself from chickening out.

As creepy and quiet as the park was, navigating through it wasn't at all a problem because all the big rides made great landmarks. There was a big Ferris wheel to the north and a curving roller coaster in the south, but the biggest landmark was easily the Doomsday Machine ride. On the wall of a boarded-up hotdog stand I found a poster that showed a group of happily screaming people plunging down the side of it strapped into a little car. As tall as the thing was, you could probably see the curvature of the earth from the top, and the really extreme thing about it was that after you dropped, your seat would still be travelling at terminal velocity when you got to ground level. From the illustrations I could tell that at the very last second before you went splat, the floor would drop out of your way and you would fall past it, into a big shaft that extended way down into the ground, and that's where you would slow to a stop. After you had been properly traumatized and/or delighted, your chair would take you back up to the observation deck thirty feet above the fairground, where you would exit into a gift shop that probably specialized in Doomsday Machine beer steins and instant photos capturing your face at the precise moment when you thought "oh my God, I'm seriously going to die."

After looking at that poster, it almost started to sound like fun, but when I put on my goggles and zoomed in for a closer look at the actual ride, I saw that the elevator track of the Doomsday Machine had either been dismantled or hadn't ever been completed. It looked like there had been an effort to convert the structure into a radio broadcasting tower, because at the very top was a metallic dome lined with golden disks that made the whole thing resemble a pepper shaker.

I may not be so good with people, but I know my electrical equipment and I could tell that was no mere decoration up there. This so-called "Doomsday Machine" was meant to broadcast extremely powerful radio signals of some kind. I was ready to bet that its use as a ride was designed as an afterthought, or maybe even a disguise. I just couldn't figure out why anyone would go to so much trouble to disguise an antenna, or why they would even need it. Out of curiosity, I toggled the controls on my goggles to look for radio transmissions, but the tower was cold. At least, for now.

I slid my goggles back up onto my forehead and used the Doomsday Machine as a landmark to find my way to the center of the park. It didn't take me long to get there and discover that a wide-open parade ground encircled the extreme ride. Here I found what I was looking for: two dozen motorcycles, all parked haphazardly on the dead grass of a picnic area. It was seven in the morning, so the owners of the bikes were probably sleeping somewhere, but they couldn't be far.

Creeping through the gum-sticky sidewalks, I made my way into the ranks of black gas tanks and chrome pipes, Rusty close at my heels. This would hurt them: they were a motorcycle gang, so these bikes must be their big thing. As I studied the bikes, however, a growing sense of disappointment crept over me. Every single one of their engines used a carburetor. Even the more recent models had been modified to swap out their fuel injection systems for the older air-flow regulator systems. It made sense that they would make these mods, because if these guys had been robbing banks with EMP-bombs, then their carburetor motors would keep running while newer, more sophisticated vehicles with fuel injectors would stall on the spot. It was the cheapest possible way to harden a civilian vehicle to a massive electromagnetic pulse.

I cursed under my breath. The only electrical systems in these bikes were the headlights and the starter switches. Sure, I could fry every one of them the way I fried the keypad on the door lock outside, but the total damage would amount to thirty or forty bucks per bike. Not exactly what I needed to hit them where it hurt and bring the Professor's plans crashing down around his ears.

I squatted there and scratched under the strap of my goggles. Their bikes were hardened against Rusty's EMP transmitter, but maybe there was some other way to hit the Blitzkriegers where it would count. These guys were bank robbers, after all, and they had stolen hundreds of thousands of dollars. Maybe the money was stashed around here somewhere—if I was really lucky, maybe they were even keeping it in large brown bags with dollar symbols on the sides to make it easier to swipe. Judging from the drifts of crumpled beer cans and cigarette butts piled outside the Doomsday Machine, I could tell that it had received a lot of attention from the bikers, so that seemed like a good place to start looking.

The building was a long, squat structure occupying the full area beneath the Doomsday Machine. It had a sign over the door that showed people strapped into the ride's seats, managing to look like they were screaming their lungs out but still smiling at the same time. Big, plate glass windows ran the full length of each wall of the building, except on the north side, closest to me, where the building shared the back wall of a stage that might have once been used by musicians to entertain guests in the park. It seemed to offer the best cover, so Rusty and I scampered over to the base of the stage. From that spot, I was close enough that I could look through one of the windows.

Even though the sun was just coming up, it was still really dark inside, and the slightly tinted windows didn't help visibility. I slid my goggles down over my eyes and switched to the lowest setting of light amplification. My breath caught in my throat when I suddenly realized what I was looking at.

Row upon row of sleeping bikers littered the floor inside the building. They were bundled up in sleeping bags, stretched out on cots, or sprawled across inflatable mattresses, their beer cans, ash trays, and potato chip bags piled between them. There would be no gold stars for housekeeping here. It seemed an odd arrangement for a gang that could steal money whenever they wanted it. If I had a share of a few dozen bank-vaults worth of loot, I would go out and buy a house, or at least a nice bed. Yet here they were, all of them snoring away together in one big makeshift dorm. Well, almost all of them.

"Hey, girly, what you doin' here?" asked a voice behind me.

I gasped and whirled in place to see a bright green shape towering over me. I yanked the goggles off to see a bald guy with a leather jacket and a stained tank-top. He was flexing his fists open and closed, as if he were trying to figure out exactly how big around my throat was.

Another one stepped out from behind the stage to block off my retreat. My stomach churned when I recognized him. It was the same shirtless creeper who had brought me the cell phone on the train.

My mind raced and my heart was pounding, but there was no escape for me. If I tried to run, they could easily grab me before I moved two steps. If I stayed there, they would do the same.

"I recognize this one," Shirtless said, lifting my chin with his grimy finger. I yanked my head away, but he just laughed.

"This one here is working with the P'fessor," he said to his buddy. Then he turned to me and rasped "Well, c'mon, then. Let's get you down there so you can get to work."

The two of them lead me through the doors and into the biker's makeshift dorm. I couldn't tell if I had just stumbled into the perfect disguise or if I was the little fly that had zoomed right past the web and directly into the spider's fangs.

Chapter 31 ~ Dean

Pushing past Victor, Angela grabbed Dean by the hand and led him next door to the shower room. She backed him up to the wall, and then opened the secret tile and pressed the down button. By the time the doors opened to the underground lab, Dean's head was spinning.

"This place," Dean muttered. "It looks like Frankenstein's lab in here. And over there—is that...?"

Dean pointed to the cage where the chupacabra sat. Its tongue flicked in and out of its mouth as it watched them cautiously.

"Your new pet?" Angela asked admiringly.

"That thing almost killed me," Dean glared at Victor. "I thought you had dissected it or something. Why are you keeping it down here? Why are you keeping any of this down here?" he waved his hand to indicate the lab all around him.

Dean wasn't quite sure what went on in that lab, but he knew it was a big secret to hide from someone who lived upstairs.

"How about we let bygones be bygones?" Angela stepped between the two of them, waving the egg in front of their noses. "As much as I love seeing Vickey get chewed out by the teacher, we have work to do, remember? Now, who can tell me why the Professor would be interested in this egg?"

There was a moment of silence as Dean and Victor shifted mental gears.

"What tests have you run?" Victor asked.

"Everything," Angela answered with a sigh. "I know it consists mostly of silicon and teslanium, but that's about all that was interesting. Do you have any ideas? Anything at all?"

The three of them were silent as they stared at the rock in Angela's hand. Dean rubbed his earlobe, which was his way of stimulating ideas, but nothing came to him. The egg was no piece of art. It had no historical value. It wasn't made out of gold or diamonds. It seemed like a cruel, meaningless joke that McKenzie had died for such a useless little lump. The only unusual thing about the egg was the faint rainbow sheen that played along its surface. That, and the weird colors it had emitted when he first took it out of the display case.

"It's probably nothing," Dean said at last. "Maybe my eyes were playing tricks on me, but I could have sworn that it was glowing, just for a minute, back in the museum."

"When?" Angela narrowed her eyes like a hunter taking aim. "Think carefully. Was there anything that might have triggered it?"

"It happened when I took it out of the case. When you had that thing of yours, your—what did you call it—your harp. Your miniature EMP-generator."

Angela and Victor exchanged a triumphant look and said, as though with one voice: "electromagnetic field."

Then it was like someone fired a starting pistol, because the two of them raced off in different directions and started pulling various items from shelves. Victor rummaged through boxes of gears and wires while Angela picked the best pieces and went to work with a soldering gun.

All Dean could do was watch. He knew his way around a toolbox, but right then he felt as useless as roller-skates on an octopus. He looked over at the chupacabra, who was leaning on the bars of his cage, looking back at him with a quizzical expression on its face.

"You and me both, buddy," Dean said to the creature, still being careful not to get too close.

The chupacabra's only response was to flick its snake-tongue in his direction.

In about twenty minutes, Victor and Angela had constructed a wand that looked like a silver billiard ball glued to the end of a length of plastic plumbing pipe. A single cord ran out its back to connect to a kettle-bell shaped gizmo in the corner that Dean assumed must be supplying the power.

"My harp emitted an irregular, broad spectrum pulse," Angela explained to Dean. "It's good for temporarily scrambling camera circuits, but you can't run a device off it. Right now, we need to generate sustained electrical induction inside the egg."

None of this made sense to Dean, but he gathered that, despite its looks, the egg was actually some kind of electronic gizmo, maybe like a cell phone that had lost its power cord. Victor and Angela had just cobbled together a way of charging its batteries without needing that cord. Why anyone would want to make a device that looked like an ugly rock was beyond him, but at least they were about to find out what it was supposed to do.

"I wish Soap were here," Victor said, readying the wand. "She's really good with wireless electricity."

Angela glared at him. "What am I, chopped liver?"

Victor ignored her and gave the dial at the base of the wand a slow twist, hunting for the right frequency. The only thing that happened was that Dean yelped in pain. He scrambled to pull out his new cell phone, which he had needed to purchase on his way back here after Angela's harp destroyed the last one. And now this one, too, was wrecked.

"You've got to be kidding! I just bought this..." Dean's voice trailed off when he looked up from his overheated phone to see the egg. Victor and Angela also stared, dumbstruck.

Shining above the egg was a slowly rotating ball of light. It looked three dimensional but insubstantial, like a ghost floating right in front of their eyes. Angela flipped off the overhead lights so they could get a better look, and their faces were cast in a blue glow as they studied the display.

Dean had to look at it for a long moment before he realized that the shining ball was actually the image of a planet, seen from the perspective of deep space. As it slowly rotated, he saw that a swirling blue ocean covered almost the entire the surface of the planet, save only a single, gargantuan continent. This landmass included gray mountain ridges, blue rivers, and small brown dots of deserts, but most of it was covered in thick, green jungles that ran from one coast to the other like bright green wall-to-wall carpeting. And there was one unnatural feature in the image: scattered across the continent were glowing red dots. There might have been a hundred of them, twinkling like little red stars.

"Aliens!" Dean said. "I knew it! I should have guessed it was aliens as soon as I saw the lizard-monster over there."

Choop rose up on his hind feet and flicked his tongue.

"Sorry to disappoint you, Captain Kirk," Angela placed a hand on Dean's shoulder. "That's not an alien planet. It's Earth. This is our planet, or what it used to be during the Triassic era, 200 million years ago. That big continent is called Pangea, and it's what things looked like before the tectonic plates broke apart into the continents we know today."

"Then what are all these little red dots?" Dean leaned in to touch one and was startled when the image changed, the globe disappearing as the perspective zoomed in on the spot he touched. It resolved itself into a bird's-eye view of what appeared to be a wooden structure in a jungle clearing. Dean pulled his hand back and the image zoomed back out until it was once again a spinning globe.

"What was that?" Dean looked at his finger and then back at the image. "What does it mean?"

"It's a treasure map from the age of the dinosaurs," Angela said, reaching out to touch another red pinpoint to zoom in on another location. "And X marks the spot."

Chapter 32 ~ Soap

The shirtless guy led me past the sleeping bikers. The place smelled like rotten milk, and I had to fight my instinct to hold my nose. One of the lounging men grumbled about it being too early to start the party, but Shirtless just told him to shut up and go back to sleep because "the P'fessor" needed me to do something. A few of them commented on Rusty, but they seemed strangely unsurprised by an eight-legged mechanical scorpion-dog clicking its way across the floor before them. Perhaps after working for the Professor they had just grown accustomed to weird things.

The building at the base of the Doomsday Machine was actually a restaurant, but you wouldn't know it from the discarded cigarette packs and the sleeping bodies spread all over where the tables must have once been. I didn't even guess that food might have been served in that area until we stepped through the swinging doors into the kitchen. That room was just as messed up as the rest of the building, with moldering pots and pans piled high in the sink and on the floor. I scrubbed my hands with some hand sanitizer as we walked, but I wished I could have applied some to the inside of my nose because of the smell.

"Through here," Shirtless said, unlocking a door to a brightly lit room in the back. This area contained only an elevator labeled "Maintenance Access." In front of the elevator doors sat the largest man I have ever seen in my life. I recognized him from the DMV photos Nikki had helped me access, but no photo could convey the impression of his true size. He looked like a titanic professional wrestler, and his body must have been forty percent fat, forty percent muscle, and forty percent granite. I know that adds up to more than one hundred percent, but it felt appropriate because this guy seemed bigger than mathematically possible. When I looked up at the florescent bulb above his shiny-bald head, I almost expected to see the light curving around him.

The big guy was evidently on guard duty, but it didn't look like he was putting much effort into it. One of his meaty hands was wrapped around a girly magazine, while his other enveloped a forty ounce bottle of beer. He glanced at me, and then, without standing up, he stretched out his elephantine arm to slap the elevator button with the rolled-up point of his magazine.

"Where's your lab coat?" he said with a gravelly voice.

"My lab coat?" I was worried that it was a trick question or maybe I needed to answer with a password. "I don't like lab coats. I prefer to wear black."

He grunted in approval before returning his attention to his magazine.

To my relief, Shirtless didn't get onto the elevator, so it was just me and Rusty going down.

"The machine's on B-2," he said to me, and I could see his tongue through the hole made by his missing tooth. "The thing's on B-1 if you want to check that out."

Even as the door closed, Shirtless was still leering at me, so I hunched over, pulled my hoodie tight around my shoulders, and folded my arms until I was safely sealed away from view.

It would have been nice to hide in that elevator forever, but it simply wasn't a realistic option. I needed to make a choice and pick one of those floors. I wasn't sure what he had been talking about when he said "the thing" was on B-1, but I liked the sound of a machine, so I pressed the other button and began a very, very long descent.

When the elevator doors opened up, Rusty and I walked down a short hallway and through a reinforced metal door. The door had a heavy bolt-lock, so I slid it closed once we were in. Somehow I felt a lot better having a barred door between me and the creepers upstairs.

I was now in a big, circular room at the very bottom of the deep shaft of the Doomsday Machine ride. The place was crammed full of electrical supplies, and when I say "electrical supplies," I don't mean computers or Blu-ray players. The stuff in that room included industrial-grade electromagnets, poly-phase induction motors, transformer cores, coolant casings, heavy-duty fuse boxes, and miles upon miles of coiled copper wire in every gauge. There was enough equipment in that make-shift warehouse to create a power plant and wire up a small city. All of it was shrink-wrapped or packed into crates, stacked from floor to ceiling, and jammed in so tight I had to empty my lungs to squeeze through some parts to get deeper into the room. Rusty had an even harder time getting around because he can't turn sideways like a person, so he had to climb over a stack of electrical cable spools and meet me on the far side.

I perused the boxes and crates, trying to find any clue as to why the Professor or the Blitzkriegers would want to stockpile items to make a power grid. Along the way, I found some rifles, bullets, and a small crate that contained something I had seen back at Topsy: earthquake grenades. Unlike all the other devices in the warehouse, the earthquake grenades had been partially disassembled and looked if someone had deactivated them and removed the few grams of teslanium contained in their power source.

None of the gizmos gave me a clue as to what was going on, until I reached the middle of the circular room, right next to the ride shaft's maintenance access hatch. I just about fell on my face when I saw the six-foot high steel kettle-bell. It was an antimatter reactor of precisely the same size as the one in the sub-basement of Topsy. Except for the improved cadmium-encased depleted uranium shielding, this reactor was an exact replica.

I rushed over to the control panel and found that the reactor was not yet operational. An open hatch on the side revealed why: the power core had not been completed. To be specific, it lacked only the components that needed to be constructed from teslanium. After working for the last two days to install a much smaller reactor into Rusty, I was pretty familiar with these pieces and I knew that all it needed were a few solid plates and some tightly-wound wire, but all of it had to be made from that mysterious superconductor. I figured it would only take about twelve more pounds of teslanium to complete these pieces, but there isn't much of that stuff to go around—all the gizmos in the secret lab at Topsy didn't have ten pounds of the stuff between them, including what I had installed into Rusty. That explained why someone had stripped the power-cores out of the earthquake grenades, but even that combined with the few spools of specially made cable stacked next to the reactor would add up to no more than two or three pounds. A little bit of that strange, pale metal goes a long way in most devices. Only the Topsy reactor had the quantity required, which must be why the Professor had sent his Blitzkriegers and the chupacabra after our reactor core.

The big question, then, was why they needed such a powerful generator. The one in Topsy had been built as an experiment and it had the capacity to generate more power in sixty seconds than all of Bugswallow used in a year. If the Professor just wanted to run the roller coasters in this amusement park, he could have done it with much, much less. He had to be after something bigger, something that would justify the attempt to break into Topsy and go to all this trouble.

There was a computer control terminal attached to the reactor, so I wiggled the mouse to wake it from sleep mode. I almost laughed out loud when I found that it wasn't even password protected. It took me 30 seconds to call up the reactor operation software that rewarded me with a diagnostic display that told me everything I needed to know. The antimatter reactor down here was linked up to the Doomsday Machine ride so that the whole thing would serve as a broadcasting tower. I had been right about the dome-shaped cap at the top of the ride: it was a transmitter, but it wasn't designed to send out radio signals. It would send out a full-spectrum EMP powerful enough to disrupt the stratosphere and alter the electromagnetic grid of the Earth itself.

I slapped my hand over my mouth to keep myself from yelping in astonishment. Now I knew why the Doomsday Machine ride had looked strangely familiar to me: it was based on Nikola Tesla's designs for the Wardenclyffe tower. It had been Tesla's failed dream to provide the entire world with wireless energy through his tower. Now, more than a hundred years later, the Professor was using the same basic design not to empower our machines but to destroy them.

If this broadcasting tower went into operation, it would induce overwhelming currents in anything with wires or circuits. That meant it would burn appliances, destroy internet and telephone communications, and obliterate power grids the world over. Not even military-grade shielding would protect from this attack, because the grounding wires and faraday cages that are used to harden equipment against EMPs are all designed to channel the unwanted energy into the earth. Given enough time, this tower could send destructive energy up through the very ground, causing all those surge protectors and grounding strips to totally backfire. Governments would fall, armies would be paralyzed, and the world would be plunged back into a pre-industrial dark age. Most households aren't prepared to go without power for more than a few days, if that. The Doomsday Machine would destroy the world's electrical infrastructure so thoroughly that it would be many months or more likely years before service could be restored.

Tesla had once said that with the right frequency he could split the earth. It looked like the Professor was about to test that claim. I couldn't see why he would want to, but he was obviously serious about carrying this thing through.

Suddenly, the whole room felt like it was spinning and I had to grip the control panel to keep myself from falling over. Just when I thought things couldn't get any worse, the screen on the computer flickered and went black. Then it came up with a video conference window. There was a dark silhouette against a white wall. His face was blacked out by some kind of software that made him look like a living shadow, but from the way he moved his arms to lean forward I could tell it was a real person.

"Hello, Sophia," the Professor's voice came through the computer speakers.

I stepped back and bumped into a stack of crates. My snooping around inside the computer's files had probably tripped an invisible alarm, which was how he knew where I was and what I'd been doing. It felt like all the warmth in my body had drained down through my legs and out into the floor as I realized there was a little web cam on top of the screen, which meant he was watching me right now.

"I know everything," I blurted out, trying to sound braver than I felt. "Except, why are you doing this? If you hate electronic stuff so much, why don't you just go live on a desert island and leave the rest of us alone?"

He laughed at me. "Look around you, Sophia. You're surrounded by the answer."

I blinked and stared around me at the crates stacked up inside the makeshift warehouse, but I knew they were only the same kind of electrical components that would be destroyed when the Doomsday Machine did its thing. Then it hit me: they hadn't stockpiled all the supplies for making an electrical grid just to watch it break. After they destroyed the world's electronics, they would be the only ones with the ability to rebuild.

I whirled back to the computer station and quickly confirmed my deduction. According to the readout, there was a smaller transmitter in this room that would broadcast a counter-frequency to protect the equipment in here from damage. It wasn't powerful, but it didn't have to be: it just had to work like the electromagnetic version of noise-cancelling headphones. According to the files, there were also several other warehouses with similar equipment stashed across North America and even more in South America. With all that, he had the seeds to start a small nation. The guns, bombs, and earthquake grenades I had found must have been so that his followers could defend these warehouses if needed. Evidently, the Professor had a lot more people working for him than just the Blitzkriegers.

"Ah, now you have it," the Professor said. "I'm not going to be known as the man who destroyed the world, I'm going to be hailed as its great savior. And when I rebuild, I'll have a planet-wide monopoly on electricity. Governments will pay whatever I want—unless I decide to replace those governments and become emperor of the Earth. I haven't decided about that part yet. But the important thing is this: in every sense of the word, I will be the only one with the power."

"You're crazy," I said. "You can't possibly know if it's going to work right. I mean, this level of electromagnetism had never been tested. There could be environmental damage of biblical proportions. Brains and nervous systems operate with electrical transmission, too— you might end up killing every living thing on the planet!"

The Professor's silhouette shrugged. "I think you're overreacting just a little bit, don't you?"

"No way. I'm not letting you do this. I'm going to the cops." Triumphantly, I whipped my Hello Kitty USB drive out of the back pocket of my jeans and brandished it in front of the webcam. Then I jammed it home into the computer and started copying the contents of the hard drive.

"Sophia," the Professor's voice was patronizing. "You are such a clever girl. Are you sure you won't come to work for me?"

"Never," I hissed. "You're a scuzz and a creeper and... and... everything else that's bad. You're worse than chewing-gum on my shoe." I was really talking my way into trouble now, but I couldn't stop myself.

The blackened image of the Professor cut me off by waving a shadowy hand.

"I'm disappointed," he sighed. "But it's probably just as well. I've alerted the Blitzkriegers to your presence. Whatever's left after they finish with you probably won't be much use to me."

Behind me, on the far side of the crates and cases, a thunderous banging sounded against the door.

Chapter 33 ~ Dean

"This is big," Victor muttered, running his hand distractedly through his short blond hair. "This is unbelievably big. If this thing really dates back to the Triassic, it may lead us to revise everything we know about human history."

"Calm down and don't get your panties in a knot," Angela said. "I've almost got the program running. Then we'll see what we see."

They had moved from the laboratory into the computer center, where they had filmed the image that the egg was projecting. As they did, the spinning blue hologram of the 200 million year old Earth made Dean's skin crawl. He couldn't imagine who had made it or what was going on in the early days of the dinosaurs that was important enough to get mapped. Whatever it was, he was pretty sure he wouldn't like it.

Angela hammered away at the keys as her monitor displayed a digitized representation of the hologram of Pangea, complete with the red pinpoints that indicated the important locations. Under her command, the software broke Pangaea into sections and re-arranged them in the form of the contemporary continents they had become. These images were then superimposed on satellite photos of the modern world and adjusted to account for new mountain ranges, rivers, and other geological features. The final result was an up-to-date map that preserved the locations of the glowing red pinpoints and cross-referenced them with GPS coordinates.

"If this thing is really a pre-historic treasure map," Dean said, leaning over Angela's shoulder. "What does it lead to? Dinosaur bones or something?"

"I doubt it," Angela said. "That wouldn't have been valuable back when there were actual dinosaurs."

"They're spread all over the place," Victor said. "They don't seem to line up with any major city or particular landmark... hey, wait. Move over—I want to see something."

Angela moved out of the way and Victor wheeled his chair into her spot. He clicked the mouse and dragged the image down to show the northern regions of the United States. He zoomed in until Minnesota filled the screen. A bright red dot pulsed in the lower corner.

"You recognize this spot?" Victor asked, tapping the red dot. "It's smack-dab on Bugswallow City. We are standing on top of that dot right now."

"It's here?" Dean asked. "What are the odds of that?"

"It can't be coincidence," Victor said. "There's a link that could explain it: Nikola Tesla. Think about it. He invented wireless power and he had possession of this egg. He would have seen the same image that we saw the first day he brought that little rock into his lab. We always assumed that he chose Bugswallow as the site for his school to keep it far away from industrial spies, but there were plenty of other backwater places he could have located the Institute. Maybe he located it here because he was looking for something."

Dean glanced over at Angela. She had her arms folded in front of her and her lips pursed, as though she were angry about something.

Victor spun around in his chair to look at the two of them. "I think he did more than just look, too," he went on. "I think he found it. The cavern two hundred feet below us—what we're using as the reactor room—is impossibly deep and impossibly ancient. It could have been built by the same people—if they were people—who built that egg. I bet all these dots lead to other deep caverns just like the one below us."

"Hang on there," Angela put out her hands. "You're making a lot of assumptions."

"We can test the theory," Victor said. "If I'm right, then these other pinpoints will lead us to other caverns. At the very least, we may get to see what the Professor was after. The first members of the Institute found teslanium down in the cavern below us. That discovery led to the invention of the antimatter reactor. I wonder what we'll find in all these other caves."

Angela leaned in towards the computer screen and moved the image around.

"It looks like the next nearest one is up north of the twin cities, near the Canadian border," she said. "It's going to be a boring, and probably fruitless trip. Tell you what: you boys hold the fort here while I go check it out. I'll be back in a few hours."

"No way," Dean said. "Nobody's going without me."

He grabbed his coat and was already heading towards the elevator. He didn't know what he would find when he got there, but whatever it was, it would give him leverage over the man who had killed McKenzie.

"Fine," Angela said with exasperation. "But don't say I didn't warn you. Okay, you boys load up the drilling equipment while I take care of a few loose ends here. Meet you upstairs in five."

Dean and Victor worked together to move the heavy equipment out of the lab. As soon as the elevator doors closed behind them, Angela rose from her seat in front of the computer and moved over to the chupacabra. The creature was huddled at the back of the cage, still as a statue, watching her with its red eyes.

She grabbed the key off its wall hook, undid the padlock, and swung the cage door wide open.

"Go back to the Professor," Angela said to the creature. "You know the way out of here. Go back to the fun park and I'll meet you there later."

Chapter 34 ~ Soap

It was a heavy-duty, reinforced door, but with the way the Blitzkriegers were pounding on it, it wouldn't be long before they got through.

The circular storage/reactor room was thirty feet underground with only one entrance and no good places to hide, but it did have one other possible exit: the ventilation shaft that ran up to the center of the Doomsday Machine. With luck, I could climb up through there and be out in the open air before the Blitzkriegers figured out where I had gone. Before I left, though, there was something I had to do.

In three minutes, I rewired the reactor's power output to split an undetectably small amount of current through a spool of superconducting cable. Then I fixed the earthquake grenades I had found earlier to various points on the wire and mounted the whole kit onto Rusty's back. This took me another sixty seconds, and the bikers had the door almost off its hinges by then. I could hear their angry shouts and rude calls to me through the widening gap around the doorframe.

"Rusty," I said, even though it's stupid to talk to a robot that isn't rigged for full language analysis. "Rusty, you've got something important to do. You've got to go save the world."

Flipping open his back panel, I performed a temporary override on his tracking protocol so he wouldn't home in on my bracelet until he was done with his next task. I entered a destination point two hundred twenty feet straight up, and instructed him to string the cable up through the tower and rig up the earthquake grenades along the way. I'd designed Rusty to move through different types of terrain and perform simple mechanical tasks, so he was already geared to pull this off and all I had to do was add in the particulars. Spreading those earthquake grenades would mean that if the Professor ever got the tes-lanium he needed to get his reactor working then it would run power up the cable to the grenades and shake the whole structure to pieces. I thought it was a pretty good plan, although there was no way to be sure the grenades would destroy the tower before the tower destroyed the world.

I finished entering the instructions, closed Rusty's control panel, pushed him into the shaft's access hatch, and powered him back up. For a moment, he just stood there looking at me with his big eyes. Then his system finished compiling data, and he nodded his head and snapped his pincers. It felt like he was saying goodbye, so I kissed him on what would have been his nose. He snapped his pincers again, pi-voted in place, and scuttled up the ladder and through the shaft, leaving a trail of wire behind him.

Following Rusty, I ducked through the hatch and closed it be-hind me just as the door clattered to the floor and the room filled with angry voices and the stomping of a dozen heavy motorcycle boots.

The shaft was at least forty feet high and stretched all the way up to the top of the building above. I could see daylight out there, but it was partly blocked out by big steel struts and metal bars protruding from the concrete walls. These were the steel bars that would send the electromagnetic waves into the Earth, but right now all they were doing was transforming my climb into an obstacle course. Rusty had no prob-lem with it, and I could see him getting farther and farther ahead of me as he nimbly moved through the maze of criss-crossing steel. I, on the other hand, was slow and I scraped my knuckles and knees something fierce as I went. I had thought it would be an easy climb, but it was bas-ically a series of pull-ups from one steel bar to the next, and my arms got stiff and shaky almost right away. About fifteen feet up the shaft, I made the mistake of looking down at the sharp angles and solid steel posts below me. If I fell, I would bounce my way down like the ball in a Japanese pachinko game.

I struggled up two more struts before I noticed a vent grate at my right. Light shone through it into the shaft, and I knew this must be room B-1, the room Shirtless had said contained "the thing," whatever that was.

Up above me, I could see Rusty place the first earthquake grenade on the tower cross beams, his narrow arms moving with precision as he clamped it into place. Below me the sounds of shouts and occasional crashes told me that retreat was not an option. I had to escape and take the data on my USB drive to the police, but if I went the same direction as Rusty it would increase the chances that we would both be caught. My robot was in the clear, but if just one of the bikers spotted the maintenance hatch and stuck his head in to look up, there was no way he could overlook me dangling up here. That meant B-1 was my best option.

I crawled on my belly across a steel joist until I was close enough to peer through the grate. Only a small portion of the room was visible from where I was, but it was enough to recognize that this room was totally different from the one below it. It was a much smaller, square room that originally might have been just a large maintenance locker. It was spotlessly clean and uncluttered, although there was a strong odor of a dog kennel coming from within.

I looked up again and gave up on climbing any higher. Even if I made it all the way up to where the shaft opened onto the roof of the building, I wasn't sure how to get down from there. My body already ached from climbing to the halfway point, and if I made a single misstep or if my fingers slipped, it would be curtains for me. I decided to go for it through the room. After all, how much worse could it be?

Very carefully, I braced myself as best I could on top of the joist and wormed my arms out of my backpack straps. I quickly found a pair of pliers, and managed to undo the screws on the vent cover from the inside. With ninja-like stealth, I pushed the grate away from the wall and lowered it to the floor, then wriggled my way through the opening and into the room.

The clean part of the room had a real hospital vibe to it. The white tiles of the walls and floors were scrubbed and glistening. By the exit door, a tray of polished flasks and beakers rested on a shiny metal table. However, the other part of the room, the part I hadn't been able to see through the grate, was much more organic. By organic, I mean slimy and disgusting. All the mess was centered around a pulsing, white membrane sack that was as tall as I was. It looked like an internal organ that had been ripped out of some epic-sized fish, and it was streaked with red and blue veins while some kind of clear fluid oozed from its skin onto the floor. This membrane sack was too big to have gotten through the door, which made me think it must have been grown right there in that spot.

The most surprising part was that Nikki Du Boise stood in front of it. She wore her pink lab coat and was glaring right at me.

"You shouldn't've come, Soap," Her voice was flat and cold.

"Nikki," I said. "What're you doing here? We have to get out of here."

She just shook her head. "They have guards outside the elevator upstairs and they'll be lookin' for you up on the roof as soon as they work out where you went. There's only one option left. Here, hold out your hand."

I extended my arm, palm up, and stepped over to her to take whatever she wanted to give me.

She snapped one end of a pair of steel handcuffs onto my wrist. I was so startled that I didn't pull my hand back before she clicked the other end to the leg of her workbench.

I yanked at the handcuffs, but the workbench was bolted to the floor. The commotion caused something inside the membrane to swish around and press at the stretchy white walls of its prison. Whatever was inside there, it wanted out.

Chapter 35 ~ Dean

Victor, Dean, and Angela were on the road for hours, resting only briefly to have lunch and to get Dean a new phone. It was early afternoon when they pulled to a stop in a secluded clearing in the forested area that formed the border between two corporate farms. Using the GPS in Victor's phone and the map from the egg, they calculated the digging spot as best they could, then set up the equipment.

The auto-shovel, according to Angela's rendition of the history of the Mechanical Science Institute, was invented by an engineering professor in response to a comment from the captain of the Langdon University debate team eighty years ago. The debate captain reportedly said "if you institute crumb-bums are so smart, how come we're still digging holes with shovels?" As it happened, that student went on to a career as a contractor who specialized in digging foundations for office buildings, which meant he dug holes for a living. If he had known about the auto-shovel that his comment had inspired, his life might have been much easier.

Although the name made it sound like a hand-tool, a fully assembled auto-shovel was actually almost the size of a small Volkswagen. It was a rounded cylinder that resembled a jet engine in its shape, but otherwise it looked like something out of a Jules Verne novel with its rusty iron body, ornate brass knobs, pressure gauges, and steam whistles. At its bottom end there were three large, grinding drills that crunched up the dirt or rock in the machine's path and fed it through its body, spewing it out its tail. The device made a nice hole about three feet in diameter, and as it burrowed down it built a metal ladder behind itself and ran buckets of dirt and rocks up a pulley system. This waste was then deposited outside the mouth of the hole, where it would eventually pile up high enough to spill back in. This meant that humans—namely, Victor and Dean—needed to shovel the debris into wheelbarrows and cart it away. Ironically, the machine required the assistance of the shovel it was meant to replace.

"How much deeper is this thing going to have to go?" Dean asked as he surveyed the rising mounds of dirt all around them. They had needed to stop the auto-shovel three times so far because it could pile up the dirt much more quickly than they could haul it off. He didn't mind the work—even with his cracked rib, it felt good after sitting behind the wheel for half the day—but the jet-engine noise of the auto-shovel was getting to him. It would have been very conspicuous in any other location, but at least they had some privacy here among the uninhabited rolling hills of mechanically tilled earth that seemed to extend as far as the sky.

"You boys are doing fine," Angela said, studying her laptop screen. "The radar readout indicates a pocket of reduced density within three meters."

"Come again?" Dean asked.

"It says we're almost there."

"That's assuming it hasn't collapsed after millions of years of geological action," Victor panted. He had been struggling to keep up with Dean at the shoveling. His face was red and drenched with sweat, yet he had only been able to move about two wheelbarrows for every three of Dean's. It was still far more than Angela had done since setting herself up as supervising technician.

An orange light flashed in the control display on her screen, and Angela immediately keyed the commands to stop the drill's progress. Half an hour later, they had reversed the auto-shovel out of the hole and completed the last excavation with old-fashioned picks and shovels to reveal a section of a broad, flat stone etched with more than just age.

Victor brushed the dust off the stone and found carvings of the same dancing reptilian figures that decorated the Topsy reactor room. Dean got down on his hands and knees to get a closer look. The late afternoon sun shed plenty of light above them, but at the bottom of a twenty-five foot hole it was too dim to make out the details.

"Those look kind of familiar," Dean said, tracing the carvings with his fingers.

"How would you have seen these before?" Angela asked. "I thought you said you hadn't been to the reactor room."

"I haven't, but look." Dean brushed dirt away from one of the figures to reveal curving barbs along its back, lanky arms, and round eyes with the slit pupils of a snake. "Does that remind you of anyone's new pet?"

Victor shook his head in denial, but he grew still as he stared deeply into the bas-relief eyes. "You might be right," he finally said. "But what does it mean—that this place was built by chupacabras?"

"Aliens," Dean folded his arms with pride at having scooped the conclusion out from under his younger, better educated colleagues.

"They aren't aliens," Angela said with unexplainable confidence. "Now, hand me one of those earthquake grenades."

Victor spread out his arms as if trying to keep a soccer ball out of the goal. "You're not going to break this," he said. "These carvings might be hundreds of millions of years old. It's a scientific treasure."

"And it's blocking the way to even more treasures," Angela glared at him. "In case you forgot, we're on a tight time schedule here."

The decision went to Dean, simply because he was carrying the satchel with the earthquake grenades.

"We need to find out what's down there before the Professor does," Dean said as he peeled back the adhesive covering and pressed the grenade's thick, gooey pads onto the center of the stone.

Victor, outvoted, had no choice but to lower his arms and give up his protest. He snapped a few pictures of the carvings with his phone before the three of them retreated up the ladder to let the grenade do its trick.

The reinforced glass at the museum had only taken three seconds to break, but this stone door took a full two minutes. It cracked in half and fell inwards, opening up a dark hole that belched out a gust of stale air. After they cleared the rubble from the broken cover-stone, they found another stone surface waiting below, but this one was smooth and perfectly round. When Dean set his foot on it, it bobbed slightly under his weight as though it were floating on water.

"It's an elevator," Angela said, joining him on the disk.

"What's holding it up?" Dean asked. There was a small gap running around the outside of the disk, and when he shone his flashlight through it he could see a smooth black shaft descending far down into the bedrock below. He could see no gears, pulleys, or any other means of support.

"It hovers the same way my flight pack does," Angela said. "It uses electrical repulsion to press against the Earth's natural magnetic field. The same thing happens when you try to push the south ends of two magnets together: one magnet always moves away from the other. Only with this, one of those magnets is the Earth."

The idea that he was standing on a floating rock with nothing solid to hold him up made Dean more than a little nervous, but the platform seemed stable enough, even as Victor added his weight to the total.

Angela located a mark on the wall that resembled a hand-print but with three long fingers instead of the typical five. When she pressed it, the disk descended at a speed just short of terrifying. Down they went, the stone walls rushing past them, the entrance to the shaft shrinking to a small dot of sky above their heads.

"How did you know to press that spot?" Victor asked after his stomach caught up to him.

"Isn't it obvious?" she shrugged.

Dean and Victor exchanged glances.

At the bottom of the five hundred foot shaft, the disk slowed gracefully and allowed the three of them to exit into a large underground room that made Dean realize he had never truly known darkness. In Los Angeles, there were always streetlights, porch-lights, and headlights, so even at midnight in the dead of winter the entire region was bright enough to chase the stars out of the sky. Even locked inside a closet, light would still find its way through the gap at the bottom of the door. Down here, however, the darkness seemed solid, like a curtain that had to be brushed aside with every step. Here, the beams of their flashlights seemed shrunken into nothing more than pale pinpricks of illumination amidst the vast sea of blackness. Add to this the extreme temperature, which Dean estimated to be close to 100 degrees, and even without the leering devil-faces carved on the walls it would have been easy to imagine themselves in the pit of hell itself.

As best they could tell, they were walking through a large vault with evenly spaced and intricately decorated pillars interspersed with free-standing obelisks. In the dim lighting, the pillars and obelisks seemed like a crowd of ghosts constantly moving, always following and forever surrounding the intruders on every side. After eons of being sealed away beneath the earth, nothing lived within the stale air of the cavern. There were no cobwebs, no scampering rats, not even a blind cave-fish. The three of them were intruders in the land of the dead, and the only sounds around them were their own footfalls echoing off the granite walls.

Dean's firefighter instincts told him that the obelisks were for decoration, but not the pillars. The spacing and shape of the columns that pressed up against the ceiling indicated that they were needed to keep the massive weight of the earth above them from crashing down onto their heads. It was worrisome to think of it, but if the cavern hadn't collapsed in millions of years then the chances were good it wouldn't fall while they were there.

"This place is way bigger than our reactor room," Victor said as he wiped perspiration off his brow. "It's a lot hotter, too."

"There's a magma flow behind this wall," Angela pointed her flashlight's pale circle of illumination at the side wall. "These caverns served as geothermal power plants. This one is still working, too—that's how the elevator had power."

"Okay, you're starting to make me nervous," Dean said. "You know something you aren't telling us."

"I know lots of things that I'm not telling you," she aimed her flashlight out into the darkness. "Keep looking around. If we find what I'm looking for, I'll tell you what you want to know."

As they proceeded, the floor sloped downwards until they came to a set of short but steep ramps leading up into an area that might have once been a temple. Inside the elevated space there were no obelisks, but squat stone pedestals projected from the floor between the pillars.

"Found it!" Angela announced.

Dean hurried over to see that she stood before one of the pedestals, her hand resting on a white metallic statue about the size of a footstool. The statue was shaped similarly to the chupacabra, with the same curving spines down its back, long arms, pointy claws, and iguana-like head. But this creature stood on heavily muscled legs that extended straight down from the middle of its body, and the weight of its torso was counterbalanced by a long, thick tail. It was almost as if whoever carved this statue had wanted to graft Choop's upper body onto a tyrannosaur's lower half, like a dinosaur version of a centaur.

"What is it?" Dean asked.

"It's pure teslanium, that's what it is," Angela responded.

Angela wrapped her arms around the statue and lifted it an inch off the pedestal before grunting and letting it fall back into place. "Phew," she breathed. "It's heavy. How much do you think it weighs?"

Dean grasped the statue around its underbelly and hoisted it up. To him, it wasn't difficult to lift, but the exertion was enough to make his biceps flare out against the sleeves of his t-shirt.

"I'd guess forty or fifty pounds," Dean said.

"Fifty pounds!" Angela's eyes blazed in excitement. "Let's get this thing to the elevator."

The three of them worked together to carry the load. Dean could have managed the weight by himself, but the shape was awkward and the extreme heat increased the difficulty of any exertion. Once they had set the statue into the center of the stone disk of the elevator, Dean turned to Angela.

"Okay, spill the beans," he said. "You promised you'd tell us what you know about this place. I still think it was made by aliens, by the way."

"I keep telling you, they weren't aliens," Angela said with mild annoyance as she moved away from them to inspect the iguana-faced carvings on a pillar. "These creatures—we call them 'progenitors'— they evolved right here on Earth. They built cities and harnessed electricity

millions of years before our ancestors had learned to fling poo at preda-
tors."

"Impossible," Victor scoffed. "Paleontologists would have
found their remains in the fossil records, not to mention signs of their
cities and tools. There would be evidence. We would know."

"What do you think this place is?" Angela gestured to the pillars around her. "The progenitors aren't going to be dug up with dinosaur bones because they never spread across the globe like human beings. By instinct, they were tied to their spawning grounds, kind of like
how salmon have to return to a certain inland river every year. In fact,
their entire civilization was confined to a single valley in what is probably now the South Pole. All of these caverns, all of the red dots on our
map, these were just automated outposts. The progenitors visited these
places, but they didn't stay. Ultimately they were all bound to their ho-
meland: bound to be born there, bound to mate there, and bound to die
there. It seems like a strange flaw for creatures of such advanced intelligence but, well, you can't fight your DNA."

Despite the heat of the cavern, Dean shivered. He had been
brought up like a good Catholic, believing that God had made human-
kind in His image and given dominion over the Earth to the descen-
dents of Adam. Agriculture, architecture, art—no other species in the
world could compete with human beings in any of these things. If Angela was right about these progenitor creatures, then it meant human
beings were not God's original masterpiece. Dean wasn't ready to grasp
the implications yet, but he had a feeling the idea was going to haunt
him for some time to come.

"If they were so advanced," Dean asked, trying to maintain his
skeptical tone. "Then where did they go? How come they aren't running
the world today and making us scrub their floors? If they had all this
technological stuff so long ago, they could have dominated the earth."

"And maybe they did," Angela turned her back to them as she inspected the pillars. "Maybe they wiped themselves out with a war or an ecological disaster, or maybe they just couldn't survive the changes in their climate. Perhaps they're still around, hiding deep below Antarctica or sneaking around the Amazon jungle, spying on the upstart human species and waiting to make their big come-back. The possibilities are thrilling. We've learned a few things from their carvings, but this is only the third cavern we've uncovered. There is much, much more to be learned."

"Wait, hold it right there," Victor said. "The *third* cavern? There's the reactor room and now this place. Did you miscount?"

"The other one was discovered by the Professor years ago," Angela said. As she spoke, she slid her backpack off her shoulders and, her back still turned to them, unzipped a pocket.

"Wait a minute," Dean said with a sinking feeling. "You never told us how you know all this."

Angela turned to show what she had drawn from the pocket of her backpack. It was a bulky pistol with six shiny barrels. Dean had never seen a gun like that before, but it looked dangerous.

"I warned you two not to come here with me," she said, flicking the wrist that held the gun to indicate they should step away from the elevator. "Still, it was nice to have you around to do all the heavy lifting."

Dean took a step towards her, but she was ten paces away and she had a steady hand.

"I've got this rail gun set to super-sonic," she said forcefully. "That means you'll be dead before you hear the shot. Now, move back. Both of you."

Her eyes burned, daring him to take another step. There was nothing Dean could do except put up his hands and allow Angela to march the two of them to the very back of the cavern.

"I really am grateful to you both," she said as they marched. "You helped me figure out how to work that egg much more quickly than I could have on my own. It made my trip back to Topsy worthwhile."

They descended the sloped floor and she indicated that they continue up into the temple area while she waited below.

"So now you're going to kill us down here?" Dean asked, his hands still raised.

"You're adorably stupid, but you've got a smokin' hot body," she said flippantly as she backed away, still covering them with the rail gun. "Vickey's pretty cute, too, plus he's as good as a doctor. I'm sure I can find a use for both of you."

"I'll never work for you," Victor called.

"You might change your mind after tomorrow," she said as she continued to back away. "You're just not going to be able to make an informed decision until after you see what happens on doomsday. I'll come back for you in a day or two. If you still don't want to join us, I'll be happy to kill you then. For now, though, I need you boys to stay right here."

Angela aimed her rail gun at the wall. The multiple barrels whirred to life and spat out a short machinegun burst of metal slugs that carved blue streaks through the blackness. Inside the enclosed space, the noise was deafening, but she didn't need to keep it up long. The first of the magnetic slugs thudded harmlessly into the stone wall, but the rest broke into the thin layer of granite, creating an opening through which oozed blazing magma. The hole widened until a section of the wall broke away, allowing a steady flow of the burning red rock to push its way out and spread along the lowered floor at the base of the temple. The temperature of the cavern immediately increased another ten degrees.

The entire cavern was now bathed in red light bright enough for Dean to see Angela's devilish smile before she turned and strode away.

Chapter 36 ~ Soap

"Nikki, please," I begged as the handcuffs dug into my wrist. It was now early evening and she had kept me locked up there all day, sitting cross-legged on the floor, trying to keep my knees away from the puddle of slime leaking out of the big, quivering white membrane sack next to me. Whatever was inside that sack, it had been moving around more and more, thrashing and jabbing at its enclosure. I was beginning to feel like a sacrificial virgin set out to feed the hungry dragon.

I also didn't know why Nikki hadn't turned me over to the Blitzkriegers, who were tearing up the park looking for me. My best guess was that she wanted to give me directly to the Professor to get a bigger reward. In the meantime, all I could do was try to annoy Nikki with my pleading until she let me go, but so far her ability to ignore me exceeded my ability to whine. She had spent her day working at the table to which I was handcuffed, swirling a green, bubbling liquid around in her flasks and filtering it through some kind of fermentation apparatus. Once or twice she filled a syringe with the liquid and then injected it into one of the veins that protruded from the membrane sack. The thing inside got really twitchy for a while after she made those injections.

"At least tell me what's going on," I begged. "You got so mad at me when I accidentally gave the Topsy key frequency to the Professor. It only seems fair that you at least tell me when you started betraying us."

She sighed as she worked and spoke without looking at me. "He contacted me after his Blitzkriegers tried to raid us." It wasn't much, but it was the most she had said to me since I crawled out of the airshaft that morning.

"Then why are you working for him?" I asked, trying to keep up the conversation's momentum. "A lot of people are going to die because of this scheme, you know."

"My conscience is clear," she said. From where I was on the floor, I had to strain my neck to see her face. She frowned as she skimmed some white gunk out of the green goo.

"People in hospitals are going to die," I said. "Just like what happened to Professor McKenzie. Also, anyone flying in an airplane is going to die. Lots of animals also need the Earth's magnetic grid to travel and live, like sparrows and pigeons and hammer-head sharks. Haven't you thought about the sharks?"

"Shut up!" she slammed the flask down onto the table so that some of the goo slopped out onto her gloved fingers and the pink sleeve of her lab coat. She took a deep breath and then wiped it away. Her voice sounded strained when she added: "I said my conscience is clear."

I was quiet for a little bit because I didn't know what to say. This time, Nikki was the one to speak first.

"You say it isn't fair to ruin the world," she said. "But some of us think it's already ruined. Until somebody makes an invention that will fill the bellies of hungry children and guarantee all of them a decent education, this here world is going to stay ruined." Suddenly, she laughed and was back to the smiling Nikki I had met on the first day of school. "Soap, darlin', this world is a vale of tears, and the people in it are nothin' but greedy and hurtful. They need to know you can hurt them, too, or they'll never leave you alone. Did I tell you about the girl in junior high who called me fat?"

I shook my head.

"I put a pressurized dye capsule in her locker," she said. "When she opened it—boom! Her face was as blue as a Smurf for a week. No more name-callin' from her."

She made a low ringing sound by tapping a steel cylinder she carried in her outer pocket. I gathered that this was one of her dye capsules and that the story was her way of telling me to be quiet before she painted me some color I didn't want to be.

If Nikki had more to add, she didn't have a chance because there was a loud knock on the door. She looked like she was thinking of not answering, but the knock came again, more insistent this time.

"Remember what I told you," Nikki said as she went to answer the door. "I might be workin' towards a degree in chemistry, but I'm majorin' in revenge."

Opening the door a crack, she peered through to speak to whoever was out there. Judging from the shadows cast by the hallway lights, there were several people at the door. The smell of grease and body odor coming from that direction told me it was the Blitzkriegers.

"What do you want?" Nikki demanded.

"We still ain't found her yet," said a raspy voice that I recognized as belonging to Shirtless.

"Not my problem," Nikki said.

"Was you talkin' to someone in here?"

Evidently, Nikki didn't answer fast enough, because Shirtless shoved his way into the room, leading the way with that big swastika tattoo on his chest. He was followed by the pot-bellied, weasel-faced guy and two more of their friends. When they saw me, their faces lit up.

"She been in here this whole damn time?" Shirtless demanded. "We been scourin' the park all day." He reached out and grabbed Nikki's wrist. "You been holding out on us, you dirty skank?"

Nikki stepped back and yanked her arm free of his grasp. "What'd you call me?" she demanded. Her voice was hard, her eyes spitting venom.

"You heard me," he turned away from her and gestured to his friends. "Grab the kid and let's go have our fun before we slit her throat."

The weasel-faced guy moved to my side, but then he saw the handcuffs.

"Can't," he lifted my wrist to show the rest of them. "Need a key."

Nikki rushed to my side. "Don't touch her," she said.

"The P'fessor said we can have her."

"Don't—touch—her!" Nikki repeated, stronger this time.

"Or what?" Shirtless stepped closer to her. "How you gonna stop us?"

I didn't see Nikki's hand move, but suddenly she held a box cutter, and she jabbed its razor tip into the skin of the membrane sack. She didn't quite press hard enough to cut it open, but it made a visible dimple in the stretchy thing.

The Blitzkriegers froze in place, their eyes locked onto that knife. They looked more scared than if she had the knife to their own throats. Thirty seconds of tense silence pressed down on us, but neither side backed down.

"Yer bluffing," Shirtless finally said.

"Try me," Nikki answered, and she pressed the knife just a bit deeper, until the thing inside sloshed around as if it was already looking for the opening.

I looked from Nikki to Shirtless and back again, not even daring to breathe. I wanted to do or say something, but I couldn't see how to get out of the situation.

Outside the door, the elevator dinged. Footsteps approached. Certain it would be more Blitzkriegers come to tip the scales in favor of murder, terror crushed down on me so hard that I thought my heart might stop. I had been clinging to the hope that Nikki could save me, but all she had was one tiny knife pointed at a strange science experiment. More Blitzkriegers meant I had no chance.

To my amazement, in strode a tall, blond woman with a black jacket, a blood-red shirt, and some kind of shining chrome device strapped to her back. Her hair was frizzed out and wind-blown, and she had a pair of aviator goggles pushed up on her forehead.

"I just flew in from Ellensville, and boy is my flight-pack tired!" she announced the moment she walked into the room. "And I found more teslanium than I had imagined possible. Isn't everyone happy for me?"

I heard Nikki whisper the name "Angela," but nobody else said anything. The blond woman strode right past the bikers as if nothing was going on, opened the fermentation vat on the workbench, and leaned her head inside.

"Look like we're almost done with this batch," she said, her eyes wild and bright. "Our baby's about to be born. Did the other lizard come back yet? I let him out of his cage, but I guess he's not that smart. Oh, and who do we have here?" She faked a surprise expression as if she'd just noticed me for the first time. "Why, you must be Sophia. I hear you're smart—maybe even smarter than me. But I guarantee you're not as much fun."

She strode back over towards the door, where she opened a closet, slid the silver rocket-thing off her back and set it on the floor, and hung up her leather jacket and goggles. Then she took down a long, black garment, and slid it over her shoulders.

"Black... black lab coat," I said in shock. Even sitting in a den of murderers, I was gripped by pure envy. "I didn't know they came in black."

"They don't," she twirled like a fashion model to show it off. It looked like it was made of fire-resistant fabric and had a long slit up the back of the hem to allow full mobility.

"You have to earn a black coat," she said proudly as she hunkered down in front of me and brushed my hair behind my ears with her fingers. "Oh, I was just like you when I started off. I was sweet and innocent with a white coat and a white soul. Angelic Angela. But I got better. I ate the fruit of knowledge and now look at how much more I've become," she turned and pointed at her back where the radiation hazard symbol had been emblazoned her back in hornet-yellow. Above the symbol were the words FALLEN ANGELA.

"But don't worry," she said, kneeling down again and patting my cheek. "Your innocence won't burden you much longer, I can tell. Soon you'll have earned a black coat just like mine."

"Hey, 'scuze me," Shirtless rasped. "We still got us a problem here. The P'fessor wants that little girl taken care of."

Angela turned on him, her face suddenly angry as she jabbed her fingers into his chest. He flinched back from her and I realized that these big, mean bikers were actually scared of her.

"Now, what would the Professor want with this darling little girl?"

"She's got information on a gizmo-thing," he said uncertainly. "She's got a, uh, a USD."

"It's called a 'USB drive,' you moron. Well, let's just have a look, shall we?"

Angela grabbed my free arm and yanked me forward. She raised her other hand high over her head and I thought she was going to spank me, but she brought her hand down softly onto the seat of my pants. Before I knew what she was doing, she slipped her fingers into my back pocket and removed my Hello Kitty USB drive.

"Darn," she said. "I was hoping for more probing, but I got it on my first guess."

She dropped the drive onto the floor and crushed it with the heel of her black running shoe. When she removed her foot, there was nothing left of my evidence but a tiny mound of plastic rubble.

Shirtless blinked at the broken drive. "But," he said. "But the P'fessor said—"

Quick as a snake, Angela put her index finger across his lips to silence him. "We're going to be forging a new society tomorrow," she said. "So let me ask you this: do you know the difference between people and dogs?"

Shirtless looked at her in confusion, and so did the other Blitzkriegers. I could see why they were afraid of her: she was as unpredictable as a wildfire.

"I said: do you know the difference between people and dogs?" she pressed him back. "No? Well, the answer is simple. Dogs are afraid of the vacuum cleaner."

Everyone in the room (including me) looked bewildered.

"Okay, so you guys don't get it," she sighed. "Let me see if I can illustrate my point."

She held out her hand to Nikki, indicating that she wanted the box knife. Reluctantly, Nikki handed it over.

"You see, a vacuum cleaner is a tool," Angela said, tossing the box knife up and down in her hand. "People—human beings—they understand what a tool is and they know how to use it. They don't have to be afraid of the vacuum cleaner because they have the power of knowledge on their side. Understand? Really? Well, then, let's run a little test, shall we?"

Angela turned slowly towards the membrane sack, keeping her eyes on us as she pressed the tip of the knife into the sack. The thing inside thrashed once, and then it held very, very still. A single drop of green fluid slipped out past the box cutter and trickled down the veined sack towards the floor.

"The Professor himself found the formula for making these little beasties," Angela said. "It took him years, but he finally deciphered the instructions from the walls of that cavern deep under Argentina. And now, tonight, it is my pleasure to introduce to you... Progenitor Replication 2.0!"

With those words, she slit the membrane clear down to the floor. It made a ripping sound like scissors tearing through newspaper, and it opened a gaping hole through which spilled a tidal wave of green fluid and clear, gelatinous gunk that smelled like the worst wet dog imaginable. I scrambled back under the table, but I couldn't avoid getting it all over my pants as the pool spread out everywhere. In the midst of this cascade, a huge, gray, slimy body tumbled out onto the floor. Like with Choop, flexible barbs ran down this creature's back, but this creature was much brawnier and had longer, sharper teeth. Its sledgehammer fists ended in bony spikes, its legs were bigger around than my torso, and its fat dinosaur tail smacked into the wall when it uncurled.

The monster rose up out of the muck of its afterbirth, its legs a little wobbly at first. It stabilized itself, flicked its tongue twice, and then it pulled in a deep breath before letting out a deafening roar. That roar was incredible. It was overwhelming. I bent down to cover my ears, but the noise still shook my guts and made me feel like my head was about to explode. It sounded like lighting, earthquakes, tsunamis, and volcanoes all rolled into one and played back through a megaphone.

The Blitzkriegers were out the door and down the hall before the monster finished its roar. It probably would have chased them if Angela hadn't spoken up.

"See?" she called after them. "This thing is a big vacuum cleaner and you're as scared as little puppies!"

I'm not sure Angela's vacuum cleaner analogy was very accurate, because I've never seen a Hoover try to backhand someone's head off. That's what this creature did, though, and that spike on the end of its fist ripped the tiles off the wall right where Angela had been standing a second before.

The monster was fast, but she was faster, and she rolled under its swing and came up neatly to her feet, where she dipped her hand inside her coat to grab something from an inner pocket. Nikki wasn't quite so graceful, because she lost her footing on the slimy floor and went down hard on her backside. She had to crab-walk backwards on her hands and heels to avoid the huge, three-toed foot that broke the tile as it stomped the floor.

That left the other two all the way across the room and me chained to a table right next to the monster. I tried to scoot myself back farther under cover, but there's only so far you can go when your arm is shackled to a steel table leg.

Suddenly, that huge face appeared right by my feet. It had red eyes and a big, squared jaw that looked powerful enough to snap me in half with its huge, pointed teeth. Its tongue flicked out again and I could feel the air currents on my fingers. The monster lifted the table, tearing the bolted legs right out of the ground with no more effort than it would have taken to lift a coffee mug. Because my arm was still shackled to the table, I went up into the air with it, sliding directly towards the beast's mouth. I closed my eyes and prayed.

There was a quick hiss and a thump, and a distinct lack of me being chewed into hamburger. The table dropped to the floor and I went with it. I opened my eyes to see the monster slump forward and close its eyes. In its back was the little red bloom of fletching that indicated a tranquilizer dart. When I looked over at Angela, she was spinning a dart pistol around her finger like she was a sheriff from the Old West.

"Get that monster into a cage and get it up to the parade ground," she commanded Nikki. "Then open a video link to the Professor and tell the troops to be ready for a midnight rally. I'm going to need seven or eight hours to get the reactor working." She paused to look at her wristwatch. "Perfect timing. Doomsday starts first thing tomorrow."

SEPTEMBER 17TH (DOOMSDAY)

CHAPTER 37 ~ DEAN

Dean and Victor had been sitting for hours, drooped against the wall farthest from the flow of magma. Only a trickle of molten rock now oozed through the gap, creeping like a red snake into the pits and through the gullies that formed as the surface of the burning moat cooled. At some point it would solidify enough that they could cross it safely, so Dean tested it by tossing a dime onto the darkest spot he could see. The coin rested for only a moment before being devoured in bright red flames.

"This place literally stinks," Dean said as he rubbed his temples. The fumes were so bad they were giving him a stinging headache. "It smells like farts down here. Really nasty, just-ate-a-gallon-of-chili farts."

"That's the sulfur from the magma," Victor said. "It used to be called brimstone, as in 'fire and brimstone.' This is supposed to be what hell smells like."

The two of them settled back into silence. Victor sat with his legs bent, his arms resting on knees, and his head hanging between his arms, coughing occasionally from the fumes. Dean leaned back against the wall, but the inward curve of the dome-shaped room did not make for a comfortable backrest. He flipped open his new phone. Of course he didn't get a signal this deep underground, but at least he could check the time. Just after midnight. They had been trapped for hours and Dean had tried everything he could think of to get out. He had searched the walls for handholds to climb across (there were none), tested various items around him to see if anything could work as a boat (everything sunk and burned), and measured off how far he could jump (he didn't come close). Now he was down to sitting and thinking, and it wasn't getting him any closer to freedom.

"Look, I don't mean to be rude," Victor said without looking up. "But are we just going to sit here until Angela comes back for us? Is that the best plan we have?"

"That's it," Dean said. "And when she gets here, I'll punch her a good one right in the nose. If you've got a better plan, I'd love to hear how to get across this lava."

"Magma," Victor corrected. "It's magma while it's underground and lava after it's forced to the surface by volcanic action."

Rather than snap at Victor to keep his Wikipedia edits to himself, Dean got up and walked to the edge of the temple area to watch the bubbles swelling and popping in the pool of fiery rock. He felt like he, as the nominal head of the Institute, had an obligation at least to be civil to his students. Even so, Victor did not rate high on his list of people he wanted to be trapped in an underground cavern with. The kid had kept the Topsy underground lab a secret, after all. It also didn't help that the first time Dean had laid eyes on him, the young man was happily strolling out of a shower with his young cousin. Sure, the shower had turned out to be an elevator, but who knows what the two of them could have been up to.

"When you came up to see me," Dean said after a long pause. "You were going to tell me something about my cousin. What was it you wanted to say?"

"Never mind," Victor coughed. "It's not important now."

Dean took a long breath of the foul air before he spoke again.

"Can I ask you something?" he said. "Tell me honestly. Do you like my cousin? I mean, romantically? I'm asking in my capacity as an overprotective family member."

Victor raised his head and looked at Dean in surprise and confusion. He must have been considering several different answers while he drew out the awkward silence.

"What difference does it make?" he finally said.

"That's not a 'no,'" Dean observed.

"Would it be a problem if the answer were 'yes?'"

Dean grimaced. Of course, he knew that Sophia's love life was her own affair, but if it had been up to him, Victor was not the one he would have picked for her. The kid was too self-absorbed and secretive. Too brainy. Maybe Dean didn't know her all that well, but he wanted the best for her, and for him that meant someone closer to her own age, more fun-loving, and maybe with a varsity letter or two.

"You don't like me, do you?" Victor looked up at him.

"It isn't about whether I like you," Dean said. "I know I don't have a say in the matter, so you kids will have to work it out for yourselves, but Sophia's young and impressionable. She needs someone to look out for her and protect her from the world."

"With all due respect, Mr. Lazarchek, I think it might be the rest of the world that needs to be protected from her. Someday she's going to turn this planet upside down—if that's what she wants."

"You don't know her," Dean said.

"Neither do you," Victor shot back.

The young man tried to glare, but a violent fit of coughing broke his eye contact. The harsh environment and the day's exertions had obviously taken their toll on him.

"The world is a tough place," Dean said to him when the coughing stopped. "You need more than brains to survive. All I'm saying is, if it were up to me, I'd like to make sure Sophia has a little more brawn to carry her through."

"Brains beat brawn every time," Victor spoke quietly to preserve his raw throat.

"Maybe in the world of books and computers," Dean said. "But let me tell you: if there's one thing I learned in the fire department, it's that all the fancy gizmos only get you so far. In the end, it's the people who use them that count."

Victor shook his head. "People don't last. People grow old and they die, and all their brawn goes away. Only their knowledge endures as it is handed down to others. Knowledge is the only thing that doesn't ever have to die."

"That's a nifty argument," Dean snorted. "When we get out of here, we'll have a fifty yard dash and see which is better, brains or brawn."

"Can I ask you something?" Victor said. "Why are you here? I don't mean here in this cave. I mean, why did you become the Dean of Students? It definitely doesn't seem like you're passionate about it."

Dean sat down heavily. It was a fair question. He might obscure the truth from President Hart and Agent Nash, but there was no reason to conceal it from Victor, especially here amidst the fire and brimstone.

"I made a promise to McKenzie," Dean said slowly. "Even though she wasn't around to hear me, I'm going to stick to that promise to find justice for her." He took a moment to touch the rings that hung around his head. His headache was getting worse, but pressing the hard gold loops against his chest felt strangely reassuring.

"Maybe the Institute isn't my thing," Dean said. "But coming here was my only chance of connecting with her again, because... because without her, I'm empty. I can't really explain it, but when she died, everything inside of me went with her. You probably wouldn't understand."

Victor studied Dean for a long while, his ice blue eyes cutting through the dim red light.

"When I was six, my parents died in a car wreck," Victor said, his voice strangely distant even as his eyes loomed large and unblinking. "I was in the back seat, in a child seat that probably saved my life. I remember watching my father breathing. From where I was, I could see his chest moving in and out slightly. And then, just before I heard the ambulance sirens, his chest stopped moving. Just like that. He was with me one moment and then gone the next."

"Damn," Dean whispered sympathetically. "I'm sorry. That must have been rough."

"After that," Victor went on. "I went to live with my grandmother. A year later, she had a fatal heart attack while we were eating dinner. My only other relative, my grandfather on my mother's side, had been battling cancer, which meant it was only a few months more before I was sitting at his bedside in the hospital, listening to his final breaths. I was orphaned three times in two years."

Dean placed his hand on Victor's shoulder, but Victor pushed it off. He seemed angry now, and his words came faster.

"You say you want justice for McKenzie, and I get that," Victor wheezed with each breath he took in, but he pressed ahead. "Nikki wants justice for the wrongs of society, and I get that, too. But everybody seems to take for granted that nature has inflicted the greatest injustice of all. How could the universe, or God, or whoever, have given us so little time on this Earth? Why is it possible to lose everything in an instant?"

Victor gasped for breath between words. He tried to stand, but dropped back to the floor.

"Take it easy," Dean said, getting worried. "I think you're making yourself sick."

Victor tried to push himself to his feet, but failed.

"Death," he croaked. "Everyone takes death as a given. Doesn't it make you want to scream?"

Dean could see that something was wrong with Victor. He pulled himself to his feet and looked out at the moat of magma. All those bubbles in its surface were releasing gasses, and who knew what was in those fumes. When houses burn, the biggest danger often isn't the flames, it's the smoke and fumes, and the same principle was holding true here. The foul-smelling vapors were having a greater affect on Victor, but it was only a matter of time before they both succumbed. Angela may have intended only to trap them there for a while, but if they didn't get out soon, she would return to find that her two prisoners had become two corpses.

The magma pool was blackening and solidifying around its borders, but it was still too far to jump. He needed another way. He went back to where Victor lay in hopes of finding something in his satchel that would work to span the gap. All he had was a pocket knife, a phone, a flashlight, and a pair of earthquake grenades. He considered making a rope out of his clothes, but there was nothing to attach it to.

Victor made an attempt to speak. Then he tried to stand again but seemed unable to find his balance.

"Save your strength, buddy," Dean knelt down to place a comforting hand on his shoulder to keep him from trying to stand up.

"It's Soap," Victor wheezed. "I'm really worried about Soap."

"Seriously?" Dean looked around at the magma oozing into the subterranean cavern and the hot vapors rising out of it. "I think you should worry about yourself for a bit."

"I don't want to worry you," Victor said. "But she went to..." he paused to cough. "She went to Happy Fun Land."

"You're worried about that? You're delirious."

"Happy Fun Land," Victor looked up at him urgently. "It's home base for the Blitzkriegers."

Dean couldn't move as his brain processed the information. According to what Victor had just told him, Sophia had marched off to a den of thugs and thieves *all by herself,* and was probably about to get herself in serious trouble if she hadn't already. The thought made him go cold. It meant Dean had failed yet again to protect the people who needed it. If he had known, he might have been able to find his cousin, send her back home, and cut out all this trouble with the egg by going straight after the Blitzkriegers.

"Victor, why—*why*—didn't you tell me this before?"

It was no good: Victor was fading in and out of consciousness. They would have to settle that score later.

The urgency to escape that cavern had now doubled, yet Dean's resources remained the same useless odds and ends in the earthquake-grenade satchel. If only he could use the earthquake grenade on the pillars next to him, he could knock one off its base and roll it down the ramp to use as a bridge across the magma. But if he broke the pillars, thousands of tons of rock would come crashing down on his head in short order. The obelisks on the far side of the magma were not load bearing and would work just as well to bridge the fiery pool, but those were out of reach.

Unless he threw a grenade.

He peeled back the flap on the gooey adhesive and tested it with his pinky. His finger stuck to it and he had to struggle to get free. With adhesive like that, even a grazing hit would be enough to attach the grenade to the obelisk and let it do its work. Once the obelisk broke, the slope of the floor would ensure it would fall towards him and maybe, just maybe, give him a route to freedom. It was far from foolproof, but it seemed like the best chance they had.

He wound up like a major league pitcher with the first grenade and ignored the pain in his ribs as he launched it over the magma moat. It struck the nearest obelisk with its rim—the one surface that had no adhesive. Murphy's Law was being strictly enforced. The grenade bounced off the obelisk and fell into the magma, where it disappeared with nothing more than a slight hiss to mark its passage.

One grenade left. Dean flicked the "on" button and took a deep breath, eyeing the target obelisk. Then he flung it backhanded, across his body like a Frisbee. The length, cylindrical shape, and moderate weight of the grenade seemed to work better with that type of throw than with the overhand baseball-style pitch, although the sting in Dean's rib was twice as bad this time around.

The grenade floated up and then down as it traced an arc away from him, revolving through the air in what seemed like slow motion. It sailed over the magma and slapped into the dead center of the obelisk, right at its base. There was an audible humming-bird buzz as the stone structure jittered loose from the floor, then a roar of wind as it fell down towards the magma, just as Dean had planned. The part that didn't go as hoped, however, was that it failed to fall in a straight line, instead twisting and cracking into one of the structural pillars.

The obelisk ricocheted off the pillar in a spray of fragments that sizzled when they landed in the magma flow. Dean threw himself down on top of Victor as the debris splashed burning gobbets of molten rock into the air. A red-hot drop the size of a golf ball thudded two inches away from Dean's head, where he watched as it warped the stone floor beneath it. Then there was a tremendous crash, and Dean turned his head just in time to see the tip of the obelisk hammering down onto the floor of the temple. The far end rested at the edge of the other side of the magma, and the body of the obelisk formed a slanted walkway. Behind it, the damaged pillar groaned and twisted in its place as several large chunks of granite fell from the ceiling above it to crash into the floor. Whatever the progenitors had used to construct this cavern must have been tremendously strong to survive millions of years, but its ability to hold the ceiling up was about to come to a very violent end.

Dean pulled Victor up and onto his shoulders into a fireman's carry.

"What're you doing?" Victor asked in disbelief, too exhausted to struggle.

"You're in no condition to walk," Dean said. "Looks like brawn wins out over brains today."

"The day's just getting started," Victor said weakly.

Dean hopped as best he could from one chunk of rubble to the next until he stood atop the fallen obelisk. The moment he got his second foot on the makeshift bridge, the damaged pillar on the far side of the burning lake collapsed completely in a torrent of boulders, and the next three pillars bent visibly as gaping cracks radiated out along the ceiling.

Dean positioned one foot on each side of the slope to stabilize himself. With each step, the obelisk rocked under him as detritus rained from the ceiling.

"What's happening?" Victor groaned, his head hanging next to Dean's arm.

"Just hold on," Dean said as he inched down the back of the obelisk. He knew that one misstep and they would be roasted in the magma, but if he took too long they would end up crushed by the falling ceiling. The raining debris splashed below his feet as he went, and the tiniest droplet landed on the back of Dean's calf. He exhaled in pain as it burned through his jeans and into his skin, but he didn't let it slow him down.

When he reached the far side, he dropped onto the sloping ground and set Victor down. The cracks in the ceiling were opening as the two men watched larger debris start breaking away. Dean flung his arm over his head protectively, and then grabbed Victor by the collar. The two rushed through the collapsing chamber as it crashed down around them, Dean almost dragging Victor along. They dove onto the elevator disc as a sheet of rock cut off the opening behind them with a thunderous crash and a choking cloud of dust.

The disc rocketed them upwards, where Dean had just enough time to grab the auto-shovel's ladder before the disc lost power and dropped away under their feet. He reached back, snagged Victor's sleeve, and pulled him to safety.

The elevator disc fell away into the darkness of the shaft. All was silent for a moment before the sound of a distant crash echoed up to them, followed later by a gust of sulfurous air.

When they finally reached open air, the night was dark and they were alone, but Dean's truck remained where he had left it.

"I guess she decided a jet pack is faster than a truck," Victor gasped, leaning on the vehicle and breathing deeply to clear out his lungs.

"Lucky us," Dean said as he slid behind the wheel and turned the key. "Load up. We're going to Happy Fun Land."

Chapter 38 ~ Soap

I've sometimes said that making an electromagnet is so easy that anybody could do it with one hand tied behind their back. I never expected that I would be making one with one arm handcuffed to a bench, but life is full of surprises. I just wish my escape plan hadn't required someone else's chewing gum.

All of us—me, Nikki, Angela, the monster, and the Blitzkriegers, were all up on the parade ground at the base of the Doomsday Machine. It had taken Angela a little longer to complete the reactor than she had originally planned, but at about three in the morning she ordered everybody out to listen to her speech. The Blitzkriegers crowded around the stage. The red-eyed monster had awakened after its dose of tranquilizer, but it was now safely locked up in a cage behind Angela. I think she wanted it up there so it would help strike fear into her audience. Above her was a huge screen that showed the Professor as he overlooked the whole ceremony like some presiding monarch. He was using the same software to blur out his face and body that he had used when he contacted me by video chat, but he spoke through loudspeakers to emphasize what Angela was saying and to boast that their moment of triumph had arrived.

The whole point of the speeches by Angela and the Professor seemed to be just to say they were ready to throw the switch to conquer the world, but it was a good way to whip their gang into a frenzy.

"Down with all of them!" Shirtless cheered from the front row as he threw a half-full beer can over his head. All the rest of his friends joined in, chanting "Bring them down! Bring them down!" over and over. They never said exactly who they were trying to bring down, but I don't think it mattered. If they got the Doomsday Machine working, nobody would be left standing.

Angela pumped her fists in the air along with them and made a noise that sounded like a cheer, but I was close enough to hear that she actually said "whatever!" It was clear to me that she was mocking them right to their faces and they didn't even know it. If only they had been smarter, maybe they would have figured out that she was just using them to get what she wanted. Of course, if they had been smarter they might have been out making a positive contribution to society instead of robbing banks and cheering for the end of the world. I guess there are inherent limits to the intelligence of criminal minions.

While all this was going on, Nikki and I stood to the side of the small stage. She had taken my backpack, removed all the screwdrivers and pliers from my pockets, and handcuffed me to the railing. Now she stood about ten feet in front of me, her lab coat draped over the back of a chair. The pocket hung open, and I knew the key to my cuffs was right inside.

First, I tried reaching for it, pulling against my shackle so hard that it felt like the cuff was going to rip my hand off. But no matter how hard I strained, the closest I could get was brushing the fabric of her coat with my fingertips. Then I came up with the idea of the magnet. I figured if I could attach a magnet to something long, I could dip into the pocket and retrieve the key.

She hadn't left me with much to work with in my own pockets, but I still had a penlight, my dorm room key, a few loops of thin copper wire, and a jeweler's screwdriver that was so small Nikki's search had missed it. I also had Rusty's tracking bracelet, but Rusty didn't have a stealth mode, and even though Angela was watching the crowd and the crowd was hanging on her every word, I was pretty sure they would notice a metal scorpion-dog traipsing up to me and using an acetylene torch to cut off my handcuffs. More importantly, Rusty was busy saving the world by rigging up the Doomsday Machine with the earthquake grenades, so I figured I had better leave him where he was.

I wound the copper wire tightly around my dorm key and fed the two ends to the battery I had taken from the penlight. That's all an electromagnet is: a wire with an electric current wrapped snugly around a metallic object. Anyway, the only item I still needed was something to give the magnet some length.

I looked around my feet, hoping to find a long twig or a stiff cardboard wrapper among all the discarded food containers and gobs of gum on the pavement. It turned out I found something even better than I could have hoped for: a long plastic stick that was used for tying up balloons. It was almost two feet long, and it couldn't have been better for this experiment if I had ordered it online.

I had enough wire to run along the stick so that I could keep the heavy battery in my hand and dangle the key-turned-magnet off the far end like the hook from a fishing pole. But the problem was that no matter how I tried to tie the wire at the far end, it kept slipping off. I needed some glue to keep it secure. I looked around again, but all I saw was garbage and gum.

Gum. Stupid, sticky gum.

There was a big glop right next to my foot, but it was too dried out to stick easily. However, it could be re-hydrated pretty quickly if someone chewed on it.

The thought made my stomach turn. My mind raced for any other option, but there was none. I was surrounded by a bunch of deranged bikers who seemed ready to graduate from grand larceny to global terrorism, and if I didn't get out of there, people were going to end up seriously dead. Compared to that, what was the worst thing that could happen to me with all those germs crawling around in that rubbery glob? Except for possibly barfing myself inside-out, my rational mind knew that my chances were worse with the Professor than with the bacteria. I tried not to think about it as I used my screwdriver to scrape the largest, most promising splotch of gum off the pavement.

Even holding it made me want to retch. It was a faded red, frazzled lump with strands that turned white and fibrous when they stretched. I tried not to imagine the microbes squirming around and multiplying on its surface, twitching their hairy little appendages and squeezing their poisonous juices out behind them. I especially tried not to imagine how I would be giving them a red-carpet welcome into my mouth, where they would wriggle and twitch across my tongue and into my bloodstream.

My stomach turned over and I gagged. The problem with imagination is that once you open the faucet you can't stop the flow.

"What's your problem back there?" Nikki half turned towards me, but I managed to hide the lump of gum and my improvised electromagnet behind my back.

"Nothing," I said, feeling bile come up in my mouth. "It's just—all this makes me sick."

She snorted and turned back to watch the show. Before I could give it any more thought, I crammed the piece of gum into my mouth. It was only about the size of a cashew nut, but it tasted strongly of rubber and dirt. In my imagination it burned like a nugget of acid with every bite. I pushed saliva at it with my tongue and then recoiled as I realized what my tongue was touching. After gnashing it nine times, it felt like it might be sticky enough (and I felt like I might go into septic shock), so I pulled it out of my mouth and stuck it to the end of the balloon stick. I gagged, and I scrubbed my tongue with my finger. I almost spat, but I didn't want to give Nikki cause to turn around. I would have gargled with hand sanitizer if she hadn't taken it away from me, even though that stuff is poisonous. I also threw away the screwdriver I had used to scrape it up because I couldn't bear to touch it any more.

It was a horrible experience, but it was done. I wished that everyone who complained about me being a germaphobe could have been there to see what I had done, but I wished even harder that I hadn't needed to do it.

As soon as I had recovered, I pressed the copper wire into the gum on the end of the balloon stick. Then I dipped the electromagnet into Nikki's coat pocket and fished for the handcuff key. For one minute I froze when Nikki glanced to her left and I thought she was about to turn around or grab her coat, but whatever she saw it must have had nothing to do with me. When she looked back at the stage, I released the breath I hadn't realized I was holding and inched the key out of the pocket.

Sixty seconds later, I was off and running through the shadows, hoping nobody had noticed me go.

My plan was to sneak out the way I'd come in and get out of that place as fast as the struggling transmission of Brett's Camaro could carry me. But I hadn't gone farther than the other side of the Doomsday Machine ride when I heard a funny, sing-song birdcall.

I stopped and looked around, but I couldn't see anything. Angela's speech was still going strong, and the Blitzkriegers were hooting and howling like they were at a rock concert. It was the middle of the night, long after birds stopped singing, so I dismissed what I heard and was about to continue on my way. Then I heard it again.

This time I looked up into the scaffolding of the Doomsday Machine ride. There was Choop, looking about as comfortable among the joists and cross-beams as a panther taking a nap in a tree. He looked down at me with those big red eyes and made the birdcall to me again.

"How'd you get here?" I whispered. "And how did you get out of Topsy?"

He chirped again and started to climb, but then he stopped and looked back down as if to see whether I was following.

"Stay hidden," I whispered. "Just stay hidden if you know what's good for you, you big gecko. Believe me, you don't want to meet your younger brother."

I shuddered at the memory of the recently-hatched monster as it ripped through a table to get at me and I didn't think it would be any kinder to Choop. This renewed my desire to get out of the park, but the chupacabra spun around in a circle, paused to look down at me, and then repeated this motion again and again.

Is it totally weird to climb a ramp into the scaffolding of a doomsday machine because a spiny reptile-thing seems to want to show you something? The answer is yes, especially when you're two hundred yards away from a pumped-up biker gang and a couple of very deadly scientists. But, in my defense, I was really curious to see where he was going.

Choop met me on the ramp and kept scampering ahead, turning to wait for me, and then scampering ahead again. He was like Lassie leading me to a boy stuck down a well. As it turns out, he really was trying to show me that someone was stuck, but it wasn't a boy. It was a robot.

The ramp led up to an open platform that would have become the ride's exit and gift shop if construction had been finished. Now it was nothing but raw wooden beams and posts, with boards making a floor over fifty square feet of what was obviously intended to have been a much bigger room. In the middle was Rusty, tugging away at his cable that was stuck between some floorboards. He was like a dog tugging at a leash, over and over again, because he simply lacked the problem-solving intelligence to do anything else, which meant he had not completed his mission. The rest of the cable and the other grenades were still stored on his back instead of attached to the tower.

When Angela hit that switch, there would be nothing to stop the Doomsday Machine.

CHAPTER 39 ~ DEAN

Dean kept his foot jammed on the accelerator and was just a little gratified to see Victor's white-knuckled hands pressing against the dashboard.

"Do you have to go so fast?" Victor asked nervously.

"I could have taken my time," Dean growled. "If someone had told me *yesterday* that my cousin was heading into a den of thugs."

The pickup squealed around a curve in the highway. At sixty, it would have been a gentle turn. At ninety, the truck almost came up on two wheels.

"I can see you're still mad at me," Victor said after the truck leveled out.

"You think?"

"You're the one who started this whole secrecy thing. Remember when we first met? I asked you about the bikers and you told me I shouldn't know. Then you never seemed to care about what we were doing, so I didn't feel like I needed to tell you."

"I saved your life back in that cave," Dean snorted. "From now on, you tell me everything."

"Maybe I can pay you back when we get to Happy Fun Land," Victor said, but it wasn't very convincing as he squirmed down as far as his seatbelt would allow while the road ripped past them.

Dean slammed on the brakes and then peeled off down the side road he had almost missed. In L.A. it would have been impossible to drive this way at any time of day, even in a fire engine blaring its sirens. At two a.m. in the boondocks, there was no one on the road to get in his way.

"Listen up and listen good," Dean said over the roar of his engine. "When we get there, you're going to stay in the car. Got it? You stay in here, keep your head low, and keep the motor running until I get back. Do I make myself clear?"

Victor nodded. "How are you going to get in?" he asked breathlessly. "The whole place is fenced off, you know."

Dean smiled grimly. "We're about to find out how a pickup does against a chain-link gate."

Chapter 40 ~ Soap

As a human being, it was easy for me to see what a robot could not comprehend. All Rusty had to do was back up a bit to un-snag the cable. I made a mental note to add a few lines of code to my next robot so that he wouldn't have the same problem. For Rusty, it was too late, because he wouldn't be coming down after he installed the earthquake grenades. It made me sad to watch him climbing dutifully upwards through that dark scaffolding. He was on a suicide mission, but it was the only way to save the world from disaster.

Choop watched the robot go, then looked at me, then back up at the robot. He had seen me with Rusty back in the Topsy lab and he must have led me here because he figured I would want to know where to find my toy. He must have been confused when I let Rusty go climbing away on his own without me.

"You have no idea that you just saved the world, do you?" I asked, even though Choop wasn't looking at me. But it was true: if Choop hadn't led me back here, Rusty would never be able to install the earthquake grenades, and there would be nothing to stop the Doomsday Machine.

Suddenly Choop spun in place and froze, looking down the ramp. Then he sprang silently into the air, landing lightly on a crossbeam from which he scampered up and out of sight.

A second later I heard what spooked him: footsteps on the ramp. I wished I could have climbed away like Choop, because a few seconds later Nikki had reached the top of the ramp and I was cornered on the platform. We were thirty feet above the parade ground, so I didn't have anywhere to go but down.

"Let me go," I said, trying to sound strong even though I didn't feel it. "I won't bother you again. Just let me go."

"Okay," she said and stood aside to leave the ramp free and clear.

I blinked. Was this some kind of trick?

"It's okay, honey," she said. "I couldn't let you go earlier because they were all out here fixin' to catch you again. But now they're distracted."

I edged towards the exit, but I didn't want to turn my back on her.

"Didn't you hear me?" she said with exasperation in her voice. "Get gone while you still can."

"Why?" I asked. "Why are you letting me go if you're working with them?" I gestured with my head back towards the bright lights of the stage where the bikers were still howling like a pack of dogs.

Nikki looked at me and sighed. "If you'd read more Machiavelli, you might've recognized that I've been on your side the whole time. It's called playing a deep game. After the Professor got to you, I knew he would keep trying until something worked, so I volunteered. This way, I've been able to control the situation."

She walked past me to the cable Rusty had stretched across the platform. He had wrapped it around a post when he went up, and it was now so tight at that spot that it twanged like a guitar string when she plucked it.

"I'm bringing this tower down," I said. "You can't stop me."

With her eyes she followed the cable up to the nearest earthquake grenade twenty feet overhead.

"Your plan might work," she said appraisingly. "But it's needlessly complicated."

"You got a better one?"

"I was just a-goin' to blow it all up," she turned to me with a smile.

I stared at her.

"I whipped up a home-brew of good, old-fashioned tri-nitrogen tetroxide," she explained. "You know: TNT. Dynamite. I fooled them all into thinking it was chupacabra chow—the idiots. I made just enough to destroy the reactor down below and maybe cause a distraction while we get away. And I can blow it with this." She drew her phone out of her pocket and wiggled it around to show me.

I couldn't believe it. All my work and fear for nothing, because Nikki had it under control the whole time.

"Well, you want to see it go up in smoke?" Nikki smiled big at me as she moved her finger towards the button on her phone. "This here seems as good a time as any. You might want to cover your ears because—ow!"

She shook her fingers and dropped the phone as if it had stung her. It clattered to the deck, where it sparked and then cracked down the middle. A red finger of flame probed its way out of the crack, waved around in the air for a moment, and then dissipated in a pathetic little puff of black smoke.

"I was perfectly aware it wasn't chupacabra food," said a well known voice. Angela was right beside us now, only she wasn't standing on the platform: she was held in mid-air by a rippling blue wave of energy that emitted from her flight pack. She descended upon us, wrapped in that electric glow while the two lower flaps of her lab coat fluttering up behind her like a pair of huge, black wings. In her left hand she held a little wand that I guessed to be the EMP generator she had used to destroy Nikki's phone. She was smiling, but her eyes burned with madness.

As she settled gracefully on the open edge of the platform, the energy from her flight pack created an army of shadows that bowed and scattered before her approach. Behind us, three Blitzkriegers scrambled up the ramp to cut off our retreat. Two of them had guns in their hands. The third man was Shirtless, who carried one of those really big knives, the kind with saw-teeth down the back edge of its blade.

I was debating whether I would be better off jumping over the ledge than letting them get me when an enormous crash echoed up from below. Dean's truck had smashed through the chain link gate at the front of the amusement park and was gunning its engine as it barreled right for the parked motorcycles.

CHAPTER 41 ~ DEAN

A two-ton pickup wins against a chain link fence. It also wins against motorcycles—even very expensive, heavily customized motorcycles.

Victor clung to the door handle for dear life. "Are you nuts?" he shouted.

"Yes," Dean said, and then he jammed the accelerator against the floor. The world became a tumble of bone-jarring thuds and jolts as the truck's smashed grill plowed through the remaining bikes. A length of handlebar careened off the windshield, instantly filling it with a spider's web of cracks.

On the far side of this newly-made junkyard, Dean slammed on the brakes and the truck skidded to a halt. Even though the truck was no longer moving, Victor still braced for impact against the dashboard as if waiting for another collision. "Do you think they know we're here?" he breathed.

As if in answer to his question, a loud crack ripped through the night as a bullet collided with the truck's engine block. At the sound of a second crack, the cabin windshield shattered and another bullet passed between the two of them with a distinctly audible "ZZZIP!"

Dean scrambled to unbuckle himself and then pushed Victor out the passenger door. The truck's headlights were off, so the two of them had the cover of darkness as they rolled to the ground and crawled through the shadows. Even so, more bullets whizzed over their heads. The truck's tires echoed the gunfire as they popped and one of the rear view mirrors shattered into oblivion. On the opposite end of the parkway, at the foot of a lighted stage, a crowd of Blitzkriegers continued to fire wildly into the night.

"Over here!" Victor shouted as he spread himself flat behind a low wall. A bullet collided with the cement next to him and kicked up a cloud of dust, but he was safe where he lay.

In the army, Dean had regularly trained to elbow-crawl through soft mud, and it had seemed miserable at the time. It turned out to be even more miserable when crawling across hard, abrasive pavement, especially while real bullets whizzed overhead.

When he got close, Victor reached out to help pull him the rest of the way behind the wall.

Dean risked a glance over the wall to see the bikers clumped together in an angry mob that was illuminated by the flashes of their pistol muzzles and the stage lights behind them. All of them stood with no regard for cover, and let their guns blaze at the truck without much care for aiming. Not a single one of them moved around to flank their target. They were not soldiers, Dean realized, just a bunch of thugs with guns. Unfortunately, thugs or not, they still had the guns and Dean didn't.

Victor slapped Dean on the shoulder and then pointed over to a row of carnival booths. "Did you see him?"

"Who?" Dean pressed himself back against the wall and looked where Victor was pointing. He saw nothing except for shadows and a cotton candy kiosk.

"Choop!" Victor exclaimed. "I don't know how, but Choop's over there!"

"You're crazy," Dean said, and rolled back on his shoulder to snatch another glimpse at the stage. He ducked back down as a bullet thumped into the base of the wall, but he was fairly certain it was a stray shot, so he leaned out slowly from behind his cover. He saw the giant, menacing form of Brick at the front of the angry mob blasting away with a sawed-off shotgun even though the truck was far, far beyond its effective range. Behind him was a stage with a big screen showing the blurred image of a man at a desk.

"Kill them, you idiots!" It was the Professor's voice, screaming through the loudspeakers to either side of the stage. "I don't want any complications during our hour of victory!"

Below the screen, there was a big cage containing a huge, gray lizard-creature. It looked like Choop on steroids, and as the Professor railed on at the Blitzkriegers, the monster gripped the bars of its cage and roared. The noise of the roar was so loud that it even drowned the sound of the Professor's voice. It muffled the gunfire, and it shook Dean's innards even though he was fifty yards away. It even caused the bikers to pause their firing.

"I'm going to get Choop," Victor sprang to his feet during the lull in gunfire. Dean lunged to pull him back under cover, but he was already sprinting away, his white lab coat trailing behind him as he streaked behind a ring-toss booth. Dean rolled to his feet to follow, but a hail of bullets thumped into the ground around him and drove him back behind the wall.

"Stupid, crazy kid," Dean muttered as shots hammered away at his cover, grinding through the bricks like chisels. Victor's sprint had alerted all the bikers to Dean's hiding place, and now they were aiming for him. At least Victor had probably reached safety. Probably.

Dean didn't dare take another look, but he could tell from the direction of the fire that the bikers were finally getting smart and split-ting into two groups so that they could encircle him. In a moment, they would get a clear shot at him—if they didn't blast his cover away to nothing before that. Either way, he would be dead within minutes, and the last thing he would hear would be the Professor's voice booming over the park's PA system.

Suddenly, Dean realized that he recognized that voice. He knew who the Professor was!

CHAPTER 42 ~ SOAP

From where I stood, I could see the Blitzkriegers firing wildly at my cousin and Victor.

"This is *so* annoying," Angela said. "Wait here. I'm going to start the machine and finish this little farce."

Then she was gone in a blue streak of electricity, sailing down to the entrance building on her way to the reactor below.

"Well, I ain't gonna stick around up here," whined the pot-bellied, weasel-faced guy. He had his gun pointed at us but he was craning his neck to see the commotion in the parade ground. "They smashed up our bikes, man. Our *bikes*!"

"You heard her," Shirtless yelled. "We're s'pposed to wait here. We need to guard these two, and maybe kill them a little, too."

"Forget that," said Weasel-Face. "Vengeance must be had, man." With that, he ran down the ramp. The third biker looked back and forth between the ramp and Shirtless and then he followed.

Shirtless yelled a load of curses after them. Then he turned back to us with a cruel grin slicing across his face.

"That's awright," He licked his lips and turned his knife so that it glinted in the dim light. "More fun for me. You skanks ready for some fun?"

"Sure, let's have some fun. Starting with this." Nikki tossed him something that looked like a half-sized can of processed cheese, the kind that has the consistency of toothpaste so you can squirt it out onto crackers. This can had no label, just bare steel sides and a white plastic tube at the top.

Shirtless caught it in one hand and looked at it with a disdainful sneer. "What's this—" the can interrupted him with a loud pop. Instantly, he was engulfed in a thick, orange mist.

He dropped his knife and stumbled backwards towards the edge of the platform. He blinked and he looked down at his bare arms and chest, and then his eyes opened wide when he realized what had happened to him.

From the top of his bald head to the hip bones that protruded out of his jeans, his skin was now neon orange, the color of a prison jumpsuit. The color was so bright he almost seemed to glow in the dark. All of his tattoos were covered, too, and you couldn't even see the swastika on his chest. Frantically, he tried to wipe it off, but it stayed so dark that it might as well have been his natural color.

"What—what'd you do to me?" he shrieked.

"Pressurized dye capsule," Nikki said. "You never looked better."

Shirtless shrieked and lunged for his knife. As his fingers closed around the hilt, Nikki plunged a syringe needle into the back of his hand. He yelped and rose to his knees, but he was out cold before he could get to his feet.

It was the syringe of Victor's special formula that I brought with me. Nikki must have kept it after confiscating the contents of my pockets.

"Too bad you only had half a vial of that tranquilizer left," Nikki said. "I suppose he'll live." Nikki's voice was so cold that I thought she honestly might not care one way or the other. She left the empty syringe protruding from his limp hand, but kicked the knife across the platform.

We both moved over to the edge of the platform to see what was going on down below. From where I stood, I could see that Victor had managed to run off, and a group of Blitzkriegers had gone to chase after him through the little alleyways of the carnival booths. The rest of the bikers were pressing forward to where my cousin was pinned behind a low wall.

Nikki swore under her breath. "Looks like the boys're in trouble. Wait here."

"Where are you going?"

"To create a distraction," she shouted back at me as she sprinted down the ramp.

A stray bullet knocked a jagged, splintery hole in a post three feet away from me, so I dropped to my belly and inched forward to look over the edge of the platform again. Nikki was dashing onto the stage, right in between the gang of bikers and the monster's cage, but I had no idea what she was planning to do.

Then something happened: every light in the park came on as if someone had flicked a switch. The rides came alive, too, swinging their plastic cars back and forth as they played garbled music. They were slow to get going, but their pace steadily increased as they received more and more electricity. I rolled onto my back and looked upwards, towards the broadcasting dome at the tip of the tower high above me. The sky all around it was lighting up in gyrating rivers of glowing greens and blues as the magnifying transmitter pushed millions of volts out into the stratosphere. Angela had started the reactor. The Doomsday Machine was warming up.

I could already feel the jostling vibration in the planks of the platform, which meant Rusty had got all the earthquake grenades into place. Now I just had to pray that they could wreck the Doomsday Machine before the Doomsday Machine could wreck the world.

As soon as I had that thought, the first of the earthquake grenades overloaded. High overhead, it blew up in a great cloud of red and black fire that sent a rumble through the whole tower. I stood up just as another grenade went off, this one below me. The tremor knocked me off my feet and I went backwards off the edge of the platform.

As I fell, I managed to grab a cross-beam, but two-by-fours are not meant to provide the best handholds. Thirty feet below, the pavement awaited me, but the orange flames were more impatient as they climbed the wooden scaffolding towards my kicking feet.

I should've known that my experiment would explode. Again.

CHAPTER 43 ~ DEAN

Dean realized with a surge of disappointment that knowing the Professor's identity wasn't going to help him at that moment. There were only three options: be gunned down where he lay, be gunned down as he fled, or be gunned down in a futile, suicidal charge at the approaching enemy.

He balled up his fists—his only weapon—and allowed himself one deep breath before opting for the suicidal charge.

He cleared the low wall and got only two steps before his charge came to a halt—not by bullets, but because the angry mob of heavily armed Blitzkriegers had dissolved into a disorganized mass of panicked rabbits. The monster chupacabra, the one that had earlier let out a roar so deafening it had interrupted the shooting spree, was out of its cage and rampaging through their midst like a bully stomping his way through sand castles. It roared again and again, swinging its spiky fist into the crowd and knocking a biker through the air to collide with two of his comrades. Faced with the thing of their nightmares, most of the bikers simply fled. A few fired their pistols at it, but without taking time to steady their shaking hands, their shots went way off target.

Dean circled around the crowd, sticking to the shadows as the monster smashed its way through the Blitzkriegers. He saw a weasel-faced biker step out behind the creature and take careful aim, holding his black revolver steadily and pouring all of his concentration into the sights along the barrel of his gun. The biker's focus was so great that he didn't see Dean's fist coming. Weasel-Face dropped heavily to the ground and the gun skidded away into the shadows.

Shaking his fist to clear it of the pain of impact, Dean caught a glimpse of Nikki standing to the side of the empty cage. She gave him a thumbs-up. Dean was taken aback even as he returned the gesture. What was Nikki Du Boise doing here? Evidently, all of the students he was supposed to protect had charged head-long into danger the minute he turned his back. Then he remembered he had another problem— Victor had run off alone.

Dean sprinted out towards the row of carnival booths where Victor had disappeared. A Blitzkrieger stepped into his path and swung at him with a tire iron, but Dean ducked the blow and caught the man in the stomach with his shoulder. His ribs flared with pain, but he knocked his attacker to the ground without losing speed. Another two bikers raced past him as the monster thundered around a corner in hot pursuit.

Dean dodged through the stampede and threw himself behind a spinning rocket-ship ride. The monster charged past him, too intent on its original prey to notice Dean's escape.

It was that moment when the lights all across the park blazed to life. Dean had to slink deeper into the alley as the bright pink and green bulbs of the cotton candy booth chased away his concealing shadows. Overhead, strange colors filled the night sky, as if someone was spewing phosphorescent paint out of the top of the Doomsday Machine.

Suddenly he felt a searing pain against his thigh, and he just managed to pull the phone out of his pocket before it exploded in vermillion flames.

"Un-freaking-believable!" he raged as he stomped his phone to extinguish it.

Before he could smother the phone, a pair of explosions rocked the Doomsday Machine. Most of the tower was steel and therefore not flammable, so as long as no one was foolish enough to be up on the platform, the ensuing fire didn't matter. His first priority remained finding Victor.

For the next few frantic minutes, Dean darted from game kiosk to concession stand as he searched. Finally, through a gap between booths he caught sight of something gray with hooping spines along its back. It was the original chupacabra, the one that had invaded Topsy on his first night there, and it was cornered against the outer wall of the park, pressing itself against the high concrete barricade as it hissed at a pair of armed Blitzkriegers.

"What do we do with it?" one of them said, his voice pinched with panic.

"Let's waste it," said the other. "Let's waste it and get the hell out of here before the other one catches us."

Dean was stuck on the wrong side of the lane of booths, which meant that to get to them he would have to run sixty feet to the intersection, round the corner, and run sixty feet back. He knew Victor cared for that animal, but there was nothing Dean could do to save it.

Then a voice shouted "No!"

Dean peered through the gap again and saw the flash of a white lab coat as Victor ran into the space between the gunmen and Choop.

"You can't kill him," Victor flung his arms out wide.

The Blitzkriegers laughed and raised their pistols.

Now that Victor was in danger, Dean knew he needed to do something. Placing his foot on a sign that read "you must be this tall to ride," he launched himself up onto the roof of the booth. His plan, such as it was, involved leaping down at his enemies and knocking them both to the ground before they could get off a shot.

The moment he pulled his full weight onto the roof, he heard a splintering crack and felt the booth lurch underneath him. The Blitzkriegers heard it too, and they turned just in time to see an avalanche of lumber coming at them. Dean collided bodily with the first Blitzkrieger, which served to cushion his fall while doubling the force with which the biker hit the ground. The second biker dodged backwards and avoided the worst of the tumbling wreckage, but a stray board hammered into his wrist and stripped the gun from his grasp.

Holding his bruised wrist, he steadied himself against the wall. He watched as Dean rose from the wreckage and dusted himself off. Then he turned and ran.

"All right, you," Dean rounded on Victor. "What were you thinking, running off like that?"

Choop pressed his head against Victor's side and chirped.

Dean held up a pair of fingers. "That's two times in the past four hours I've had to save you."

"Can we make it three times?" Victor held up a shaking finger to point past Dean.

The roar from behind him told Dean what he would see before he turned around. The monster filled the lane with its bulk as it watched them with burning red eyes that flicked back and forth between Victor, Dean, and Choop.

Dean stood rigid. He sensed that this creature wanted to rend and maim with mindless ferocity. It was paused now, but probably only because it was working out how to kill one of them without letting the other two get away.

"What do we do?" Victor whispered tensely.

Dean didn't have an answer, but Choop did. The smaller gray creature slid past them to crouch just out of reach of his larger counterpart where he chirped a bird-like song. Compared to the raw, destructive power of the monster, Choop seemed even more skinny and sleek than he had before. It was like a ninety pound panther squaring off with a four-hundred-pound-gorilla.

Choop chirped again and the monster's eyes widened. For a moment it appeared that it might respond. Then suddenly it raised its fists, roared, and leaped at the smaller version of itself.

Springing sideways to avoid the monster's spiked fists, Choop evaded the bigger creature long enough to slip past it and escape around the row of booths. The monster roared after it and then turned to face Victor and Dean.

Dean leaped to the center of the lane, blocking the monster's path, looking for some way to buy Victor more time to escape. To his surprise, it was Choop who again came to the rescue.

Just as the big monster seemed about to charge, Choop bounded in from behind to rake his sharp talons down the rampaging reptile's tail. The monster howled and spun around, and Dean could see deep red gashes where Choop's claws had split the gray skin.

Bellowing again, the monster lunged forward in a blur of talons, fangs, and spines. Here again, Choop's speed and agility saved him as he sprang into the air, bounded off his attacker's back, and dashed away, letting out another low-high-low birdcall as he went.

The monster bolted after Choop and almost had him. But each time it got close, Choop managed to evade its attacks. In a frenzied moment, the two creatures were around the corner and out of sight.

"Was he..." Victor began in disbelief. "Was he protecting us?"

"It looks like he was protecting *you*," Dean said, pulling Victor away down the alley. "But I know he just kept both of us from getting pounded into pâté. That makes us even for the cavern, so now you only owe me one for the Blitzkriegers—"

Before Dean could finish, he was yanked off his feet from behind. The bright lights of the amusement park spun around him in a violent circle until he crashed face first into the sidewalk. A lance of pain shot through his head. Rolling onto his side, he squinted through double-vision to see a mountain of a man standing over him.

"You owe me a new bike," Brick boomed as his size 16 motorcycle boot crashed into Dean's side. There was another explosion of pain as he heard another rib snap. Agony paralyzed him. He couldn't see, and he couldn't breathe.

"I'm gonna send you to find your dead girlfriend," Brick roared.

"Fi... fiancé..." Dean could hardly hear his own voice as those gargantuan hands clamped onto his shirt and hauled him into the air.

CHAPTER 44 ~ SOAP

I kicked my legs through the air below me, but my toes didn't find any crossbeams to stand on, and I could feel the heat of the flames searing my feet. That meant it was a race to see whether I would die by falling or burning. Oh, wait, there was also a chance that the whole Doomsday Machine could come crashing down on my head and crush me to death, so I had lots of options.

One of my hands slipped off the two-by-four, which made the fingers on my other hand slip even closer to the edge as I swung like a rag-doll. On the back-swing, I managed to grab the rail again and re-position myself, but it wouldn't last. I realized my hands were now close enough for me to re-activate Rusty's homing bracelet, but I knew I had maybe thirty seconds before I fell and Rusty would take ten times as long to navigate down from the top of the tower.

"Help!" I yelled, but I doubted anyone could hear me. I braved a look over my shoulder. The lights in the amusement park were now overloading and exploding into darkness. In a few places fires were beginning to eat away at the gaudy paint of the parks attractions. By the light of the swirling cloud of illumination that now stretched across the sky, I could see that all the Blitzkriegers who could still move were either riding away on their bikes if they still had them, or else just running off into the night. In a moment, I saw why they were running: in a flash of motion, Choop scampered out from behind a concession stand with the big monster close on his spiny tail. It looked like Choop was hauling flat-out for the Doomsday Machine, probably because he intended to climb it to get away from the bigger, clumsier beast.

"Help! Up here! Help!" I yelled, even as I slipped another inch.

Choop didn't slow his gallop, but he did glance up in my direction and veer slightly my way. He couldn't run in a straight line for very long or the monster would catch him, so he had to keep doubling back and zigzagging to avoid getting pulverized. I slipped down to just my fingertips and realized that even if Choop was going to come to my rescue, he would never make it to me in time.

Suddenly a strong hand clamped onto my wrist and hauled me up onto the burning platform. I rolled over to see which of my friends had come back for me and was shocked to find Angela glaring down at me, her lips pulled back in a frightening grimace.

"What did you do?" She grabbed the collar of my hoodie to yank me to my feet, and then shoved a shiny, six-barreled rail-gun into my face. "What did you do to my tower?"

Although the fire was burning through the scaffolding and the wooden platform where we stood, the working parts of the Doomsday Machine would easily survive the blaze. But the whole structure was already quivering as the earthquake grenades amped up the harmonic resonance. I could feel the vibrations in the floorboards below my feet, and at that moment a screw fell from high above and bounced next to me. I could hear the grinding of metal reverberating through the steel struts. In another few minutes the whole tower would pull itself apart, but if I told Angela what was causing it, she would be able to cut the power, stop the earthquake grenades, and go back to destroying the world. On the other hand, if I didn't tell her, then she would blow my head off.

"Tell me!" she shrieked. I closed my eyes, ready for the burning magnetic slugs to slice through me.

She held me at arm's length and put the gun up to my chin. I don't know if she really would have pulled that trigger, but she stopped to look over my shoulder. I squirmed around in her grasp to see Choop perched behind me at the edge of the platform. He cocked his head like a bird, looked from me to Angela, and then glanced back down the way he came.

"Get out of here, you stupid lizard!" Angela waved him away with her gun. It startled him enough that he bounced up higher into the scaffolding and climbed up into the darkness.

If Angela had wished for no more interruptions, she was disappointed only a moment later. The soft clangs of Choop scaling the tower structure above us were replaced by the heavy thumps of something else coming up from below. A thick, spiked claw appeared over the edge of the platform, followed by another that wrapped around a cross-beam with the grip of a python. The monster wasn't nearly as good a climber as Choop, but what it lacked in agility it made up for with brute strength. It moved not so much as though it was pulling himself up as if it was trying to pull everything else down.

The monster's head appeared over the ledge, and then the rest of it emerged from below. It struggled to get its thick, powerful hind legs over the edge, but then it rose to its enormous height and glared at us. Angela dropped me to the side and stood before the monster, seemingly unafraid. When it roared at her, she didn't even blink.

"Yeah, yeah, yeah," Angela said. "I've heard that before." Then she thrust out her rail gun and fired.

A steady stream of thunder split the air around us as her magnetic projectiles broke the sound barrier. The noise was horrible, and it drilled into my skull even though I clamped my hands over my ears. However bad the sound was, the sight was even worse.

The monster's charge was arrested as countless red gashes opened in its chest and arms. It stumbled backwards, wobbling on its legs just like it had done when it first emerged from the egg sack. When it looked down at its own body, the hoods over his reptilian eyes trembled. Even I could see that it was feeling pain and confusion.

I felt like someone had packed my heart in dry ice when the monster raised a hand towards Angela to show her the red droplets trickling from its claws.

"Eep?" it said. It was the first noise other than a roar it had ever made, and it was such a small sound to come out of such a big creature. In that last moment of life, I couldn't see it as the depraved killing machine it was designed to be. It was just a lost baby, utterly alone in a strange world, abandoned by parents who died millions of years before it was born. And now it was being murdered by its very own midwife.

Angela shot it just once more, this time through the head, right between the eyes. The big creature went limp and slid off the platform, all the power and energy and life extinguished from that mighty body. I ran to the edge to see where it had landed, but I had to turn my head away after I saw it stretched out on the pavement below.

"You killed him!" I shouted at Angela, hot tears burning my eyes.

"That creature was defective," she said, the gun at her side as she walked towards me. The fire rose up behind her and made her hair shine red while dark shadows played across her face. Half way across the platform, she tripped, just a little, just enough to make her look down and see what had caught her foot. It was the tightly-drawn power cable that led to the earthquake grenades.

Her eyes blazed in the reflected light as she inspected the cable and saw that it went up into the rails above. Then she laughed, scooped up the knife Shirtless had dropped, and slashed the cable at her feet. There was a blue flash, and the shuddering vibration beneath my feet settled into nothing.

I cried out and lunged for the cable, but it had been stretched so tight across the floor that I couldn't bring the severed ends together to close the circuit. If there had been even an inch of wire or a chunk of metal in my pocket I could have made the connection, but I had nothing left.

Angela stood over me and laughed. "Well, Soap, it looks like you've finally outlived your usefulness."

CHAPTER 45 ~ DEAN

Brick hurled Dean into the center of the skee ball court hard enough to crack the machine's casing. Then the big man was on top of him, pinning him to the ramp with one ham-fist and slamming down onto his skull with the other.

The first blow created a miniature universe of pain inside Dean's head. When he finally managed to get his eyes open, he saw stars everywhere.

"I was going to beat you to death with a crowbar," Brick rumbled. "Now I think I'll just use what God gave me: fists and boots."

Dean wanted to ask about why boots qualified as God-given while crowbars did not, but the question was unlikely to work to his advantage. Also, he wasn't able to catch his breath to speak. All he could do was watch the big fist coming at him again.

"Leave him alone!" Victor grabbed Brick's arm in an attempt to stop him, although he might as well have been trying to hold back an avalanche.

Brick shook him off as though he were a fly. "Go home b'fore I smash you up, too." He rumbled.

"If you want my Dean of Students, you'll have to go through me first."

Dean tried to tell Victor to get out of there, but his voice came out as nothing more than a pained exhale as the world around him spun and faded in and out of his vision.

Brick, seemingly amused by the audacity of his new enemy, dropped Dean to the ground and turned to look at the young man. He drew in an enormous breath, making his already-massive chest swell to titanic proportions. "I got no problem killing you first, if that's what you want."

"Why are you even doing this?" Victor asked desperately. "Why would someone like you want to work for someone like the Professor?"

"I'm just in it for the money," Brick chuckled and took a menacing step forward. "Bought me a badass hog—which you wrecked. So now I'm gonna wreck you."

"I warn you: I'm pre-med," Victor said, stepping backwards. "I'll be able to name each and every bone you break."

Brick just grunted and cocked his fist.

"No, really. These over here in my hand are called the metacarpals," Victor held his left hand far out to his side and wiggled his fingers.

Brick sneered at the hand that waved to him. When he did, his head turned for only a second, but it was long enough for Victor to use the broken length of two-by-four he had been hiding behind his back in his other hand. He whipped the board around, jumping up just enough to connect with the side of the giant's neck.

With nothing more than a grunt, Brick's eyes closed, his head lolled back, and he crashed to the ground.

"You K.O.ed him," Dean said as he struggled to his knees. "You K.O.ed him in one blow...?"

Victor checked Brick's neck for a pulse and nodded with satisfaction. Then he wrestled the giant's limp arms behind his back and bound his wrists with medical tape. "I did warn him about being pre-med," he said with a hint of smugness. "A blow to the carotid artery causes swelling that momentarily interrupts blood flow to the brain. If that happens, you're taking a nap, no matter how big you are."

Dean winced as he stood up. "Okay, we are officially even as far as saving each other's lives. But you have to admit you just proved that brawn wins out over brains."

"What? No way. This was pure physiology. Plus, check out the two-by-four," Victor tossed the broken length of lumber to Dean. "That wood is compressed and chemically treated. Very high tech. Tons of science."

Dean realized that this was the first time he had seen Victor smile—and that it was the first time he had smiled at Victor.

Their moment was interrupted by a series of rapid-fire shots echoing across the park.

"Sounded like a machine gun," Dean tried to sink low into a soldier's crouch but found his legs almost giving out under him.

"It was Angela's rail gun," Victor said. "And it sounded like it came from up in the tower."

Then Soap screamed, and without another word the two raced across the forty yards between them and the Doomsday Machine. All the bulbs in the rides and streetlamps they passed had burned out, leaving the park in shadows once again. The only illumination came from the small fires sprinkled throughout the booths and attractions, as well as the eerie glow from the bizarre borealis effect in the sky.

As he moved, Dean clamped his right arm over his side to reduce the shifting of his broken ribs, but the pain was still oppressive. His agonized breathing, combined with his other injuries, slowed him to little more than a limp, and he did not arrive at the Doomsday Machine until well after Victor. There they both stopped, looking at the curtain of flames that blocked the only ramp that led to the platform.

Victor threw his arm across his face to protect himself from the heat and the smoke. "How do we get up there?" he asked frantically.

The ramp was burning and getting worse fast. Dean estimated that it was only about as hot as a thinly-packed camp fire, and the danger zone was still only a few yards wide. He had run through bigger blazes than this—but only while wearing an insulated suit, a helmet, and respirator gear.

With protesting ribs, Dean stripped his bomber jacket off his arms and slung it around his head and shoulders.

"Wait here," he told Victor.

"What are you doing?"

In answer, Dean pointed to the fire department logo on his t-shirt. Then he buried his hands into his armpits to protect his fingers and charged into the blaze. Uninjured, he might have been able to cross the burning area in two great bounds. Limping as he was, it took a dozen shuffling steps, each one blistering his feet. The skin of his arms and face reddened as though his body had received an instant sunburn, and the heat and smoke wrapped around him like a suffocating blanket. He gritted his teeth in pain, but he pressed on through.

The moment he broke out of the flames, he collapsed to his knees and slapped his palms against his body to smother a dozen embers on his clothes. As he did, he could smell the burned rubber of his shoes, but he did not detect the salty stink of cooked human flesh, which was a good sign. Still, all the hair had been burned off his arms and the skin was dry and red. He might need hospital treatment. But first he needed to rescue his cousin.

He reached the platform to find Soap kneeling next to a severed cable. It looked like she was trying to get the two ends together, and from the expression on her face, she must have thought it was really important. Angela loomed over her, clutching a big silver gun.

Dean stepped up onto the platform. "Let her go. Just fly away on your jet pack and let her go."

"And leave you behind to destroy my doomsday machine? I don't think so." She grabbed Soap's arm and pulled her up and around in front of her, holding her tight and pressing the six shiny barrels of her rail gun to the side of the girl's head. "Look at that, Soap. Your cousin is here to save you. I see passion runs strong in your family. I have to admit, I find it really sexy."

With Soap clasped tightly in front of her, she backed to the far edge of the platform, her gun never wavering. Soap's eyes went from her cousin to the cable, as if she were trying to tell him something.

Dean held out his hands to show he was unarmed. "We can talk about this. Your guys have all run off, so it's just us."

Angela laughed. "My guys? You mean the smelly little pawns? Frankly, after they had completed enough heists to fund our operation here, they were expendable. We've got far better people than that. We've got a whole nation."

Dean wasn't sure what she meant by that statement, but he guessed it might be a bluff. At that very moment, it didn't matter, because it wouldn't bring him any closer to saving Soap.

"I've got something else to tell you," Dean took another step, his hands still high. "I know who the Professor is."

Angela's eyes widened for just a second. He could see that she was trying to play it cool, but he had caught her off guard. He used her surprise as an opportunity to take another step.

Behind him, he heard Victor call out to Nikki. Evidently, Nikki had been searching the building below for something to help, because a moment later Dean heard the unmistakable FWOOSH of a fire extinguisher. He knew that an extinguisher couldn't save the burning structure, but it could subdue the flames on the ramp enough for the two of them to join him. Dean rolled his eyes: he had told them to wait where it was safe, but he might as well have told moths to stay away from a candle.

"The Professor could only be one person," Dean said, inching forward again. "He had to have intimate knowledge of the Institute's secrets. He had to know about this whole EMP thing and design an EMP-bomb for the Blitzkriegers to use in their heists. Also, he must have had the information to know that there might be more of that special metal in the progenitor caverns."

As the spurting sounds of fire extinguishers worked their way closer, something metallic climbed down from the scaffolding towards Soap and Angela. Dean's mind raced to understand what he was seeing: a mechanical monster with eight spider legs, pincer arms, and flickering eyes. Thinking that this must be another of the Professor's weapons, he went to dive forward to pull both of them away, but the gun Angela pressed against Soap's head checked his action.

"Look out!" he called.

Angela and Soap both turned their heads to see where he was pointing.

"Rusty!" Soap exclaimed as the robot came to her like a well-heeled dog.

The angry look dropped from Angela's face for just a moment as she studied the robot. "You designed that? Not bad." Despite her compliment, she pushed Rusty back with the tip of her running shoe. During the distraction, Dean took one more step forward.

Victor and Nikki had now arrived at the top of the ramp, and Choop had joined them. They stopped at the edge of the platform when they saw the gun at Soap's head. Choop made a birdcall, but then pushed his head into Victor's side as if to hide in the pocket of his lab coat.

"Oh, how heartwarming," Angela said sarcastically. "The whole Mad Science Institute is here at last. Hey, I got an idea. Let's roast marshmallows and sing Kumbaya for the next two hours while my doomsday machine rips apart the magnetic balance of the planet."

"For a little while, I thought the Professor might have been you," Dean pressed on. "Except then I saw him speaking live on the big screen while you were there. Besides that, he needed contact with criminals to recruit his thugs."

Dean was now on top of the cable. Without lowering his hands or dropping his gaze from her eyes, he placed one foot on each side of it, so that the severed ends pointed towards each other and protruded an inch past the melted soles of his shoes.

"Of course, I recognized the Professor's voice almost as soon as I saw him up there on that big screen. I'd heard that voice before, when I'd video conferenced with a man in prison—what better place to get in touch with a gang of bank robbers?"

"Does this little lecture have a point?" Angela barked.

"It has two points," Dean said. "The first is this: the Professor is actually Bill Helmholtz, former Dean of Students of the Mechanical Science Institute."

"What?" Victor said in shock.

"I'll kill him," Nikki said flatly.

Angela sighed. "Pretty good detective work for a firefighter. But it doesn't change the fact that tomorrow Professor Helmholtz is going to be the most powerful person in the history of the world. Unless your second point addresses that fact?"

"My second point is simply...this," Dean twisted his feet together to drive the ends of the cables towards each other. His feet moved, but the cables didn't stretch far enough. "I mean... this. No... this." He re-positioned and tried again and again, but each time he achieved nothing. The closest he could get the ends was still a half-inch too far apart.

"That thing you're doing with your feet," Angela said, not bothering to look down. "Stop it."

And then she shot him.

CHAPTER 46 ~ SOAP

I saw my cousin crumple and fall right on top of the power cable. For a moment I thought he might be electrocuted on the severed ends, but when I saw the dark red stain spreading out along his thigh, I knew he had other troubles.

Victor made a move to get to his side, but Angela trained the gun on him.

"Back on your end of the platform, Vickey," Angela said. "If I severed an artery, it's his own fault."

When she shifted her stance, I tried to worm free, but her arm was so tight around me I couldn't get my arms away. Even if I managed to escape, she could have just gunned me down. I might have been able to lunge backwards and drive us both over the edge, but she had a flight pack and I didn't, so that idea seemed seriously flawed. I was stuck, but at least I had managed to slip Rusty's homing bracelet off my wrist, thread it through one of the buttonholes in Angela's lab coat, and click it closed. I had another idea, but it would take good timing and even better luck to make it work.

"Why're you doin' this?" Nikki cried. "You're goin' to send the human race back to the dark ages."

"No!" Angela shouted, suddenly furious. "I'm sending the human race ahead into a golden era! For too long we've sheltered ourselves from danger, and that means the weakest, stupidest individuals keep having more and more weak, stupid children. They're breeding faster than their smarter, stronger counterparts. It's a reversal of Darwin's laws, and we need to get it under control if our species is going to advance."

"What are you saying?" Victor asked in outrage. "You want to establish a master race? Is that it? There was a guy named Hitler who tried that, you know. It didn't work out so well."

Angela flicked her gun dismissively. "Science clearly shows that the Nazis were idiots. What I'm talking about doesn't have anything to do with skin color. Every race has geniuses and morons. This Doomsday Machine is going to hit the reset button on the world so that the smartest and strongest among us will survive and the rest will die off. It's nature's law. By protecting the weak, we make ourselves unfit for survival."

"Wrong," Dean spoke up from where he lay on the ground. It sounded like his throat was all dried out, but his words came through strong and clear. "By protecting the weak, we make ourselves strong."

By the end of his sentence, he was having trouble speaking. It was like he was being vibrated. Then I felt it, too, as the floorboards began to rattle under my feet. A crashing and a grinding of metal echoed down the tower as a huge cross-beam broke away high above and smashed through other beams as it plummeted.

Dean rolled slightly to one side and then I saw what he had done. As he had been covering the cable with his body, he had managed to work something in between the severed ends to close the circuit and activate the earthquake grenades. At first, it was too dark to see what he had used. Then a blue spark jumped across the gap and I saw how he had made the connection.

The break in the cable was filled with two golden engagement rings set side by side. Gold is a fantastic conductor.

Angela shrieked and threw me to the side. She raised her gun to shoot Dean again, but my finger was quicker.

"Rusty," I said, pointing to her flight pack. "Blast this."

Angela had set up the Doomsday Machine's broadcast to affect almost everything except teslanium-based circuitry, which is why her flight pack, my robot, and the earthquake grenades had remained functional after the tower had been activated. Rusty's beam had no such safeguard, and at my command he sent a swift EMP kick right up Angela's backside.

Her rail gun spewed off the last of its ammunition harmlessly into open air as her flight pack flung her straight upwards. She shrieked and flailed her arms, but she was as helpless as a mouse in a tornado. Rusty maneuvered under her, dutifully homing in on the bracelet that was looped through the buttonhole of Angela's lab coat. Just like the autogyro I had once played with in my apartment back in New York, when Angela flew up to a certain height, she left the range of Rusty's EMP and fell back down towards him. As she got closer and her pack got nearer to the magnifying transmitter again, she would go zooming back upwards, her arms and legs pin-wheeling helplessly as she careened through the air. Up and down, up and down she went, screaming and swearing as Rusty followed her bouncing trajectory down the ramp and out into the park.

We just made it off the platform as big chunks of wood and metal came crashing down. The whole tower tilted and then snapped in half, with the broken top part falling away to crush the Ferris wheel and a whole bunch of other rides. It was so loud and kicked up so much dust that I had to cover my ears and close my eyes.

When I looked again, the Doomsday Machine's borealis effect was fading from the stratosphere and the stars were becoming visible again, bright and clear against the black sky.

SEPTEMBER 20
(A PERFECTLY NORMAL DAY)

Chapter 47 ~ Soap

"Please, Soap, you have to forgive me."

Brett sat on the corner of my dorm-room bed, leaning forward to talk to my back. I was trying to work: I wanted to develop a miniaturized version of Angela's electrogravitic flight pack to install into Rusty so he could carry more weight.

"Sure, I forgive you," I said as I wound a white wire around a power cell.

"I mean it; I'm so sorry. I didn't even think I had that much to drink. For me to pass out like that and then for you to get kidnapped—you can't even believe how sorry I am."

It made me feel a bit guilty to think it was actually my tranquilizer injection and not his drinking that had caused him to pass out. But what could I tell him? I had to stick to the official story we had given to the police, the FBI, and the press. We told everyone that the Blitzkriegers stole Brett's car with me in it and then my cousin Dean tracked us down to Happy Fun Land. In real life, we didn't want any government interference with our own secret reactor, so we stripped all the teslanium out of everything in the park before we called anyone. Even without the whole doomsday thing, there was still plenty of evidence to arrest the entire gang and Angela, too. They were taken in on charges of larceny, abduction of a minor, criminal conspiracy, and more stuff I can't remember, plus I think the FBI guys were working on an angle to get them classified as terrorists because of the way they used their EMP-bomb in their bank raids. Oh, and as far as anyone knew, they were also the ones who wrecked the transmission in Brett's Camaro. (Sorry, Brett!) More importantly, the cops dropped all charges against my Dad and instead opened a huge investigation of the Professor—now known to be Professor Helmholtz—and his criminal conspiracy.

I had just about finished coiling the wire around the power core when the door to my dorm burst open and Hanna came in with a big white box in her hand. I could tell immediately it wasn't a present for her because she had a very sour expression on her face. She'd been wearing that expression a lot during the last few days, ever since she found out that the charges against my Dad had been dropped, which meant President Hart had no choice but to reinstate me as a Langdon University student. My initial theory was that she was just jealous of the attention we had been getting. The Mechanical Science Institute was all over the blogs and news shows with stories about the star-crossed lovers, a firefighter and a college professor, and how he went on a quest for justice after her murder. People from Hollywood kept offering my cousin big money to make it into a movie, but he turned them all down, saying he didn't care about that. I happen to know that there was something else he cared about, because I found a stack of printouts of news stories on his desk, and saw that he had gone through every single page and underlined the word "fiancé." I don't know why, but for some reason it made my cousin really happy that the whole world was now saying that McKenzie had been his fiancé instead of just his girlfriend.

Anyway, when Hanna walked into my room with the big box in her hands, she saw Brett sitting next to me and her frown got even deeper. She grumbled something about the box blocking the door, and then she dumped it on my bed and walked back out of the room.

The box was large enough to hold a sheet cake, and it was unmarked except for my name written in black ink in the middle of the lid. I opened it carefully and there inside was a lab coat. A long, black lab coat, made from thick fire-resistant fabric and lined with dozens and dozens of pockets. On the back, embroidered in glossy black thread just barely visible against the black cloth of the coat, was the crooked arrow in a triangle that represented the hazard warning for high voltage. Above that were the words "FUROR. EXITIUM. SCIENTIA." There was a note in the pocket that said those words meant "Madness. Destruction. Knowledge."

The coat was so beautiful that I almost started crying when I put it on.

And that wasn't all. In the front pocket I found a phone. I was hesitant to turn it on after my ordeal with the Professor's calls, but when I did I found a text message from Victor. I opened it up and read:

Victor: Look out ur window

I went over to the window and at the foot of the bridge that led to campus, there were two figures looking in my direction. One wore a long pink coat and one wore a long white coat. I waved, and they waved back. Then my phone buzzed with an incoming text.

Nikki: like the coat? I made it 4 u
Soap: Best! Coat! EVER!!!
Soap: Come up 2 my room
Victor: Need 2 get back 2 resrch
Soap: r u going to tell me what ur resrchng?
Victor: Not yet. The Institute still needs some secrets ;)
Nikki: Meet us @ topsy when ur ready
Victor: c u soon

The two of them turned and strolled back along the path. As they crossed over the bridge, a flock of ducks flapped out of the reeds and into the air above them.

"Yeah, so, anyway," Brett cleared his throat. "How about you let me make it up to you? Let me take you out to dinner."

"Sure, I guess," I said, even though I wasn't looking at him when I said it. I was looking out the window, watching a certain white lab coat disappear into the orange sunset.

Chapter 48 ~ Dean

There weren't many people in the prisoner visitation room when Dean sat down to await Professor Helmholtz. He had been surprised when the Professor agreed to his visitation request, but perhaps the mad genius who hatched the scheme to destroy the world had been a little desperate for human contact. After all, he was now being held in solitary confinement as prosecutors and investigators unraveled his network of criminal influence that stretched across the country.

It was coming to light that he had been working on this scheme for years, originally using the money embezzled from the Institute to fund the construction of the Doomsday Machine at Happy Fun Land in order to disguise his device. After President Hart cut off his revenue source and had him arrested, Helmholtz had recruited from his fellow inmates and their friends to help steal the necessary funds to complete the project. President Hart was now spinning his actions as heroic, but at least he wasn't inclined to hassle the now-famous Mechanical Science Institute now that the applications were pouring in. This meant Dean would soon be free to return to Los Angeles while someone better qualified took over as Dean of Students.

As he waited for the guards to bring out the prisoner, Dean drummed his fingers and wondered why he had wanted to speak to the man who had almost destroyed civilization. For starters, it would be his opportunity to gloat over his enemy's downfall. But the truth, he realized, was because he needed to see that the Professor was suffering. Even if he were, it would be a small comfort to Dean: McKenzie was dead, and Helmholtz could never be punished enough for that crime.

At least he still had her memory. To remind himself of that, he touched the rings that hung from his neck. The electricity that had passed through them had melted the metal, welding the rings together into a double-looped symbol for eternity. It was an appropriate symbol, Dean felt, for the unending bond he shared with McKenzie.

Two guards escorted Helmholtz into the visitation room. The Professor looked thinner now, and the orange jumpsuit hung from him like an oversized sack. Yet the man's face was calm as he lifted his telephone receiver.

"Should I congratulate you?" Helmholtz asked. "Or would you prefer that I rant about how I would have succeeded if it hadn't been for you meddling kids?"

"You can say anything you want," Dean said. "You're still getting life without parole."

"On the contrary. Do you think I agreed to meet you because I longed for your sparkling conversation?" Helmholtz looked up at the clock and then leaned towards the glass, his smile transforming into a savage grimace. "Rather, it was to ensure that I would be brought to a certain visitation room at a precise time."

As he spoke, the lights flickered violently. There was a flash and a pop, and then the visitation room went dark. The sounds of chaos swiftly followed: shouts in the distance. Someone screaming. The guards cursing their silent walkie-talkies.

Suddenly, muffled shouts and thumps erupted from the other side of the room. A series of electrical discharges allowed Dean to catch a glimpse of men using stun-sticks against the unprepared guards. These men wore night-vision goggles, and one of them was using a bolt-cutter to free Helmholtz from his chains.

Dean sprang from his seat and slammed the bottoms of his fists against the glass partition, but it was pointless. Somewhere above, helicopter blades beat the air, ready to carry the Professor safely away to freedom.

About the Author

Sechin Tower is a writer, game designer, and teacher. He lives in the Seattle, Washington area with his beautiful wife and adoring cat. In his spare time, he prepares for the zombie apocalypse by running obstacle courses and practicing Brazilian Jiu Jitsu.

Visit his website:
SechinTower.com

CPSIA information can be obtained
at www.ICGtesting.com
Printed in the USA
FSOW01n0329310316
18570FS